"STAY WITH ME, PILOT ONE, ON MY MARK!"

"Tezar, there is disagreement here. Four hundred lives, highly trained physicians and technicians—"

"Pilot One! On my mark! I'll lose you otherwise."

Rear screens showed Palaton that the cable was vibrating. The transport ships sought to cast themselves off without his guidance.

"A Choya in burnout . . ." a voice cut in, overriding the pilot. Palaton heard authority and skepticism in the stranger's voice. The cable bounced. The escort slewed in response as the heavier transports dragged slightly on it.

He drew on his talents and hurled his own voices of command at them. "Stay with me!" He had no way of knowing how well the comline transmitted his words and tone, but there was momentary silence at the other end. Alternating between sight and blindness, he calculated wildly. Then, "Mark!" he shouted. And he freed the cable as he sheared the escort off violently, accelerating rapidly.

But the escort did not respond properly and, with a shudder, he realized that the transports had quite possibly released the cable before he did—slinging themselves into nowhere, never to escape from the patterns of Chaos. . . .

CHARLES INGRID'S
Magnificent DAW Science Fiction Novels:

RADIUS OF DOUBT

THE PATTERNS OF CHAOS #1

CHARLES INGRID

DAW BOOKS, INC.

DONALD A. WOLLHEIM, FOUNDER

375 Hudson Street, New York, NY 10014

**ELIZABETH R. WOLLHEIM
SHEILA E. GILBERT
PUBLISHERS**

First Printing, October 1991

2 3 4 5 6 7 8 9

DAW TRADEMARK REGISTERED
U.S. PAT. OFF. AND FOREIGN COUNTRIES
—MARCA REGISTRADA.
HECHO EN U.S.A.

Printed in Canada

Dedicated to my father,
who flew for his country and loved it,
and to fellow classmate Roy Corrigan,
who flew because he loved it also,
even though it was the death of him.

And to Sheila, for remarkable coolness,
in the face of fire.

PART I

THE HOUSE OF STAR

Chapter 1

High winds tormented the descent of the incoming shuttle, buffeting it from the moment it entered the atmosphere of the planet called Sorrow. Passengers aboard the vehicle in the freight section clung to their safety webs and harnesses. In the forward cabin, only two first class passengers endured the bad ride. The Choya got to his feet, heedless of the bumps and dodges, and began to pace. His fellow passenger, the Daranian, closed his eyes and began to recite religious verses in a high-pitched hum. Through his thick lashes, however, the Daranian continued to watch the Choya pace. Though both beings were bipedal, like most of the sapient races, the thick, furred body of the Daranian could not compare with that of the Choya. The Choya was tall and slender, yet broad-shouldered, his double-elbowed arms sinewy with grace ... and there was a natural arrogance to his stride, the self-assurance of one who was a leader among aliens, a role to which a Choya seemed born.

The shuttle vibrated with a high-pitched screech, nearly out of range of their hearing. The Choya stopped in his tracks and looked upward, his thick brown hair cascading backward from the coronet of horn that crowned his head. His attitude of watchful listening held for another second and then the shuttle plunged.

The Daranian fell from his seat and dangled at the end of his safety line, but the Choya kept his feet with little effort as the shuttle leveled off with a tremor. As the Daranian hauled himself back into his webbing, it struck him that the Choya had acted as if he'd known what was coming.

The Choya threw him a glance. "I think," he said, "we've had enough." With economy of movement, he crossed to the "Authorized Only" door locks leading to the control cabin.

The Daranian concealed his grimace of triumph. The Choya *was* a *tezar*; he'd been correct in his estimation of his fellow passenger, and the legendary *tezarian* pilots would no more tolerate this buffeting than cross-marry outside their Houses.

The Choya disappeared beyond the bulkhead. The Daranian closed his third eye in supplication and increased the fervor of his chanting.

Palaton forced the second bulkhead open. He was exhausted, having come off a year-long contract, and now the rules of approach to the Halls of the Compact subjected him to the indignity of being transported by an inferior pilot. His horn crown prickled with the intuition of something violently wrong in the control cabin, and as the air lock came open, the hysterical voices within hit him like a blow to the face.

He hadn't wanted this assignment and wouldn't have taken it if his elder hadn't ordered him. Two weeks in the predatory political atmosphere of the Halls was not what he considered a well-earned vacation. His *bahdur* talent flickered with fatigue, warning him of a dangerous drain on his psychic abilities, and then the hysteria of the pilot and navigator slammed at him. Palaton flinched, gathered his reserves, and lashed out.

"Who's in charge here?" he said, flexing his arms and folding them across his chest.

There was an immediate, stunned silence in the cockpit as the pilot and navigator swung about to face the intruder. The pilot, a quad-armed brachiator, wrinkled his pelted face while the navigator, one of the flighty, winged Ivrians, settled to a perch. The Gorman pulled his lips back from his canines, snarling, "You're off limits."

"And you're off track. What's going on?"

The Ivrian clacked his flexible beak several times in menace display before sputtering, "Storm center has us. We're caught in the leading edge."

Storms above Sorrow were no simple matter, but a professional should be able to handle it. Compact rules of approach stated that only neutrals could pilot in from the orbiting stations where the deep space ships berthed, but Palaton was not going to accept any rules which would subject him to any more abuse.

"Let me in," he said.

His words were soft, but his dual voices were low with intent.

The shuttle caught another thermal drop and plunged abruptly. Palaton shifted his weight to the balls of his feet and his knees flexed, but the Ivrian went sliding off his perch in a flurry of feathers. The pilot grabbed his webbing with a groan and shook his furry head. Palaton finally caught at the wall to keep his balance, narrowed his eyes, and glared at the control board.

There was no automatic pilot here—computer sentience was against the rules of approach to Sorrow, to avoid having drones sent in to wipe out the multiracial city. But it didn't change the fact that a competent automatic pilot could have handled this shuttle.

The Gorman shoved over violently. "Here," he grunted. "Take it." And buried his face in all four of his hands. Palaton would get no prettier invitation. He came forward and sat down in the second's chair. The Gorman's presence felt like a light, greasy film over the controls and he forced back a shudder as he took the guidance system in hand. He sent his *bahdur* spiraling outward, feathering the edges of the storm, with its highs and lows, its turbulent clashes. For a moment, his abilities dimmed, flickered as if lightning had struck, and his heartbeat pounded fiercely in echo.

A *tezar* was nothing without his *bahdur*. It happened to all of them, sooner or later, guttering out like a primitive tallow candle, but he wasn't prepared for it to happen to him. He shook off the icy shock traveling through him and reached again, and this time he found the prescient knowledge he needed.

The shuttle came into his control like a child going to its mother and settled there, in comfort. He, in turn, took it and cradled it, skirting the furious winds which had tossed them about and finding clearer skies. The shuttle answered awkwardly, like a young bird with a crumpled wing.

"You've got mechanicals," Palaton said aloud, as soon as he identified the source of the problem. "Probably a chip gone bad. Anyone would have had difficulties."

Anyone but a tezar. He did not say that out

loud. He did not have to. The Gorman raised his face. His broad, almost flat nose sniffled.

"I thank you, *tezar* Palaton," he said.

"Think nothing of it," the Choya answered. "I'll bring it on in, if you don't mind, considering the malfunction." He gathered up the shreds of his energy, pushed worry aside, and functioned on pride. He could not possibly have felt his *bahdur* flicker. Not possibly.

"I would be honored."

The Ivrian said nothing, but its wing agitation settled from a furious buzzing to a languid fanning. The second-class passengers in freight knew nothing about the danger they'd been in, and even the Daranian had only his guesses as to what had happened.

There was another violent plunge of the shuttle, then it leveled out once more and the turbulence disappeared. The Choya did not return from the control cabin, but the Daranian rode out the rest of his passage in peace.

Palaton suffered the effusive thanks of the Daranian upon arrival, reminding himself it was the due of a *tezar*. He watched as the Daranian fumbled off about his business, choosing the confined interior of a cabcar to ride the rest of the way into the Halls. He himself felt like a claustrophobic freed and as he turned his head into the wind, where the scattered clouds of a milder storm spit-spattered him, he took a deep, steadying breath. The fear that had lanced him was finally loosening its grip, but Palaton was left unsettled in its wake. Even fatigue had never dimmed his power before. Without his abilities, he was nothing. He was a Choya without lineage—a thing almost unheard of and seldom spoken of publicly—and without his *bahdur*, he had no career, no calling.

Every *tezar* was faced with the inevitability that his talent would one day burn out. That was the nature of psychic ability. But in the Choyan race, psychic abilities were not a come and go talent. They were as steady as any of the five more common senses sentient races shared. They kept the nature of their abilities hidden from other beings, as much to keep the upper hand in galactic politics as to avoid being exploited, but only those abilities needed to pilot the soulfire, or *tezarian*, faster than light drive, carried a debilitating genetic disease with it.

He was too young to be ill. Too new to be used up. He could not be facing the beginning of his end. The high winds of the upper stratosphere that had telegraphed a restlessness to the planet's surface now whipped a chill wind at him. It brought the sting of tears to the corners of his eyes, but he stood on the obsidian plains until his head cleared. The wind spoke of storm and the storm reflected his own inner passion. Standing near the shuttle berths, smelling the burn of the recent landing, listening to the creak of metal as it cooled and settled, the shouts of the multi-lingual crews working over the berthing cradles, all these soothed and polished and buffered him. When he was ready, he turned to the transportation alcove and defiantly chose a jet sled over the conventional vehicles. He did not like feeling staid.

The crystal canals leading to the massive city known as the Halls of the Compact were empty of traffic in the early morning light. He left the helmet off—one size rarely fit all, particularly not when it came to the Choyan race, whose dual brain pans and horned crowns were of a large and proud size—and a few spattering rain drops dampened his face. Palaton bared his teeth in annoyance at the weather. He would not go gently into the storm, but as the jet sled took him over the canalways, the rain faded.

Sorrow smelled of an early spring. The weather held the edge of a newly tempered sword blade. Palaton enjoyed the passage of winter into spring. He drank the air in now as the rapid glide of the sled along the canals flung it into his face. If he looked down, he would see what was imprisoned in the crystal and recall all too clearly why the planet had been named Sorrow. As he neared the Halls, the canals converged into a solid lake, self-bridged by a separate, flawless arch of quartz, whose glassy interior remained unstained—but the death encapsuled below it was reflected in its mirrorlike surface. All those who wished to enter the Compact had to pass over that bridge—and those resolute enough occasionally looked down.

An entire race of people had died within those crystal confines. Massed together, frozen forever within the canals and lakes of this part of the continent. No member race of the Compact held within its history a clue to who these people had been or what had happened to them, but their death was a stark memorial to the awfulness of the event. Had it been war or suicide? Destruction or preservation, waiting for the day when the crystal could be split and the people offered up again into life? No one could hazard a guess—but the technology of it remained beyond anyone's ability to duplicate or undo. The common theory was that it had been an act of war, and it was in the hope of avoiding another war like that one that the Compact had been woven.

Thus far, in a limited way, the weaving had been successful. There had not yet been another war of such destructive scope. Palaton did not see how there could possibly be. No member race in the Compact knew how to construct a weapon which could do what this one had and he did not think any would even dare try. The view from the bridge was a daunting one. It was the children which bothered him the most.

He took the bridge at an incredible speed, with the sled monitor warning him of reckless endangerment, and the governor kicking in to slow him down. It mattered not. As a *tezar* he knew exactly how fast and far he could go. The sled did what he wished—he came off the arch in a high jump. For a moment his heart soared. Then the sled slammed to the canalway and he braked rapidly as he neared the traffic of the more conventional roadway and then reached the garages. Like the rain clouds which were skittering away, the wind and the speed had purged him. He turned the sled into transportation and passed through the security portals.

"That's him," the Daranian said to the being who stood in the shadows beside him. "I came in with him on the transport. He saved our hides. The turbulence damn near brought us down."

The shadowed being said quietly, sibilantly, "He should have saved me the trouble."

"I don't want to know," the Daranian answered. "I pointed him out to you. My part and obligation in this is done."

"Of course," the shadowed one responded,

but the Daranian had already hunched his head
into his shoulders and lumbered away. The dark
one looked after him through slant eyes accus-
tomed to seeing in the night and smiled. He
looked down again from his vantage post as the
Choyan prey passed below. Then he sprang out
and down, landing effortlessly, and he, too,
passed through the security portals, his weapon
of hollowed bone perceived as organic and
harmless. With a grim quickening of pace, he
caught up with his prey and trailed him into
the Halls of the Compact, biding the time to
strike.

The tongue-lashing he got from the garage
officials restored Palaton's cloak of arrogance.
He needed it to survive within the Halls, he
more than any other Choya who might have
been sent here. But there was no ground-tied
being who could tell him what to drive or how
fast to drive it. He was a *tezar*!

Rejuvenated, the fear of his talents dimming
blunted and pushed as far back as he could
force it, Palaton readied to pick up his assignments. He registered at the front directory and
waited in the lobby until his map could be
printed out and his itinerary handed him, but
even as he took it, he already knew where he
would be going. The contracts wing was easily
accessible to the fore of the city complex. He
would be among more businessmen than politi-
cians and he preferred it that way.

Moameb's uneasy health had shoved him into
this assignment, weary though he was from his
last contract, but he would only spend two
weeks in this hellhole. There would be a pouch
of contracts to pick up and a dozen or so to

finish negotiating personally. There were always more jobs than pilots and the *tezars* could pick and choose as they wished. They were the lords of Chaos. They alone could navigate the realm beyond faster than light speed with any degree of accuracy. They were the main commodity of the Choyan people in this butcher shop of a galactic alliance. And no one alive within these Halls would know the shame that Palaton carried within him, a shame far easier to hide among strangers than among his own people.

Palaton found himself smiling grimly as he strode along the walkways to the contracts wing. He had resented Moameb's blatant maneuvering at first, but knew the elder had a reason for everything he did, even now, as disease-racked as he was. The elder's patient leadership by example as well as by haranguing the cadets seemed aimed more and more specifically at Palaton. "Consolidate your position with the Compact," he'd insisted. "You need more than your reputation." He'd ignored Palaton's rebuttal that he was not a politician, that he could not ply the arts of compromise.

"Compromise is nothing more than following thermals. You're a pilot, aren't you? Then, by God-in-all, go with the flow!"

The walkways about him were thronged with bodies, each moving in a pattern and direction known only to itself. Yet there was a deference shown to Palaton. He could not help but sense it. He was a *tezar*, and they gave way to him. He let his guards down a moment to bask in the subtle respect, a childish indulgence but one which his ego needed. The warmth of the touch comforted him. Still, he was no psychic vampire, he would not feed off the unsuspecting, and he prepared to put his guards back up.

A clammy, vile brush of emotion grazed him. Palaton choked as if he'd swallowed wrong and fought to maintain his outer pace. Something wrong, something evil paced him. The enmity followed him, but as his *bahdur* passed over it the feeling slipped away. Palaton felt sudden unease. His talents did not include telepathy or empathy to any great degree, but he had sensed something; he was sure of it. He turned away quickly as the corridors and wingways of the business section grew more crowded.

Once out of the crowd, he was able to appreciate the beauty of the glass and stone building. A view of the nearby snow-capped mountains, amid a dark blue sky so virgin and rich with moisture as to be nearly purple backdropped the Compact buildings. He looked for a reflection behind him and saw nothing. He scanned the passing beings, most bipedal and walking, a few in adapted carts. Nothing unusual or sinister met his survey. Palaton paused, not liking his inability to trust himself. Alone in non-Choyan territory, he had only himself to trust.

He would have to turn the corner whether he liked it or not. The corridor floors began to separate into business halls and he sought out a lift.

Once inside the lift, he spoke his floor number and conference hall identification code. The lift glided into motion, separating him from the crowd, moving to a final destination. He looked out and downward and saw nothing cut off from its pursuit of him. Palaton clicked his tongue inside his mouth. He was becoming overly cautious. Then, thinking of the hair-raising jump off the bridge, grinned madly at himself for even thinking such a thing. He was still grinning when he emerged from the lift and saw the being waiting for him outside the conference rooms.

The Abdrelik had his back to him, but Palaton's jaws clamped shut and his gorge rose all the same. He hated the amphibians, could not tolerate their personal habits or their worldviews. He almost turned away and left. The Abdrelik had heard him, however, and swung about. He was compact, squat, with a massive body that could survive in land or sea. His purplish green skin had a sheen approximating slime and on his lumpish head, a sluglike creature sat like a sideways hat, or a living wig, busily feasting on the tiny parasites and fungi which Abdrelik skin was prey to. It made sucking noises as it fed.

The Abdrelik facing him opened wide his two lidded eyes. He made a grimace approximating a Choyan smile. "Palaton," he said, his voice booming. "What an unexpected pleasure." Drool escaped from the corners of his mouth as GNask spoke.

Nothing an Abdrelik found pleasurable would please Palaton. He came to a halt. Before he could respond, two figures came between them. He recognized neither, knowing only that they were humankind, small and awkward in their movements, and when they spoke Trade, their accents were stilted.

"A moment, Master Palaton," the taller human said. "We've been waiting ... we have a contract. . . ."

The interruption was a gross breach of Compact protocol, but there was a desperation in the two that Palaton found he wanted to answer.

The Abdrelik bristled. His voice rumbled outward, a warning of the eruption soon to follow. "Palaton, we have an appointment."

If the humankind annoyed GNask, Palaton would find a need to speak to them. He bowed forward. "A moment, GNask, is all they ask. I am, after all," and his glance flicked over the chronogram, "early." He stepped aside, drawing the two beings with him, out of the Abdrelik's reach. "What can I do for you?" he asked, without taking his eyes off the bulging amphibian.

The Abdrelik's anger was plain. Even the symbiont stopped its feeding, putting out two tiny stalk eyes to look about in disturbed curiosity. Palaton suppressed a shudder as he bent to hear the humankind speak.

Humankind were new in the Compact and he'd never had to deal with them. As he looked down now, his gaze met theirs and Palaton found himself momentarily struck dumb. The eyes, he thought. The eyes were so like a Choya's that he could scarcely look away, large and luminous and expressive, eyes that he'd never thought to see in another species. *Eyes were the window of a people's soul.*

"Master Palaton?"

"I'm sorry," he said, abruptly brought back to an awareness of his surroundings. "Begin again. You have a contract?"

"We've been waiting weeks for a *tezar* to review it for assignment. No one will give us an appointment."

Humankind had no seniority in the Halls, had not yet won true acceptance in the Compact. No one would employ favors to smoth their missions. In the peculiar way of their kind, even their most senior ambassadors were transient, rarely serving more than a handful of years. One scarcely had time to introduce oneself before the humankind was gone and replaced by another. Moameb often complained of the fleeting reliability of such ambassadors. And, as the Abdrelik's expression so keenly conveyed, they were considered one step ahead of the food chain and if that became a misstep, they would be at the mercy of many of the aliens who formed the Compact.

But they had found sympathy in Palaton. He reached for the diplomatic pouch they carried. "You've had your contract evaluated by the Combine?"

The smaller one flinched. His single tone voice rose higher. "What evaluation?"

"Ah." Palaton took his hand from the pouch without retrieving it. "You've missed the most important stage of hiring a pilot. The Combine has to review all contracts and approve them before you can make an appointment for assignment."

The taller man flushed. "No one told us. I beg your pardon, Captain Palaton."

He was unfamiliar with the honorific the humankind used, but he heard the respect in the voice tone. He bowed his head slightly. "I'm glad to have been of some service. When you come before the board in the Combine, tell them you have a Class Zed priority. This means that you come from an underdeveloped system and can claim front line assistance. You'll save yourselves time that way."

They withdrew. ". . . weeks!" the smaller one's pallid voice drifted back to Palaton's hearing.

·"Help now . . ." the taller one answered mildly, as they disappeared around the corridor's curve.

GNask said nothing as they passed him, but a string of drool cascaded from the corner of his mouth to the corridor floor. He mopped his lips absently on the back of his hand.

The ambassador looked back and met Palaton's gaze. "And now, *tezar*, if you're finished playing with the lower life-forms. . . ."

"Ambassador." Palaton passed into the conference room. He paused a moment in the doorway and looked back thoughtfully. His horn crown prickled with sensation as though he could hear something normally beyond his range of hearing, but he did not actually hear anything. It merely felt as though he should be able to. He had to let the moment go. Frustration ruffled through him. He could not doubt himself, not in front of the Abdrelik, but he felt a thin edge of desperation. Was he feeling the first symptoms of the disease which would first take his *bahdur* from him, leaving him a burned-out hulk, then slowly cripple the remnant left?

He could not deal with this. But he had to. There was no one else to deal with it. Palaton took a deep breath and pushed onward.

GNask brushed past him. The room security sealed itself. He dropped his diplomatic pouch on a conference stand, thick fingers manipulating the locks, and pulled out the contract documents. The screen lit up as Palaton sat down.

"I have a need," GNask said, "for only your best. That's why I made an appointment with you, specifically, when I heard you were replacing Moameb temporarily."

Apprehension made Palaton circumspect. He

stretched a hand out on the tabletop between
them. "My presence here does not mean I will
be the *tezar* fulfilling your assignment." He
looked at the split screen delineating the contract first in Abdrelikan and then in Trade. He
kept his expression neutral, wondering if his
eyes, like the humankind's, betrayed him. Did
they show the disgust and revulsion he held for
the kind of work the Abdrelik offered? Did they
show his fear?

The split screen offered a wartime contract.
The Abdrelik gave him time to view it before
commenting.

"Lucrative," GNask said, "for us both."

"You don't need to make FTL jumps to fight
a war." Palaton looked away from the screen.

"This one must be. The Kirlians are well
armed and defended. We can't neutralize them
as the Compact has directed us to without it."
GNask paused. "We've been unable to set up a
command post within the system from which to
strike. We have to come at them from without."

"They're efficient."

"And bloody." GNask pulled his lips into a
smile. "I relish the challenge."

"You armed them."

"Of course. They wished to fend off the
Ronins."

Palaton's dislike deepened. The Ronins were
assassins in the singular and butchers in the
plural. The quills that made up their head-
dresses were far from hollow in their natural
state, filled with a deadly toxin that could drop
a foe at ten paces. Before a Ronin could go off-
planet, it had to be disarmed, but that did nothing for its naturally ferocious nature . . . or its
murderous tendencies. The Choya tapped a nail

on the tabletop, considering the subtle manipulations of the situation. "I suppose the Ronins cried foul."

GNask's flat, dark eyes sparkled. "Once again, of course. So we will disarm the oversupplied and overzealous Kirlians, and then take contract to defend them against the Ronins who will once more attempt to subjugate the Kirlians if they can avoid getting their paws burnt."

"As you say, a lucrative proposition." Palaton took a deep breath. His scalp crawled with distaste, and he took care to keep his voices pitched neutrally. "The Combine agrees you need the *tezarian* drive, it is not necessary that I agree, and so it will be supplied. I do agree that half a dozen pilots will be necessary and you'll have your assigned *tezars* within three planet spans. Satisfactory?"

"No," replied the ambassador, leaning across the table on forearms nearly as thick as Palaton's thighs. "I want a Choyan of your caliber. And I want you."

"I am not available."

"Squeamish, Palaton? Or up to your neck in local politics?"

"My personal concerns are none of your business." Menace prickled in the air of the conference room. Palaton had felt afraid that GNask would pierce his armor. Now that the Abdrelik was attempting it, rage replaced the fear. Rage was easier for Palaton to deal with. His tone became steely.

The two locked gazes.

"I disagree," said GNask. "I have a vested interest in the fall of the House of Star."

"The Wheel turns," Palaton answered evenly, though the aura about GNask seemed suddenly to flare crimson, obliterating normal vision. "That is life."

"In six hundred years of FTL flight, there has always been a House of Star at the helm." GNask considered his blunt nails. He looked up briefly. "There must be considerable upheaval and concern among your fellows. *Tezars* live a brief but spectacular existence among the Choyan, but Star has ruled since the inception of the *tezarian* drive. You are not only losing an emperor, you are losing an entire ruling House!" GNask's voice sank into a hoarse whisper.

Palaton thrust himself to his feet. "I don't speak to you of egg layers and warm water silt. You don't have the liberty to speak to me of my brethren."

The purple hue of GNask's hide deepened. His two lidded eyes blinked rapidly as he followed Palaton's movement. "I think I do. What I witnessed here this morning intrigues me, combined with the rumors."

Even though he knew he was being baited, Palaton could not help himself. "What rumors?"

"Rumors of illegal traffic between humankind and Choyan. I could scarcely credit it myself. Yet you yourself seemed drawn to them. Perhaps what I've heard is true . . . that the Choyan are culling them out and educating them."

Such a breach of Compact regulations was unthinkable, yet he had also heard intimations, but in-fighting among the Choyan was kept intensely private. What had humankind to do with it? Palaton drew a deep breath. *The eyes*, he thought, *damn those eyes!* "Your contract," he said softly, "is in peril." He heard the undertone of danger in his own voices.

GNask pulled back rapidly. "You threaten me?"

"I warn you only that no contract the Combine puts out is beyond review or appeal."

The Abdrelik smiled grimly. "You can be convincing. I see I tread on boggy ground. You can afford to be arrogant, Palaton, because no one pilots like a *tezar* and no one has a drive as reliable as the *tezarian* drive. But you'd do well to remember this is a yoke which none of us wears willingly and with the House of Star falling . . . none of us may have to much longer." GNask got to his feet and snatched back his diplomatic pouch. "I have taken no offense from your personal remarks."

He lied. But Palaton told the truth as he leaned over the tabletop and said, "But I have taken every offense from yours and if I find your or any other Abdrelik claw meddling in the works of my or any House of the Choyan, I will take your hide off you, GNask, and give it to your heirs for an egg basket."

The amphibian ambassador froze, eyes bulging. His jaws open to reveal tusks that could shred Palaton, horn crown and all. His intent to murder shimmered through the room. Palaton needed no *bahdur* to read it. GNask lifted a shaking hand as if in appeal, but it was fury which trembled in him.

Then the assassin struck.

Chapter 2

Palaton dodged before he heard the *pfft*. GNask moved also, barking out an order for the lights to go dark, and the room plunged into blackness as Palaton hit the floor. He lay still a moment, listening. His *bahdur* augmented senses overwhelmed him with the Abdrelik's fear and anger. The ambassador's perceptions flooded whatever he might have picked up from the assailant. Palaton took a deep breath and concentrated, filtering out the Abdrelik's emotions. Death was in the room, a palpable smell and chill—Palaton took hold of it, though his skin crawled as he did so—and found what he searched for. Above—he was above and moving confidently along the conference room balcony. Palaton could almost taste the assailant's bravado. Darkness did not hamper his perception.

"He can see us," he told GNask urgently and began to move under the shelter of the room's screening. The Abdrelik was on his own and Palaton wasted no more energy tracking him.

The ambassador's abrupt darkening of the room was to the assassin's advantage but Palaton had no intention of signaling his action to reverse the advantage by ordering the lights to glaring intensity. He'd have to do it manually and risk drawing the assassin's fire.

With himself and GNask in the room, Palaton had no idea which of them was the target. If he were a betting Choya, which he was not, he would have bet the Abdrelik ambassador was not a popular man. Still, his *bahdur* had been nagging at him all morning. No, Palaton thought, he himself might well be the target and as such, he would do well to keep moving.

Palaton got to one knee, shifting away from the wall screen, and mentally outlined the room's features in his mind. He knew where the manual lighting controls would be located ... near the door and at the podium where GNask had displayed the contracts.

Any target could be expected to bolt for the door, breaking the security seal and making for freedom. The assassin would do well to watch the doors. The *tezar* put his cheekbone to the flooring where the marble tiles laved his face with coolness. Palaton took a breath and moved, not quickly, but deliberately, with all the grace and elegance a Choyan body was heir to, and gained the podium. Another *pffft* split the darkness, passing his crown, skimming so close he felt it touch his aura. A comet tail with the stink of poison wafted past his nose.

Light flooded the room again, white light, white hot, so brilliant he thought his sight might be burned from his eyes. He narrowed his glance in reflex even as GNask let out an involuntary yell of surprise and annoyance.

Something fell from the balcony behind him. Palaton swung about, saw the lithe body twist and land supply on its feet. It was dark, carried about it an aura of evil, and more darkness cloaked it. There was a ripple around its edges where reality shimmered like air off hot pavement. Palaton recognized the distorted effect of illegal shielding.

The assassin had weapons and shielding; they did not. He had *bahdur*, but the facets of his talent were limited, and nothing he wished to reveal in front of the Abdrelik ambassador. The Choyan kept their secrets. He quickly sifted through his options as the assailant made another move across the width of the conference room.

Palaton pitched his voices low, demanding, using *control*, saying, *"Run"*. He gave a mental push as he spoke and looked up to see the being across from him, a dark cloud of menace, focusing on him.

Within that black cloud, he could see a denser outline and knew the assassin had hand and blowgun to its lips. Palaton's mouth went dry. "Run," he husked, voices breaking. It was accented by the faint trill of the security alarm, and Palaton realized it had been going off ever since the action started, and he had not heard it, having filtered it out. Now the noise drilled through him. Patrols would be on their way in response. The being's window of opportunity was closing rapidly.

"Run," he said a third time, and the assassin dropped its hand and weapon from its mouth.

GNask kicked the sundered door open and fresh air swept in. Their stalker's nerve broke entirely.

The assassin answered by way of action, fleeing out the rear doors of the conference hall where the security locks had been broken. The noise of the busy traffic in the outer corridors flooded in. Palaton reached into the podium and turned the lights down to normal.

"You must be a popular being," he said mildly to GNask.

The ambassador rolled heavily to his feet and got up, surprising muscular strength hidden by his bulk. His large lipped jaws worked, without immediate reply. "I owe you nothing," he said finally.

"Nor I, you."

Footfalls pounded down the corridor and Compact security police poured into the room. The patrol leader to the fore snapped out, "There's been a breach of the security locks on this conference hall. For your safety's sake, we will escort you to another meeting room."

"I'm not surprised," Palaton said dryly. He put his booted foot down on the poison dart near him, crushing it to powder. "The doors appear to have been forced open. However," and he swung about to look at GNask. His brow arched. "I believe our appointment has been concluded without incident."

They traded a look for a long moment, then the Abdrelik appeared to make the same decision Palaton had. Neither wanted to face a grueling Compact investigation into the matter. Palaton had no wish for the Compact to know he'd drawn the attention of an assassin and as for the Abdrelik, he would have multiple reasons of his own for avoiding inquiry. GNask retrieved his diplomatic pouch. He stated, "The distinguished *tezar* is correct. We've no need for further conference. Perhaps Palaton has need of your escort to his next appointment, but I do not." He brushed past the patrol and left, the room darkening for a moment as his massive body filled the doorway, shutting off the sunlight outside. It was just a momentary dimness, however, and then the Abdrelik was lost to view.

Mulling over the Abdrelik's remarks, Palaton realized that the ambassador had not made the assumption that he alone could have been the assassin's target. GNask had let Palaton know that he knew the *tezar* could also have been the prey. It bothered Palaton only in that he wondered if GNask could have made him the target.

The security force hesitated, then did a trotting survey of the privacy room. The patrol leader stopped at the door whose seal had been forced. He ran a four-fingered gloved hand along the seal.

"Subtle," he said. "*Tezar* Palaton, did anyone attempt to force entry?"

Palaton smoothed his expression. Too neutral and the patrolman would know he lied. "Not to my knowledge. We had a disagreement and the esteemed ambassador kicked the door. Quite hard. You will probably find traces of the marks from his boot heels. I think the seal may have popped under the blow. However, the integrity of the conference has been maintained and I've no complaints."

The patrolman motioned his force out the door. "Thank you. Do you wish escort . . . ?"

"No. That will be quite unnecessary. And," and the corner of Palaton's mouth quirked, "my next appointment should not be so hot tempered as an Abdrelik." He gathered his map and itinerary from the tabletop and left, the patrolman closing the door behind him. The smoothness of his exit belied his frame of mind.

The assassin had only desired to do bodily harm in an endeavor to take Palaton's or GNask's life.

GNask's guileful maneuvering had been aimed at nothing less than his soul.

He canceled his other appointments, feeling suddenly fragile, although he was certain the assassin had fled the Halls and was probably making his way off planet. His memory of the lithe body within the shielded darkness and the grace with which the assailant had regained his balance despite falling from the balcony led Palaton to the conclusion that the assassin had been one of the Nortons. The feline beings seldom hired out as assassins, but within their own tribes murder was an accepted method for attaining promotion within the ranks. The more he considered the nocturnal sight and sly movement, the more he felt he was right.

But his intuition would not tell him why. Why had he been marked? Or had the Norton been sent to kill the *tezar*, any *tezar*, who'd shown up for the contracts appointment?

And knowing this, had one of his own people sent him to the death trap?

The Wheel turns, he thought. Within the Halls of Compact, he was a *tezar*, a pilot who brought order to the patterns of Chaos, a driver who challenged the limbo of faster than light. Within his House, he was a product of the unthinkable, born of a cross outside his lines, and his mother refused to name his father, leaving Palaton to bear the brunt of her sin. Was he to be a target for her choices?

And how had GNask been able to hint slyly that the Abdrelik had known his secrets? Or had the ambassador merely been plying what he knew of all living nature, that everyone carried secret burdens and guilts? Palaton chided him-

self for letting the Abdrelik get to him. All the
ambassador could possibly know of him was
that he was a superb pilot, even among a race
of superb pilots, nothing more. He told himself
that, and did not believe it. His inner dialogue
clenched itself like a fist in his stomach.

He wandered through the conference wing
and found himself outside, where the storm-
drenched air was laced with a clean scent and
the sun shone brilliantly through slate gray
wisps. He pivoted on his heel to stare at the
roofs of the temple buildings and he found himself suddenly drawn.

He made his way against a current of flesh
hurrying the other way. The crowd deferred to
him, his passage parting a sea of beings. He
took his due as they gave it to him, assuming
the mantle of importance being a *tezar* gave
him, and used it to shield his rapidly crumbling
facade of invulnerability.

The temple wing of the Compact city was no
less impressive than the business wings, though
the politics here were often far more subtle ...
and mortal. Palaton pulled up and took a deep
breath, then recognized the outline of the Choyan
temple, and made his way to the chapel.

Once within the grounds designated for the
Choyan sanctuary, he saw only his own people.
He dodged the secretaries of the Prelate. There
were politics and workings here that would
make the gears that drove the Halls of Compact
look like a child's toy. He had come to rest in
the chapel, certain that he would be alone in
his worship.

Across the green lawns, he saw the flagstone
A-framed building, its doors open, a faint glowing light issuing from within. His stomach

eased a bit. Palaton strode inside, ducking slightly to pass under the door frame and paused at the interior altar. There he left his boots.

The quiet murmur of water permeated the building. A bird flew across the high peaked ceiling, driven in earlier perhaps by the rain, unwilling to leave or perhaps unaware that there was an exit. The secretaries of the Prelate would drive it out later, gently, waving palm fronds at it to avoid injury. For now, both the bird and Palaton were free to seek sanctuary.

Under the bare soles of his feet, the wood decking felt highly polished. He padded to the edge of a brook, eyeing the island it encircled. There were rocks here, meant to be used as seating, but it was the island he sought, and so he stepped into the brook to wade across.

The water was chill, invigorating and cleansing. The brook had been measured, and he took his own measure within it. Seven strides to the island. Seven steps of contrition. The water warmed as his feet stirred it. He climbed the island bank and stood, his mind emptied, his heart full.

He sat cross-legged in a hollow lined with dried leaves and flowers. They gave out a faint aroma as he settled down. He closed his eyes, thinking of home, his home, which had been denied to him the day his *bahdur* had been tested and he had been shown to have the qualities needed for a *tezar*. Those qualities were the only thing which kept his life from being a living hell and yet ... he thought of his mother and the Household in which he had been raised.

There were three great Houses of Choyan. The Houses of Star, Sky, and Earth. The House of

Star held the predominant number of pilots,
though the abilities were also found in Sky and
Earth. Within the Houses were divisions signifying the different Choyan positions upon the
Wheel of Life. Ascendant, then Right Wheel,
Descendant, then Left Wheel. There were mil-
lions of Choyan within the Houses and their
portions of the Wheel. Each knew his *bahdur*,
each knew his abilities and tendencies from
birth. Each strove to fulfill his potential. That
was the lifelong struggle of a Choya.

Alone among *tezars*, Palaton knew only half of
his heritage. Marked by bastard birth like the
lowliest of the Choyan classes, he knew little of
the genetic legacy he had been born to fulfill.
Although he was a pilot whose sense of direction was infallible, he himself felt lost. When
the *bahdur* failed, he would be lost, without a
heritage.

Had that bastard birth marked him for death
as well as failure?

The bird inside the sanctuary fluttered from
rafter to rafter as Palaton looked up at the noise
of its wings. The bird skimmed the top of a flo-
ral trellis and came to rest on the flexible
branches of an evergreen seedling, bouncing a
little on the willowy branch.

Palaton put a hand to his brow, rubbing the
base of his horn crown, where the weight he
bore sometimes pained him. Water splashed
abruptly behind him and the Choya sprang to
his feet, heart pumping rapidly.

There was one of the humankind in the
stream. He looked ridiculous, stick figure stiff,
trousers rolled up to his knees, and he froze in
place as Palaton stared at him.

The being smiled tentatively. "Some place,

huh?" he said in Trade, his words a little slow as if he thought in his native language and then spoke in rough translations. He did not have the Trade slang exact, but Palaton's *bahdur* augmented the Choya's hearing of the humankind's speech and made up the difference.

Palaton did not move, frozen by shock at the being's trespass.

"Do you come here often?" the humankind offered up, as he crossed the stream of water.

"No," said Palaton mildly, feeling the other's aura. He recognized the aura of the taller humankind who'd appealed to him for help before his appointment with GNask. There was nothing but benevolence approaching him. On a scale of paranormal ability, this being scored only slightly above a stone wall. Humankind reportedly set great store by such abilities, but rarely possessed even an iota of them. He relaxed as he interpreted nothing sinister about the trespasser.

"I do," said the man. "It's quiet and out of the way." He sat down on a nearby rock, put his head back, and breathed deeply.

Palaton watched as the other partook of the sanctuary's atmosphere of well-being. He came to the conclusion that this one had no idea he trespassed, no idea that this was Choyan property, no idea that he was in the heart of a temple. He contemplated sending the being out, but his curiosity kept him from this automatic response. He forced himself to resettle. "There is," he remarked, "a peace about this place."

"I can't take it outside. The canals, the lake . . ." the being's single voice faded. "None of my briefings described it the way it is. Why do you . . . why do you build the Halls here?"

"To remind us. Sorrow was found this way. We crossed its path long after its people reached their sad destiny. We don't know why or how—we only know that we, too, could reach the same destiny if we do not stop to negotiate among ourselves. Perhaps you have something similar in your history?"

"I don't—" the being halted. "Pearl Harbor," he said, "I guess. It's a war memorial. Off an island shore where most of the Pacific fleet went down. After a hundred and some years, the sunken vessels still leak oil and the men aboard are buried within their hulks. It's sobering."

"Sometimes we need to be sobered into making peace."

The man nodded. He rolled his pant legs back down, hiding his pale skin. "You're the *tezar* who helped us earlier, aren't you?"

Palaton smiled wryly. The awe of his office no longer had the being tongue-tied. Perhaps it was because they both sat, wet and barefooted, within the parklike confines of the temple. "I am."

"I want to thank you for your aid. The protocol of the Halls is something I'm still struggling with. I'm John Taylor Thomas and I'm newly elected."

"As are all your people." Forty years was a minute amount of time in the Compact. Palaton did not wonder that the beings were struggling with understanding their place within it and its workings.

The man fell silent. Palaton was struck by the similarity of their hair locks, though the humankind's were far shorter and he had no horn crown to protect his skull casing. The being looked up. "I just met a Quino," he said, "who claimed to have known one of our long dead American presidents. It sort of rocked my sensibilities."

"Don't let it," Palaton replied. "He may well have, though the Quinonan aren't known for their truthfulness. More likely, it was one of his hive which had done so, and he retains the memory. The Quinonan were exploring your system for centuries before they reported your presence to the Compact. Such exploration is illegal and the effects of it will color proceedings for decades yet to come." Palaton personally did not like the insect beings, with their undead white skin, bulging heads, and immense flat eyes, but he most resented the psychic shield they projected, intended to generate abject fear in others. He felt the Quinonan to be compassionless bullies. The hive conscience was not a favorite of his to deal with. He offered a further bit of wisdom. "The politics of the Halls are not confined. They spill out everywhere. It is not wise to let your guard down."

"If not here, where? If not with friends, with whom?" the man answered. He stood. Palaton looked into those remarkable eyes.

"You're aware you trespass?"

The other shrugged with a fluidity of movement Palaton had not expected these angular beings to possess. "And will you ask me to leave?"

Palaton laughed dryly at himself. He should have known no motive was so uncomplicated. "Now you know why Choyan have crowns of bone. Otherwise, it would be easy for an enemy to sneak up and brain us. You are persistent, whoever you are. You have tracked me to ground. What do you want?"

"The stars," the man answered intently, suddenly meeting the Choya's gaze, and the expression on Thomas' face struck a blow to Palaton's soul. "Give us the freedom of the stars."

"It's not mine to give."

"The *tezarian* drive. Surely you can install it in any vessel you wish."

"There is no *tezarian* drive without a *tezar* to pilot it." Inwardly, Palaton felt intense sorrow. Here was another race which would dig at him for his secrets, which would despise him for keeping them.

"Without it, without access to contracts, we're hostage in our own system. The Abdreliks consider us part of the food chain, the Quinonan use us for barter like devalued coins."

"I cannot give what you cannot understand, even if I would break the laws of my people." Palaton spread his hands. "We contract ourselves to your will, insofar as the Combine will allow. I can give you nothing more."

"You mean you will give me nothing more." He ran a hand through his hair, a gesture of futility that Palaton read well. "Now you've seen what all the Compact talks about, a human begging for crumbs of help. You have it all, and we're dying, and none of you will help us. You take our children and give nothing back." The humankind paused, swallowing back what else he might have said.

That pricked sharply at Palaton. Here was another who hinted at what the Abdrelik had insinuated. "What do you mean? What children?"

"My child," said John Taylor Thomas urgently. "I don't want to give her up. Tell them for me."

"We don't take children. You're talking about

the grossest kind of exploitation. It's against our laws as well as those of the Compact."

John Taylor Thomas gave him a scathing glance. "I thought," he said slowly, "you were different. A captain among the Choyan, disinterested in political games. Our children leave. Choyan take them. They never come back. All we have in their wake are vague promises of help, of advancement. But even that we don't receive. I want our children back, *tezar*. I thought I could ask you for help." Without further word, the man recrossed the brook and gathered up his shoes.

"What children?" Palaton called after him desperately, but the man kept walking. Palaton read the lines of his stiff stick-figure form and saw nothing of defeat there. Guileless creatures, direct and frank. What had the ambassador meant? What had GNask befouled by mentioning it with his sly innuendo? What had Moameb known that he did not?

Chapter 3

John Taylor Thomas made it back to his compound where security guards stiffly saluted him and watched him enter. He could feel them staring at his back. He wondered if they could hear his heart thumping inside his chest. He slapped his palm over the lock to his private quarters, felt the briefly irritating wash of the retina check pierce his eyesight, then was inside, safe, alone.

He collapsed on the bed, feet dangling over the edge, gaze fastened on the ceiling, and waited for his heartbeat to return to normal. His ears rushed with the *swish* of adrenaline driven pressure. Slowly, he regained control again.

The Choyan had a natural self-assurance that bordered on arrogance. He could accept that. He thought perhaps that he had found one who would level with him, one who would listen and respond in kind, devoid of the political dance that seemed to permeate everything said and done within the Halls of the Compact. Disappointment keened through Thomas that he had not. The *tezar*, though gracious, had been as opaque as any of his race.

Thomas sat up on the bed. He loosened his diplomatic tie from around his neck. His compound window overlooked the rugged purple mountains, a far better view than that commanded by his office window. He stared at the horizon as if it could offer him the advice he most desperately needed.

He'd run for office on a techno-eco cleanup slate and now he was in danger of losing his backing, a volatile constituency if ever there was one. Only the e-t ambassadors were elected, but the reasoning there had been good. No one branch of government, national or international, nor any one country, could then control the fate of the world by mere appointment. Campaigns, however, were financially risky. He could not have done what he did without surreptitious backing. For himself, he had never questioned whether the price was too high. He'd been prepared to pay it. Earth needed technological assistance to clean up its ecological messes, and the aliens could provide that, if they would. It was time to take a stance of strength in the Halls of the Compact and demand assistance. He would demand that assistance. He could show that strength. He would pay the price.

But now his backer had contacted him and told him the debt would be called in and how, and he realized he'd given away his first born child.

Thomas blinked fiercely at the window, his tie clenched and crumpled in his knotted hand. There was no one to rant and rail against. He'd never had a means of contacting them, they contacted him when they wanted him to know something. He'd been warned to maintain silence. He'd broken it today in his overpowering need to save his daughter, and the *tezar* had either feigned ignorance—or Thomas was dealing with a fringe group of Choyan, a splinter group, and there would be no help for him because there was no open knowledge of these activities.

He did not think Palaton had been lying. There had been an intelligent openness in the alien's eyes which had bespoken silently what could never be said aloud. So where did that leave Thomas now? What options had he?

He could fall back on a strategy the Americans had perfected: if a people will not help you, perhaps their enemies will.

Thomas reached for his communications line and signaled his secretary. She answered briskly.

"Betty, get me an appointment with Ambassador GNask. And make sure it's after lunchtime or whenever that thing's eaten."

"Yes, sir," the woman said without missing a beat. Thomas closed off the line. His knotted hand relaxed and the crumpled tie fell to the carpeted floor where it lay, unheeded.

GNask lowered himself into the semi-sludge bath awaiting him. The tepid waters felt both cool and warm as they washed silkily about his body. His legs trembled a moment as the water and the seating took the weighty bulk of his body. He gave a long, breathy sigh. His *tursh* had settled upon his forearm, feeding, and as the bath made it more mellow, it simply lay contentedly. GNask stroked it fondly. His *tursh* was of the family line, a lineage traceable as far back as Abdreliks traced their symbiont, perhaps even to the first partners. An Abdrelik was only as good as his *tursh*, his family liked to quote, and theirs were as prominent as any. He sorrowed for the lesser classes and for the armed forces who could not take their symbionts with them, settling instead for topical creams to keep their skin clean and pure. No. A *tursh* provided more, much more, and he owed much of his success to his. He stroked it a last time and sank back into his bath, resting the heavy folds of his neck against the rim of the soaking tub.

He had been basking for the better part of an hour, water swirling about his bulk from time to time as the tub recirculated and warmed it, when the wall screen illuminated. His heavy-jowled secretary filled the window.

"Your appointment is here, your honor."

GNask positioned himself more solidly upon the podium seat inside the tub. "Admit him," the ambassador droned, rousing from the calm stupor he'd allowed himself to be lulled into. He cooled the water temperature, bringing himself back to alertness.

With a click and a nearly inaudible whoosh, the wall panels opened to admit a small and diffident figure. He frowned and felt a rumble of anger and hunger boiling up from deep within him as the junior ambassador of the humankind stepped in. GNask stifled his reaction and reached for his *tursh*, stroking it to calm himself. He did not occupy the position in the Compact that he did by allowing base emotions to rule his judgment. He would not ruin spans of work in one imprudent moment.

The man looked pale, but then, most of his kind did, even those with skin the color of fine mud. He glanced around the bathing room and then perched upon an upholstered guesting chair without being invited to do so, and GNask felt his jaw tighten. What was it about these beings that so inspired the worst in him?

Perhaps it was their huge eyes and their fearful look, the look of prey flushed out of the shallows, unable to think of a way to fight free. No sporting game these, but fodder, nothing more and often much less. They had soiled their own waters almost beyond redemption and had the nerve to come whining to the Compact to be saved—they, a race which had achieved space!

His symbiont quivered in agitation under his stroke as it absorbed the humors of his temper. GNask opened his eyes wider, knowing the voluptuous folds of his face would be emphasized and spoke. "Good afternoon, ambassador."

The man nodded, saying, "I understand I owe you an apology, ambassador, and have come to deliver it in person."

GNask's attention was piqued. The being had some spine and sensibility, after all. GNask liked spine. It made the meat easier to pull away from the smaller bones. "Your apology is noted, John Taylor Thomas, and also the admirable point that you have delivered it yourself, in person."

"It seemed the proper protocol." The humankind shifted. He seemed paper thin, but GNask could see a wiry strength in the way he moved. He would be fast, on foot. Flailing, in the water. His guts rumbled a second time. "I don't expect you to sympathize, your honor, but politics on my world are complicated. My predecessor does not care if I disgrace myself or my world. Few rules of protocol, or, indeed, briefings of any kind on procedures, were left for me." A fleeting expression passed over the humankind's face, an expression that unfortunately reminded GNask of a Choyan smile. "I must resort to learning by experience and I regret deeply if any of my clumsy attempts have offended you."

"The matter is forgotten." GNask waved his hand. He found himself fast losing interest in the being. He reached out and retuned the water temperature before dropping his hand back into his bathwater.

"I know your honor has many appointments, but might you indulge me with a question or two before I leave?"

His *tursh* purred slightly on his arm. GNask's gaze flickered over it quickly. The humankind must have enough of a personality to please it. That thought alone brought his attention back to the man. He looked up, meeting the other's expression.

"If I can enlighten you in minor matters, I will do so."

"You are one of the founders of the Compact, are you not? The Abdrelik race and the Choyan race."

"Yes. Not myself personally, but I have lineage going back to those first days."

"Who discovered Sorrow? I've done a little research on it, but the roots are obscure."

GNask felt his face folds crease with irony. "No one is certain. It may have been a Quino explorer, or a Choyan *tezar* or one of our raiders."

"And the ... people ... of Sorrow ... were like that always?"

"From the moment of scouting. A terrible enemy, eh, to have done that to a people and then move on? It is one of the reasons we came together in Compact. There is an enemy out there perhaps greater than any of our petty rivalries."

"But no one knows what happened."

"The quartz which binds them has been difficult to date, to analyze, even to penetrate for core samples. Modulation readings are about all we can get . . . and that is affected by the matter trapped within it."

A fleeting look, a tiny shadow, passed over the man's face. Gnask knew nothing of its inner meaning. He wondered if it indicated deception. He would have to take time to study this race's body language. The vocal nuances of Trade would be too difficult to pin down with this one's poor accent. "If you are interested," GNask offered, "I can have my secretary access background material from our archives, material not normally available to general audiences although it is not classified."

"That would be greatly appreciated."

GNask felt a surge of pleasure. This one might be easy to introduce to the Abdrelik viewpoint, so different, so much purer, than that of the Choyan. Although this man carried no weight in any of the greater committees, a prudent vote here and there, even in lesser decisions, was always a plus. "Why do you ask?"

The man shifted. "A morbid interest on my part, I guess. The interference of discoverers upon new entry worlds . . . the tampering. . . ."

"Tampering? Do you think Sorrow has been tampered with?"

Another shift of weight. Uneasiness, perhaps? GNask leaned forward slightly. His *tursh* put out stalk eyes, reflecting the change of temperament. The humankind said, reluctantly, "My people tend to think of themselves first."

The Abdrelik followed that train of thought swiftly, answering, "The Quinonan behavior on your world is to be regretted. However, you have moved past that. There were sanctions offered as recompense on your behalf, as I recall."

"There are others. . . ." John Taylor Thomas' voice trailed off. He cleared his throat. "My predecessor left a task for me, a task that he was unable to complete, a task that transcends our inherent rivalries for power. If we prove our case, there will be other compensation due us— aid we desperately need. I'm sure you're aware of our plight."

GNask nodded, letting his eyelids fall slightly, looking less alert, more bored, not letting his subject know that he hung on every word, was dissecting all he could from the man's behavior as to the truth and reasoning behind the facade of his words. "There are committees to help your research," GNask prompted.

"The ... subjects ... of my research are greatly revered. I have been blocked at every attempt and don't think I'll be getting much more help."

The silted water in the bath surged with GNask's abrupt movement. The man would not have been so bold as to come to him, accusing the Abdrelik of tampering. Therefore, he came aware of the uneasy balance of power forever seesawing between the Abdreliks and the Choyan. Without saying so, he accused the Choyan. No doubt, he hoped the Abdreliks had been keeping a careful watch on their rivals in power ... which they had. There had been shadowy reports of Choyan in territories where Choyan never ventured, Choyan who could not be traced back to Cho or their predominant Houses. Now here was another nebulous suggestion. He had pondered much over the assassination attempt on the *tezar* Palaton which had posed a threat to himself as well. Perhaps there was a motive here which could be uncovered and used against the Choyan bloc. He did not think the humankind had the courage to order an assassination, but if the Choyan had been tampering, there were other races which would. GNask interrupted the man before he could utter another word.

"This matter will take some thought and consultation on my part. My committees take a great deal of my time, but perhaps there is a member of my junior staff who might be able to give you some insight. I suggest, ambassador, that you make an appointment with my secretary as you leave. Give me some time . . . a day or two . . . we'll see if we can't find some cooperation for you."

John Taylor Thomas stood up. "Thank you, your eminence. I am in your debt."

Their gazes met. As alien to him as the humankind was, GNask felt the sudden surety that this being knew what it was to incur such a debt—and to pay it. He nodded. The humankind bowed and left.

GNask sat there, contemplating his next move until his bathwater turned quite cold and his *tursh* climbed to his head, retreating from the chill.

Chapter 4

The dance of manipulation and profit that marked the Halls of the Compact exhausted Palaton by the time he left and made the outward-bound FTL jump for home. A connecting flight brought him closer and he rented a cabcar to finish the journey to Blue Ridge.

There were three main flight schools: the Commons, where those of the general population who were tested and proved talented were trained; the Salt Towers, named for the nearby gigantic salt cliffs and the site where most of the elite scions of the ruling Houses were trained; and Blue Ridge, his destination. Every *tezar* had an affinity for the school which had trained him. Palaton was no different and he found the anticipation building as the conveyance brought him closer to the home he was fondest of. He got out as the cabcar settled to the driveway surface and took a deep breath in relief. A windstorm had swept through, leaving behind its spice-scented fragrance, for the winds had come across the hills where the groves and brush grew wild and abundant with the pungent flower called *tinley*. The aroma almost made up for the damage, swirled banks of fine dust here and there, green feathery branches of the fragile thara trees down everywhere.

Located on the outlying borders of the city holdings, the barracks looked as if Blue Ridge had borne the brunt of the wind's fury, but it had been constructed to do so and the cadets were out sweeping walkways and grafting to limit tree damage. They paid him little attention, though he could almost feel them staring after him as he walked up the drive.

His master was waiting for him at the front doors. The elder smiled broadly. His hair was silvered about his horn crown, and the lines in his face nearly obscured the jewelry he had imprinted under the healthy bloom of his skin, yet his dark eyes flashed with amusement. For an ill Choya, Moameb looked remarkably fit. Palaton felt his brow furrow in irritation as Moameb spoke.

"It must have been a successful trip," he said. "I heard you nearly got yourself killed."

"You're looking well," Palaton answered dryly. He wondered why the other had pleaded invalidity, sending Palaton to the Halls of the Compact in his place.

Moameb had the grace to flush, bringing out the tracing of his facial jewelry in bright contrast. He scratched at the base of his horn crown, above the right temple. It was a quick, diffident gesture, like a twitch. Then he answered, "You'd be surprised how quickly my health returned after they grounded me."

The mildness of the elder's words belied the punch behind them. Palaton felt as though he'd been gutted as he sucked in his breath. Grounded. Never to fly again. His *bahdur* so extinguished that he would never again do what he'd been intended to do. The disease had eaten at him until he was terminal . . . but he might as well already be dead if he could not fly. He got words out past a suddenly contracted throat. "I—"

Moameb cut him off. "I don't want to hear it." There was an edge to his Choyan double voice which told Palaton that the elder didn't lie. He did not want to hear pity or sympathy. He stood aside in the doorway. "Come in and tell me what happened."

Behind them, the soothing strains of a *lindar* recording floated almost inaudibly on the air. The hall smelled of fried bread and Palaton almost smiled, thinking of the cadets' evening meal. He stepped inside and felt the homeliness of the hall wrap about him like a cocoon. Here was where he had been taken in, when his mother's Householding would not have him, and here was his House, if a *tezar* could ever make a barracks a House. But this was not his alone, he'd shared it with eighty cadets and of that eighty, sixty had lived to become *tezars*. Attrition wore at their numbers daily . . . death and burnout, so that there were never enough. The great barracks were never full, but they were never empty either. From this cocoon issued forth beings of incredible ability and terrible destiny. If they did not die of the disease, they died of its consequences, lost in the limbo of an FTL jump, lost in Chaos, drawn into its patterns without hope or end.

Moameb pushed him into a chair by the solar hearth and while he basked in its warmth, which Palaton felt a little too keenly but managed to ignore, knowing that older bones needed more heat, he told his instructor what had happened. He mentioned the ambassador's sly innuendo of collusion with the humankind, but did not tell him of the disturbing trespass in the chapel. He wanted to have Moameb's reactions to the Abdrelik's accusations first.

Moameb looked at him keenly. "As you describe it, the Abdrelik was at least as worried as you."

"I think so."

"Then he could not have sent the assassin."

Palaton's brow quirked.

"Don't discount the ambassador," Moameb warned. "He's as likely a murderer as I've ever met. But neither do I think you have to walk about looking over your shoulders. The chances are that the Norton's target (if it was a Norton which sounds likely, thank your stars it wasn't a Ronin) was the *tezar* who'd come to negotiate the new contracts. It could as likely have been me as you . . . or any Choya."

"And I was flattered."

Moameb laughed. "A jaded response if ever I heard one, which means I would have given anything to have seen the look on your face. You hide yourself well, Palaton. As for Choyan involvement with humankind, there may be some minor meddling—what new race does not intrigue us? But nothing to the extent that the Abdrelik suggests. The Quinonan are infamous for that, not us. How fatigued are you?"

Palaton considered the empty glass of brew in his hand which had helped to lubricate his tale. He was somewhat, although not altogether, satisfied with Moameb's response. He determined not to let the man's last words haunt him. He'd come home, and he needed the respite. "I'm more mellow than tired," he evaluated.

"Then come with me. I've been grounded, but I'm still an observer here. I'm due at the plateau in a few minutes. Come watch a run or two with me. There'll be no one about to do business with before this evening anyway." Moameb fingered the observation glass hung upon a thong around his neck.

Palaton considered the proposal. The raw edge of excitement and adrenaline a new cadet lived on could be contagious. He needed that feeling, he thought. The newness of flight and all its abilities. He stood up. "Let's go."

They caught a skimcraft to the plateau and then a cog rail up its side to the great, wind flattened mesa, where nothing grew that had not made its peace with that invisible current. The grass and brush were wiry, limber, and tough, growing low and twisted. As the railcars crested the plateau's edge, Palaton felt the wind in his mane. As it had been on Sorrow, it was spring in this hemisphere of his planet, spring just past the edge of winter, and there was a chill to the breeze. He could see the rows of thrust gliders and the cadets milling around them as their instructors sent them about their various duties around the dual launchers.

"First launch?" he asked. He was not empathic, but he could feel their nervousness and excitement clear across the expanse of the plateau. He would have to be as dead and dull as stone not to.

"No . . . this should be their third run."

"Ah." The third run was the flight which separated the *tezars* from the cadets. They'd flown with all their senses as well as their innate talents. Now they would be sensory deprived and their *bahdur* alone would keep them aloft and safe. They would be monitored, but there were always fatalities from here on out in the training. The knowledge was sobering.

Moameb took his elbow. "This should be the largest graduating class since yours," he said.

"The attrition hasn't even started yet."

"But their test scores are high. We hope to lose the smallest percentage ever." The silver-haired Choya lengthened his stride. "They're waiting for us."

Palaton drew salutes and sidelong stares as he joined the class. He could tell from the crimson patches on their sleeves that this was the second wing, the second ranked grouping among the cadets. Blue wing must be flying from the campus in the mountains where crashes were invariably fatal, and it was possible green wing was not yet off the simulators back at the barracks holding.

Thrust gliders were basic: catch a thermal once catapulted, and you were free until landing, and that should not be too difficult from these heights. The more complicated aircraft and shuttles and deep space liners would come seasons down the line. First came your senses, your ability to trust in those genetic, innate talents bred into you . . . then came the machinery invented to give sustained flight.

They looked younger than he remembered. Palaton hid this rueful thought as he paced among them. They moved in waves, first jostling forward to touch him as though he imparted luck, then dropping back out of deference, only to eventually grow bold again. Tall even for a Choya, he looked over the tops of their heads and met Moameb's gaze in amusement.

He looked away as he wondered what role his old mentor could now possibly play in the development of this wing when he had not even the *bahdur* to help keep a cadet aloft if he or she failed. He watched as Moameb bent to the equipment bins, which had been battered by the years and initialed by the various classes until they were beyond repair, and began to issue deprivation helmets.

All the cadets, male and female alike, had worn their hair down, simple and without adornment, because of the helmets. Now they came forward shyly as their names were called and took the gear. The helmets were fierce-looking, dark and hooded. Palaton hid a shudder as he looked at them and remembered how he'd hated them. Not for himself—but for his friends who'd died wearing them. A cadet usually did not wash out of the wing at this stage. He usually died in training.

There were cadet graduates with purple starstrike badges on their shoulders waiting beside the noses of the thrust gliders. There was one graduate for each plane . . . the graduate would be the safety net for the plane's pilot. Their *bahdur* should be strong enough to assist any pilot in trouble. It was a good net in theory, but the reality was sometimes far from it. The graduates had not yet passed their final exams; in fact, part of that exam was working here with the new flights. And, with two catapults loaded and ready, the flights were about to begin.

"Who's up first?"

Palaton turned at the clear, concise voices of the wing instructor. He wasn't mistaken, it was Kedra coming out from behind the catapult where she had been checking the launch mechanism. He thought he might have flushed, for he had once had an affinity for this tall, striking

female, her bronzed mane long enough to curl
to her waist in the back. She looked at him and
smiled fleetingly before turning away with her
stylus and automatic pad poised in her hands.
"Well?"

The red wing was suddenly mute, their bravado fled. The first launch would be a terrible
thing to witness. They stood with their dark helmets tucked under their elbows, the neutral colors of their flight suits stark witness against
their skin, highlighting their fear.

"I'll go," Palaton found himself saying. "I
haven't blind-flighted in a long while. It's good
for the soul."

Moameb gave him a triumphant smile as he
tossed out a helmet and now he knew why the
elder had brought him up to the plateau.

Learn by example, the elder had always taught
him. And he'd been brought up to this wind
flattened mesa to give that example. Palaton
gripped the helmet between his palms until the
material was no longer chill, then he turned and
strode to the plane that was held in the catapult
launch.

Kedra gave him a leg up onto the wing. The
purple star-strike badge of the graduate flashed
as he reached up and gripped Palaton's boot as
well. The instructor stepped back and let her
student say, "I'm here if you need me."

"As a *tezar* will always be for another," Palaton
replied automatically, and the young Choya's lips
tightened with pride as he nodded and backed
away. Palaton settled himself in the pilot's seat.
He moved it back for his legs, but there was
little he could do about the spread of his hips
and shoulders. With a more mature body than
most of the glider pilots, he fit in the cockpit as

well as he could. He checked the wing flaps and the tail rudder and stick control. Then he picked up the ebony helmet from his lap and secured it over his head.

Instantly, there was no light except the faint spidery red flickering from his own eyes which faded as his sight adjusted to the total darkness. Horn crown obscured by the helmet, he lost his hearing as well. He smelled nothing but old, rank sweat worn into the helmet's lining. Taste gone except for the sudden, dry cottony feeling in his mouth. He tried to lick his lips in surprise. Fear? No ... surely not. Anticipation, rather.

The thrust glider shuddered. He recognized it as the catapult arm moving into release position. He felt a feather light touch of his guide's *bahdur*, acknowledged it and sealed it away. If and when he needed another's eyes, he would open up for that *bahdur*, but he would not be a *tezar* if he needed it.

The mechanism launched. The thrust glider arced forth with a gut-wrenching suddenness that abruptly shoved his head back against the headrest. He found he'd been holding his breath and as the glider hurtled forward he forced himself to relax.

Palaton opened up his *bahdur*. He did not need to see the ground to sense its aura, but it was the wind he reached for, moving the stick and paddling his feet gently on the controls. He did not care if he was off the mesa's edge or not—the wind was there for him, tamer after the previous windstorm, and he rode it.

There was a purity in glider flight, like sex without any precautions or entanglements of intention. His heart beat faster in exhilaration as he felt the glider take the thermal and soar, far, far above the mesa and the ground below it. The auras bloomed like a rainbow after a tempest.

He wanted to hang glide all day, and he could if he could find the right thermals, but he knew the red wing below was watching him and aching for the freedom he now had. He began to bring the glider down, wafting gently until the dry lake bed at the mesa's base sent him a message of its aura and he came down. Three bounces and he was skidding to a stop.

There were instructors on the lake bed as well, waiting to load the glider onto the railroad and take it back topside, and one of them knocked on the canopy. He took off his helmet and popped it open. The Choya grinned at him. Palaton grinned back foolishly.

They were lined up for their chance when he gained the mesa again. He'd seen three go off after him, as the cog rail cars painstakingly geared their way up the side of the plateau. The first two had gone off achingly pure and fine. The third had wobbled and taken a heart-stopping plunge before settling.

Moameb was waiting for him and took the helmet from his hands. "You set them back on their heels," his mentor said with a fierce pride in his voices. "You should have seen the look on their faces."

"It felt good." He took a bottle of juice from one of the graduates and drank deeply. "What about that third launch?"

"She panicked, but the senior cadet got her straightened out." Moameb's tone dropped into neutral. They both knew the cadet could not afford any more distrust. Either she had the instinct—or she didn't.

Palaton watched as five more launched. Then, his concentration disrupted by a vague sense of unease, his attention was drawn to one of the purple star-strike badges. She stood rigidly, the cords of her slender throat tight, her eyes closed, and he knew she was locked into her talent. But the glider had not yet left the second catapult. It was scheduled to go next.

The thrust glider trembled, mimicking the panicked movements of the pilot within it. Locked in yet trying desperately to get out. He looked to it and saw the cadet clawing at the canopy. The glider shook heavily and he saw the catapult arm react, going back to release it prematurely, while the other plane was still in its airspace. He caught Moameb's arm and yelled, but the catapult shot forward and the glider arced upward. The cadet assigned to it keened aloud, swayed, and dropped.

Chapter 5

The errant plane pitched skyward. There was a heart-stopping moment as the senior cadets broke rank, running to the fallen Choya'i. The crimson wing froze in place, torn between the unconscious female and the two pilots in immediate jeopardy. Palaton took a deep, gulping breath as he flung his chin up and watched the gliders.

He thought for a moment they would collide, but then the second hit the faint backdraft of the first and veered away slightly. He was reminded of fighting hawks as they neared and sculled away. But the pathway of the first had been invaded enough as it plunged off the mesa's edge that it bucked into a thermal, then a wind shear hit it and it tumbled dramatically.

Moameb put his glass to his eye and let out a sound. "He's hit his head. He's unconscious."

Kedra called out, her imperious voice cutting across the panic, "Give it lift!"

The senior cadets had been grouped about their fallen comrade. Now they looked to their instructor. Simple levitation would not keep the glider aloft ... it would take the combined efforts of those who possessed that talent. It would mean abandoning the other pilot in the runaway glider.

Every instant counted. The second plane had, by good fortune, caught a warm thermal, despite its wing waggling, and rose off the mesa. "I've got it," Palaton said, in spite of himself.

The cadets with the purple star-strike on their shoulders leaned together, clasping hands, and he knew their talent arrowed after the first plane. A joyous shout told him they'd steadied it, they had it cradled, even as he sent his *bahdur* streaming after the panicked pilot. *Bahdur* couldn't feel cold, could it? Yet his mind seemed lanced with ice as he reached after the Choya. He found the cadet still thrashing under the canopy, unable to get his helmet off, clawing at the straps under his chin, his horn crown swelling with the battering and the helmet becoming ever tighter.

The Choya felt Palaton's bright touch. It flared into the darkness surrounding him like a beacon. For a moment, Palaton felt panic himself as the other latched onto him, then he carefully separated himself and the student. That was what he must have done to his observer, leeching away her soulfire, driving her down, and that was what he would do to Palaton if he let him.

A parasite like this deserved to die. Palaton's thought filtered through the battle to reach the other, and he pushed it away. He had no right to judge. Determinedly he reached out with just enough *bahdur* so that the other ought to be able to see the auras and thermals and guide the glider.

But the panicked pilot seemed unable to take those threads. It was all or nothing. Palaton felt the cadet clawing at his mind shield even as he must still be flailing at the glider's restraints.

There was real power behind the cadet's desperation, power which frightened Palaton in spite of his experience. He thought of drowning Choya who could pull their would-be rescuers down with them.

Moameb's hand fell heavily on his shoulder, breaking Palaton's thought, as his mentor said, "Do what you can. The other's down safely."

Palaton blinked. He'd been locked in the other's visual deprivation, in total darkness, as if he once again wore the helmet. Now he could see the glider spiraling downward and knew the cold wind icing across them carried a wind shear at the mesa's edge. Once the plane hit that—

"He's fighting me," Palaton got out, and his throat hurt, and he knew the cords of it were standing out tightly. The base of his crown was stipled with sweat.

"Do what you can," the other repeated.

Palaton took a deep breath and went sightless again as he delved into the other's dilemma. He felt it as the pilot grabbed the stick and oversteered, experiencing the downward plunge, unsure of how to right it, unable to distinguish up from down or even right from left. The glider swooped, its responses set for the slightest touch, overreacting with the terrified cadet's heavy-handedness at its controls.

His *bahdur* flared orange in the darkness. Palaton let as much of it go as he could afford to, giving the desperate pilot whatever he needed and more. He felt himself being swallowed up and knew that drowning sensation again.

Then his *bahdur* went out. He lost it all. His jaws yawned in a shared silent scream with the Choya as the plane went down.

Moameb's touch brought him back. Palaton found himself on his knees in the wiry prairie grass, its bruised scent rising around him. He looked up. Moameb had paled.

"An ugly way to lose a cadet," the elder said, and held out his hand. "There was nothing you could have done. *Bahdur* or not, his actions brought the glider down as surely as the wind shear."

As suddenly as the wind had come up, it dropped away. Palaton looked across the mesa edge where dust rose in a smoky cloud and he could hear the thin shouts of the landing crew. Now there was no wind shear. Another minute or two longer. . . .

Shaken, he got to his feet. Moameb's hand was warm and he kept his clasped inside it for a moment. His *bahdur* had failed. Again. Bile rose inside his throat. And the cadet was dead because of it. He needed to tell the elder of his failure. It must have shown in his eyes.

"There was nothing else you could have done," Moameb said and squeezed his hand tightly before letting it go.

Kedra strode across the plateau. She put a hand to Palaton's temple, brushing back a stray lock of hair and wiping away the perspiration of his effort. "Thank you," she murmured gently, "for trying."

He could not respond at first. How could he tell her of his failure? That his *bahdur* had gone, leaving them both stranded? That he was no more a *tezar* than the dead Choya? "I—" he got out, but no more. Kedra dropped her hand and turned to shout instructions.

"Get the Choya'i down from the mesa. She's in shock." She looked back to Palaton. "That glider downed more than one cadet." She paused as a litter bearing the Choya'i was carried past them, her classmates solemnly encircling it. She waited until they were out of earshot and loading the railroad cars. "She's been paired with him before. She knew he was leeching and told no one. She thought she could handle it. The crash was her failure as well as his death."

"Lovers?" Moameb said.

Kedra shook her head. "No. Not yet. But indications are that she augmented his *bahdur* to help him get by."

Or that he just took it from her, as he'd tried to take Palaton's before Palaton's talent had abruptly abandoned them both. He stood on the mesa and felt like a blackened, flameless, burned-out torch, listening hollowly to them speculate over the accident.

Kedra put her hand on his wrist. "Let's go down," she said. "There's nothing more to be done here." She looked across the plateau, staring off at the horizon. "Perhaps it was for the best," she murmured, thinking aloud.

Palaton feared to correct her.

The heady smells of dinner permeated the barracks by the time they got back down. The skimcraft ran in shifts, taking twelve at a time until all of the crimson wing, the purple star-strikes, and instructors were brought back. Palaton's stomach churned at the odors as he walked into the hall.

He ate because he should, chewing mechanically, seated among diners who kept silent in a way that was unnatural for the cadets' hall. The first death of the new classes always had that effect. He'd forgotten it. Forgotten the honor of the new *tezars* at fulfilling their destiny and the starkness of the reality that even that honor might not always be good enough. Not only had a pilot died, but one of the graduates had failed a portion of her passing exams. It was not enough to be able to fly. A *tezar* had to be able to support his brethren in any way he or she could. This was their strength.

He watched the Choya'i once or twice. She held herself rigid on the bench, picking at the food on her platter, pushing it around with her two-tined fork, not eating, but busying herself so that she would not have to meet the pitying glances of her fellows. He wished he had words to comfort her.

As the long, rough-hewn tables were cleared, the inner doors blew open, carrying in the pungent scent of deep space liners and landing fields where the sands were turned to obsidian by the heat. Instinctively, the pelt hairs rose at the back of Palaton's neck as he turned to see who'd swept in.

Nedar stood in the archway, his black mane wind-tossed between the wings of his horn crown. The gaze of his dark eyes ranged across the immense room. He stripped off his flight jacket and let it drop to the floor. A green wing cadet scurried to pick it up and hang it in the corner.

Nedar was of the House of Sky, a *tezar* with the instincts of a predator, a survivor, one of the best combat pilots the Choyan had ever spawned. He strode forward arrogantly, hailing Moameb.

"Elder! A round of brew to remember the fallen. It's too quiet in here." He straddled a bench.

Kedra pushed herself away from the instructors' table at the head of the hall. The servers were poised, waiting for confirmation of Nedar's order. She frowned a second, then gave a brisk nod. They ran to get kegs and tankards. She crossed the hall.

"Nedar, a pleasure to see you." Her voices communicated that pleasure, with an undertone which reminded exactly who was in charge of the cadets' barrack and who was an interloper. Palaton admired the subtlety, though he thought it would probably be lost on Nedar.

"The pleasure is all mine. The pilots' hall is too empty tonight. I heard Palaton was breaking bread with the cadets and I came to keep him company." Palaton lost his mental bet. Nedar took a foaming tankard and downed it.

More likely the pilot had come to bring Palaton back, anxious to learn what new contracts were being offered. Palaton had not yet posted them. Their eyes met as Nedar thumped his empty mug on the table. Moameb stood. A tress of silvery hair fell into his eyes. "Palaton, you've been gracious for far too long. I detain you from your duties and your rest."

Palaton pushed away from the table. Nedar's voices cut across the growing talk and the clamor of the kegs being uncorked and trays of tankards filled.

"Let him stay, elder! I didn't come to drag him away."

"Nevertheless, it's time we both left. The wings need time alone to salute their fallen."

The two *tezars* stood, eyeing one another. Tradition left the wings to themselves while they assessed their lives and their losses. The older brethren like himself and Nedar who'd already passed the rite of passage were intruders. Palaton had been waiting until after dinner to excuse himself gracefully, but now Nedar's brashness was carrying him away. Nedar snapped his fingers, and the cadet who'd put away his jacket now bolted to bring it back. His mug had been refilled and he quaffed this one in three long hard gulps. He let himself belch when he thumped it down empty, said, "To tradition!" and took the jacket from the nervous Choya holding it. "Come on, brethren. We've work to discuss." And Nedar led Palaton away from the cadets' barracks.

Nedar paced as Palaton worked on the interlink to post the new contracts. The *tezars'* hall was entirely different from the cadets' barracks. It was not an immense, open hall, but a series of smaller rooms, some for meditation and some for negotiation, many for gaming and entertainment, several smaller dining halls, and rooms such as this where work could be done on the interlink. The walls were studded with memorabilia from famous flights and fliers. Palaton worked under a portrait of Quesan, one of the House of Star, who'd begun as a *tezar* and ended as an emperor.

Nedar paused to read over his shoulder. "A garbage run," he sniffed. "Have we nothing better to do than that?"

Palaton did not answer. He hadn't yet come to GNask's contract and knew the other would seize it the moment it came up on the reading board. Across the planet, the interlinks would post the same contracts at other *tezar* halls, though this was their main holding. The emperor's staff would receive notification and from thence it would go subspace on Choyan interlinks for those *tezars* already on contract but interested in transfer or just in the latest news.

A *tezar* generally knew when and where a war was going to start before its participants did.

Another pilot entered the room. He was chestnut-maned, chunky, and short, the epitome of the House of Earth, which ran to shortness and solidness. He grinned widely as he saw Nedar hovering over Palaton.

"Nedar! When did you get in?"

"And since when do I answer to you?" Nedar thumped the other on hefty shoulders. "This afternoon, if you must know."

"And when are you going out again?"

"As soon as I can."

Burly Hathord stopped at Palaton's elbow. "That's a mess of contracts you're posting. Rumor has it that Panshinea is going to request all contracts be reviewed by him prior to posting." Only the name of the emperor drew reverence out of Hat's voices. All else was game to be made fun of.

Palaton's fingers paused over the keypad. He looked up. "Seriously, Hat?"

"Dead serious. The emperor doesn't want his best *tezars* off and unavailable if he has to defend the throne."

Nedar's expression became speculative. "Where did you hear this?"

"And when?" Palaton added.

"Yestereve, from my sister."

Hathord's sister was an administrative diplomat. His source was impeccable, for she was a somber Earthan, not give to humor or flights of fancy. Palaton would believe anything she said, even if she declared the sky to be yellow and the grass white. Nedar had filled a small glass goblet with hard liquor. He swirled the amber liquid about the bowl.

Nedar did not have to think aloud for Palaton to guess his thoughts. If the emperor imposed such control, the reaction of the *tezars*, whose independence was both legendary and necessary, would be split. Panshinea might well find himself immersed in the civil war his weakening powers invited. It was not up to the *tezars* to defend a ruler whose time to abdicate had come.

Nedar took a sip of the liquor instead of speaking. Hat added carelessly, as if unaware of the charged atmosphere in the room, "I've never heard of a Descendant Wheel so determined to hang on."

"We don't know that he's Descendant. He could be Right Wheel," Palaton said. He returned to his processing, but his fingers moved slowly so he could talk with Hathord as well.

Nedar cleared his throat. "His actions speak for themselves, Palaton. The House of Star is far from what it was. The Wheel has turned, it's that clear. The throne must . . . evolve."

Hat let out a short bark of a laugh. "And it's a Sky who'll push it every time." He squelched his humor as Nedar swung around to look at him. He cleared his throat. For an Earthan, he was remarkably inept at balancing.

Palaton hid his smile as he turned his attention to the Abdrelik contract, which he was now setting up to feed to the interlink. As he'd predicted, Nedar's attention was riveted on the screen.

"That looks promising."

Hat was half a beat behind him, eyes squint-

ing in his furrowed face. "God-in-all, but those
Droolers love a fight."

"It keeps us employed," Nedar replied absently. "It keeps me *alive*." He finished his
drink. "What do you say, Hat? Join me in
battle."

"Not me. Look at that set up. Disarming an
overarmed Class Zed system . . . they could take
your head off your shoulders coming in." Hat
shuddered. His whole squat body vibrated. "I
like freight runs. Nice commission and nice dull
expectations."

"Ummm." Nedar spread a hand open across
the top of Palaton's, halting his processing. "Put
my name up for that when you've finished
inputting."

"You've just come off contract," Palaton said
mildly.

"Never mind. This is what I like to do. It's
like honey to children."

"You'll burn out."

Nedar's dark eyes narrowed. "Do you live in
my head? No? Then I'll choose what I do."

Hat sensed the enmity. He sputtered, "It
won't be final, Nedar. Not until the panel autho-
rizes it."

"They'll authorize it. The Abdreliks need seven fliers. How many do you think will put in
for this contract? The panel will fall all over
themselves okaying the volunteers and grit their
teeth assigning brethren to fill the remaining
posts. Put my name in, Palaton." There was a
blaze deep in his dark eyes that reminded Palaton of what his unseeable *bahdur* felt like to
him. The Choya tilted his head defiantly, black
mane of hair tossing back through his horn
crown.

"It's a slaughter."

"It's a contract."

"You'll not be able to Household. You'll be wherever the Abdreliks staff you."

"And you'll miss my tender company, eh, Palaton?" Nedar showed white teeth in a smile. "The Droolers pay well."

He kept protesting. "The work is intense. You've just come off a contract without leave. You've not had your medicals yet—"

"Lay off." The hand overspreading his grew tense. The veins stood up tightly through the back of Nedar's skin. Palaton could count a pulse rate through their throbbing if he wished. "I am not you, nor you me. My *bahdur* burns brightly. Don't cozen me, brethren," and he said the last with an ugly twist that told Palaton they were not, nor could ever be, brothers, but they were most definitely and eternally enemies. He had often thought Nedar held a hatred for him. Now he knew. *We hate what we fear most.*

Palaton stared down at the back of Nedar's hand until the Choya moved it away and he could continue processing. When the contract had been fed in and was accepted, he entered Nedar's name as requested.

"My thanks," Nedar said smoothly. His breath smelled faintly of the liquor he'd imbibed.

Palaton closed down his posting to the interlinks. "Don't mention it," he answered.

Hat shuddered again. He looked from one to the other, fighting his inborn Earthan tendency to make peace. Palaton put a hand on his shoulder. "Reviews will be in the morning."

"Who's reviewing?"

"Moameb, for one, I imagine. He's been grounded."

Flying *tezars* were not allowed to review or make assignments because of possible conflicts of interest. Nedar's brow went up in surprise and Palaton felt a stab of gratification. Evidently Nedar had not known that Moameb's affliction had progressed to that stage. Palaton dropped his hand from his friend's shoulder. "It's been a long day, brethren, and I intend to put an end to mine."

He left the posting room for his quarters in the sunset wing.

His old rooms had been sealed while he was gone these last three seasons on assignment. They smelled slightly stale as he opened them up, despite the herbal potpourri he'd left behind to keep both moths and staleness out. His flight bag had been left leaning against the closed door and he kicked it across the now open threshold. He did not like what he'd seen in Nedar's eyes and he walked now to the small oval reflective hanging over the bureau. He leaned forward and looked closely.

As he'd suspected, he had the same driven look. The compulsion to fly, no matter what the cost. The terror that the day when that could be taken away might be closer than ever dreamed before. Did Nedar have secrets he feared known? Palaton closed his eyes tightly for a second, then he opened them, took a deep breath, and ordered his quarters' door closed behind him.

There was a message posted on his private interlink. Palaton sat down and massaged the back of his neck before opening the comlink.

It was dated several days ago, though it was in Moameb's voices. Palaton listened and read the printout confirmation, then sat back in stunned silence.

His mother had died. His only hope of learning the truth about his genetic destiny had fled with her. How could he honor his destiny without full knowledge? And why had Moameb said nothing to him about the tragedy?

Chapter 6

He dreamed of Sorrow. Of figures cast in crystalline coffins, of a planet vein-shot with canals and lakes of the dead. Of their silent message, which he tried to hear and could not.

He woke, covers twisted about his horn crown and face, lips dewy with sweat, and lay for a moment in the darkness. He thought of Kedra and that it would have been sweeter to have gone to bed with her, but it had not been offered and he had not asked.

He drifted to sleep a second time. Like a stray wisp of cloud, he dreamed of entering his mother's Householding and came to ground, and walked, searching for her.

Or perhaps he *was* her, the dead, for there was nothing living as he walked. The auras had gone out of everything he passed, colors faded to sepia. The potted trees weeping in the courtyard might have been synthetic for all the life-glow he caught from them, but he knew they were not when one bud opened and bloomed before his eyes as he walked slowly past.

His footsteps brought no ring from stone or wood. His touch was ice. His heart thudded heavily in his chest with the fear that he might be trapped here forever, but Palaton told himself he dreamed and hoped for the best. The

Choyan spoke of other races, other beings as "the walking dead," for most of them had not the sensitivity to know what was living and what was not. They could not sense the God-in-all. Perhaps he walked as one of them, alien, among his mother's rooms.

A door swung open before he could put the palm of his hand to it as though the wood, once living and still vibrant, could not bear his touch upon it. As he ducked below the lower archway of a Choya'i's quarters, he could hear his mother's voice. Tresa sat, curled on a large sedan pillow, embroidery in her lap, and spoke to an unknown Choya. Neither of them sensed his entry.

Her artistry in embroidery had been well known and Palaton recognized in the half-finished canvas across her lap a wall hanging that now resided in Emperor Panshinea's palace. She had pricked a finger and now sat, contemplating letting the blood stain the thread and canvas, a seal of the artist's suffering, or sucking away the crimson drop and keeping her work free of blemish.

She decided on sucking up the drop. She looked up from her finger to say, "I do not want him tested."

Palaton knew without being told they discussed him. The Choya sitting across from her was massive across the shoulders and even inside his loose shirt, muscles visibly bulged and shifted with his movement. "There will be only the singular consequence and none other."

Her facial expression was stubborn. "But you *will* try, regardless. If I will not tell you who his father is, you'll try to find out however you can."

"The testing is only for his talents," the Choya persisted just as stubbornly, and a surprised Palaton realized this was his grandfather, a Choya he had always perceived of as elderly. But this Choya was still in his prime, his voices rumbling with low thunder. "If he's accepted as a *tezar* candidate, he has some hope even if you keep your silence."

His mother took three deft stitches. When she looked up, her sadness had been gathered back and only her eyes reflected it. "I have no choice," she said. "Silence is my only recourse. And if you think his *bahdur* is his only recourse, then so be it. He's so young. . . ."

"We'll not send him out until he's older, but to even know if he has a place among the cadets will aid in his education."

"I wanted him to be a priest. I wanted a chance for him to do some good in the world," she said, as if not hearing her father's reassurance. She put down her canvas a second time.

Palaton listened in amazement. In all the years he'd lived with his mother in the Householding, and in the brief returns he'd had after entering school, she'd never spoken of her hopes for him. She rarely spoke to him at all. He started forward to force his presence upon them, dreamsmoke or not, but his grandfather thrust himself to his feet and began a diatribe against the priesthood and Palaton felt himself jerked away. The silver cord of sleep yanked him abruptly out of the room, out of the past, out of hope.

Palaton woke panting. He threw his mangled covers aside, damp with sweat, and stared upward at the ceiling.

He was not dead, she was. He was not bereft of

hope, she had been. And he knew then, though no one had informed him, that his mother's sudden death had been a suicide. As for the rest of the dream, he had no way of knowing if he had manufactured it from a childhood memory of eavesdropping, or if it had been a farewell sending from his mother, or if it had sprung full-blown out of his own restless desires.

It was with relief that he sensed the faint bloom of life from the wooden bureau across the room, the aura of his own figure lying in the bed, the dim auras of reality that surrounded him. At least outwardly, he was no longer alien among his own people.

He slept past review. Moameb left word for him to join him in the east dining room, a small, intimate room glowing with antiques burnished with polish and attention over the hundreds of years the school had been open. The tables were small, scarcely bigger than writing desks. Perhaps that was what they had been at one time, before the interlinks. The tray between them held mugs of steaming *bren*, flier's juice the cadets called it because of the many pots of *bren* all of them consumed. The *bren* had been brewed strong, its aromatic steam welcoming, its color dark as poet's ink. Palaton pulled up a chair and palmed a mug gratefully.

"I'm sorry," Moameb said. "I couldn't find the words to tell you face-to-face. I thought once upon the mesa, but—"

"It's all right," Palaton told him. And it was, and the silver-maned Choya relaxed. "What did I miss in review briefing?"

"Nothing much. Nedar has already left to fulfill

GNask's contract. We felt that there would be little to gain by denying him."

"And the other six?"

"Four volunteers and two assignees."

Palaton thought of burly Hathord. "What about Hat?"

"He's going to stay here at the school. I'm training him to replace me."

Palaton did not have to feign pleasure. Hat would be perfect taking in the young fledglings. He sipped cautiously at his mug. "And me?"

"A combat contract, but not for the Abdreliks."

Palaton balanced the mug in front of his face, leaning on his elbows on the small tabletop. "Where?"

"A small system, one you're probably not familiar with. A chance to go exploring, and do some good in the worlds."

The echo of familiar words stung Palaton and he hid his startlement behind the mug of *bren.* "I'll be leaving soon, then."

"A week or so to rest. You booked for some retreat time at the temple, you'll get that, and a few days to pursue whatever other, ah, interests you have." Moameb got a slightly foxed look on his face.

Palaton ignored it. He took a strong draught and let the *bren* burn its way down his throat and into his stomach, the aromatic oils rolling off the back of his throat and rising into his sinuses. There was a mild rush. He savored it. He set the mug down. "How long is my stay?"

"Six seasons, our time." Moameb paused. "It's a civil war. Could be longer, could be less."

"And I'm on the side of the good guys," Palaton said dryly.

His mentor's face wrinkled thoughtfully. "I hope so," Moameb answered. "I certainly hope so."

The seven steps across the temple brook at Sorrow represented the seven senses purified by those who attended to the God-in-all. There were the five senses of sight, hearing, taste, scent, and touch, the sixth sense of paranormal ability and the seventh of the soul.

All those who were *tezars* knew that there was no purification of the sixth sense for them, that once the neuropathy began, there was no turning back, but that had never stopped Palaton from being religious. There were rituals within the temple that both lifted and comforted him. The brook had been only a temporary rite, now he sought the full services of the temple.

The temple on the school grounds had probably been there before the school, from the looks of it, granite cut blocks fit into one another so solidly a knife blade could not be slipped between, yet the raw wind off the plateaus could find its way through. The underground mineral springs and natural mud baths within lent a warmth that would be stolen away the moment a bather rose out of the basins and the wind could get at him.

For days, Palaton did all that was required of him. He meditated, fasted, bathed, composed a new melody for the *lindar*, edited a book another acolyte had written on a mathematical analysis and played five-team kickdown, a process which chipped a tooth which he had capped, but that did not matter because he'd gotten one of the winning goals. When he was ready, finally, completely ready, he went to talk to the Voices of the God-in-all.

The chamber was dimmed, as it was supposed to be, and Palaton entered cautiously, using his aura sense to tell him where the low benches were, found one to his liking and lay down upon it. The sense that this bench had been worn down through the centuries by those who had lain upon it touched him. He had been settled and still only a moment when the whisper of the Voices entering swept across the stonework, flooding his senses: the hem of a robe touching the ground, the pad of a slipper, the scent of herb soap and a faint, sweet smell. Palaton smiled to himself. This Voices had a sweet tooth and had eaten a candy before coming in.

The Voices of the God-in-all shifted about for a moment, seeking a comfortable position. It might be one of the acolytes or the Prelate himself or any of the other religious officers in between. It mattered not, though Palaton wondered briefly whether it was the Choya who'd wrestled to block him on that final goal. The Choya had walked somewhat stiffly. From age or athletic contest? He could not ask, of course, and knew he would not be told. He let go of the wonderment. It fluttered away like a dry leaf in the wind.

The Voices spoke, a Choya, tenor and high baritone, the sounds of his voices pleasing and soothing. He gave the ritual invocation and Palaton responded and they slipped into the rite of Voices and Listener which was somewhat of a misnomer because the guidance of the Voices would be to listen when Palaton opened up. He wanted to talk of his fears of losing his *bahdur* and knew that he could not, because even in the confidence of this ritual, the incident would be reported. He lay trapped in uncertainty. The Voices grew still.

Then, gently, "What do you think of when you prepare to sleep?"

Palaton felt his face warm, then knew the Voices did not ask about sexual fantasies or accounting worries. "You mean when I need to sleep and can't?"

"Yes."

"Pure flight." The words left his mouth before he'd considered, but he knew the rightness of them.

"Pure flight?"

"Flight without cost or exploitation, without mechanical augmentation." Without the torch-like burning of *bahdur*.

"Like one of the thrust gliders, or do you mean levitation?"

"Not levitation." Palaton spoke slowly. "I'm in a plane. But there is no fuel expense or the hum of motors—yet it's not a glider. It's as though *I* drive the plane. I pilot it and it's only a shell, a second skin. It's like a glider, but not dependent on thermals. I can cut across wind currents, through storms, whatever is necessary. And the glory of it is—I know where I've been, where I'm going, and *why*. I know what the destiny of my flight will be and all its consequences."

"Omnipotence?" suggested the Voices.

Palaton felt uneasy at the interpretation. "Perhaps."

"If not, then . . . enlightenment?"

"Enlightenment." Palaton felt the stone bench under his hips, cupping them, pillowing his shoulders'. He felt the press of his horn crown against the rock, his hair a thin mattress underneath it. He had had a dull headache earlier. It had gone and he had only noticed the change now. He repeated a second time, "Enlightenment. Maybe."

"And why do you seek this pure flight?"

"Because that's the way it's supposed to be," Palaton said, and was surprised to hear his words edged with impatience.

There was a noise, as if the Voices closed a notepad at his knee. "Child," the Voices said. "Do you know what you search for?"

"I'm not searching," Palaton answered slowly. He amazed himself again. "When I dream. . . ." He paused again remembering the dream when it came to him. "I've already found whatever it is. I'm complete. Fulfilled. Pure."

"Then you are fortunate. Most of us know only that we must search." The Voices moved a little closer, and Palaton smelled the faint sweet haze of his breath again. "You probably need us less than we need you. You dream of journey's end while most of us dream of the hazards of the journey. You must ask yourself if this is because you wish to avoid the journey—or if this is because you know your destiny already and know the journey will be successful. Most of us live day by day coping with our failures. Have you already learned this difficult lesson or have you acknowledged this weakness within yourself?"

"I don't know," Palaton answered uneasily.

There was a feather light touch upon his brow, a benediction. "You must search. Palaton, you have completed the Purification. You're free to leave the retreat whenever you wish. I understand your contractors are awaiting you. Good-bye."

Palaton felt unfinished. Did this dream interpretation mean the priest knew of his difficulty with his talents. Or perhaps that he would outlive his *bahdur*? Or even that he might be that rarest of *tezars* and not contract the disease? It had been known to happen once or twice. He sat up in the dim cave. "But how do I know?"

"By making the journey. Only at journey's end will you know."

"Wait—" and Palaton groped outward, grasping for the Voices, hoping to catch an arm or a bit of robe. There was only emptiness beside him. The cave was totally empty save for himself. There was no faint aura of warmth or presence beyond his own. He sat up. He told himself the Voices had merely teleported out, even though the normal implosion of air which would follow such an event had not occurred.

"God-in-all," Palaton muttered. "Who in the dark aura was I talking to?" He brushed his hair off his forehead and back into the swoop of the natural tiara of his horns. He left the cave dissatisfied, not knowing if it was for the lack in himself the Voices had hinted at or the listener's ignorance of the answers he needed.

Chapter 7

GNask ordered the room sealed until they three were alone, the humankind ambassador, his squirming get, and himself. The ambassador's child looked like a pallid, plump grub and fought determinedly to remain at large, running around the room on legs that seemed too frail to propel it at such a speed. The Abdrelik watched with the fascination of the hunter for prey, knowing he could not strike.

John Taylor Thomas said nervously, "I'm taking a great risk in meeting you alone like this."

GNask answered, "The risk is mine. There is no other way to accomplish what we must."

"Why do you need to see my child?"

The Abdrelik could not take his eyes away from the glistening, darting movements of the toddler. He said heavily, "My sources have been drained. I cannot find the information we need to secure her future. Therefore, in the interest of our alliance, we need to make adjustments in our plans."

Thomas had put a hand out as the toddler careened about the small room, but she eluded him with a squeal and kept running, her fine halo of hair standing on end. He drew back his hand and looked fearfully at GNask. "Adjustments?"

"If the Choyan want her, they will take her. However, we can take steps—"

"No. That wasn't what you told me. That wasn't what we agreed upon, ambassador."

GNask shifted his muscular bulk. He was taller than the man and nearly three times as broad. He feared nothing from the being although the other's tone spoke of stress and a great effort to maintain control. "We agreed that I would help you. I am helping you. My tracers upon Choyan activity show that there is a circumspect line of traffic which we cannot pinpoint as to origin or destination, traffic which does not seem to be related to any of the three major branches of Choyan society. However, the planet of Cho has been kept veiled for many centuries and, try as we can, we are not as expert as we'd like to be."

"They're not taking my daughter!"

"They *will* take her, ambassador. That seems reasonably inevitable, for they are a cunning and capable people. Since we cannot prevent their action, we can only take steps to ensure her traceability. A simple implant—"

Thomas' complexion blanched. He ran a hand through his hair. "They'd detect it. They'd dispose of her before they'd allow it through the system."

The Abdrelik puffed in distaste for the rampant emotionalism of the humankind. Then GNask caught himself and said, "An ordinary implant, yes. But not this. It's organic. It does not transmit. All it will do is stimulate the subject itself to reveal its whereabouts. The Choyan will have no control over your daughter's behavior, over her innate desires, however they may wish to indoctrinate her, because we will have been here first."

The room's austere interior held only the three sentient life-forms and a small, sterile table. GNask now reached out to that table. The slug symbiont resting on his wrist began to slither downward, tracks glistening, undulating toward the tabletop. John Taylor Thomas watched in fascination, mouth half-open.

Finally, he uttered, "What are you going to do?"

GNask said only, "Bring the youngling here."

Thomas hesitated, but the toddler had run out of steam and came staggering over to her father and sagged against his trouser leg as she embraced him knee-high. GNask patted down his waist pouch until he found the instrument he wanted and withdrew it.

Thomas looked at the compact, precise laser knife. "What are you going to do?" he repeated tensely.

"Imbue her with what she needs to assure her survival and the success of our alliance. You need her returned. The Compact needs the Choyan to cease and desist subversive activities." GNask showed his tusks. "We do what we must." The laser's tip glowed and, as the symbiont rested on the tabletop, the Abdrelik sliced down, quickly, cleanly, so unexpectedly that the *tursh* hardly quivered at all with the movement. A finger-length segment curled away and lay heaving with a life of its own.

GNask reached out and took the child away from her father. She gasped as he swung her into the air and sat her down upon the tabletop. Before she could scream or scramble away, the Abdrelik had lifted her mane of hair away from the nape of her neck and made a quick, cutaneous incision. He placed the *tursh* segment upon it.

"God," Thomas cried helplessly as the slug segment thinned and disappeared within the slice on his daughter's neck.

"A year at the most," GNask told him. "Your kind is not a sufficient host for longer. But the *tursh* will do its work. There will be no scarring when this heals and the *tursh* will assimilate itself further into the body. When it begins to die, it will return to this area and an abcess will form. That will have to be treated carefully. Do not call on your doctor. Contact my office. Once the abcess is healed, the indoctrination will be imperceptible by any means. This is not a psychological indoctrination that can be detected by testing. Her entire makeup is being altered. The Choyan would have to read her mind to know what we've done."

"And when they take her, she'll ... she'll want to come back?"

"Want is not strong enough. She'll not rest until she is reunited with us. She will betray the Choyan conspiracy by any means she can and return to you." GNask watched the man closely. With his *tursh* attempting regeneration in her body, she would also be imbued with those basic memories and drives that were of his lineage. Even though the symbiont would eventually die rather than propagate, the links would be permanently forged for a symbiotic relationship. He wondered how that would affect the radically different humankind.

How, for example, would she curb her desire for the taste of human flesh?

GNask turned away in his musing. "It's done.

I will leave you to your daughter. Enjoy her in the time you've left. Enjoy the great enterprise we've begun together. Her lifetime will bring to fruition the efforts of more than just the three of us." He picked up his *tursh*, made soothing sounds of apology to it, and returned it to his scalp.

The toddler sat stunned into quietude on the table. Her father stood uncertainly, arms open, unable to reach for her as if repelled by what his daughter had suddenly become. He cast a last look at GNask. The Abdrelik thought darkly of Choyan eyes, which he detested.

"We are allies," the Abdrelik said. "We will not let one another down. To the end."

The expression on John Taylor Thomas' face was unreadable and he did not make a sound until the Abdrelik had unsealed the room and left, fresh air flooding inward in his wake, filling a vacuum of sourness and hatred. "The end has begun," he murmured and reluctantly took his daughter into his embrace.

She neither cried nor welcomed his touch. Her too bright eyes seemed turned inward, to other stimulations.

What had he done?

Chapter 8

The smell of the mechanics' bays leaked into the wardroom. The air was permeated with the din of the robotic arms at work, the staccato of metal being drilled and polished and refitted, the *whirr* of instruments, the smell of burning plastics, the sludge of oils and lubricants, and the pungent sting of fuels. Palaton had grown wearily used to it and found it as necessary a part of his morning as a steaming mug of *bren*. It was more irritating to hear silence and smell the solvents used to clean idle bays.

He sat at a table with his bare feet propped up—he'd not yet put his boots on—the obligatory cup of *bren* in front of him. It left little brown rings on the tabletop and some of the liquid had soaked into the edge of the charts he was reading over. He absently put a finger down and mopped the rings into another direction on the sloping and warped tabletop and sucked a tooth for a moment, the capped tooth, and thought of where his best entrance window to the system would be. He made a stylus mark at a possibility.

There would be satellite mines along the approaches and other deterrents, but that would not be his worry. He was to pilot through Chaos from this station to that system and then open

up the belly of the mother ship and deliver his
load of attack vessels. Then he would pull back,
out of range, until recall and swoop back to
gather them up. He and five others were going
in, delivering a wing of nearly five hundred vessels, yet even that would not win this war. It
had not these five seasons past and there was
little hope it would in the future.

He saw the specter of defeat more clearly
than he did the chart he narrowed his eyes at.

Palaton sat back in his chair with a sigh. The
wardroom was empty. He was up early with his
habitual Choyan restlessness, and he savored
the solitude. He wrapped his hand around the
mug and drew it to him, warmth spreading
through his palm.

He had not discussed the possibility with his
contractors nor they with him, but he knew the
course had been run and they had lost the risk
they'd taken. It saddened him.

It had been a racial war, the Threlks and the
Gurans, with the Gurans scrambling to avoid
genocide, and the Compact maintaining a neutral position. Palaton did not pretend to understand the politics that would dictate neutrality
in one situation and meddling in another, but
he knew he did not wish to see the Gurans
wiped out. They were a generally cheerful,
ingenuous little people, and he held a respect
for them that had nothing to do with his
contract.

Moameb had promised him he might make a
difference and he was deeply troubled that he
had not. Not in the long run.

Palaton stared at the charts in front of him,
charts showing the webwork of the planet's
defenses over strategic holdings, particularly

over the shieldings and mine nets that kept the Gurans from utilizing their surface strongholds effectively. Early morning fuzziness obscured his vision. He rubbed his eyes.

Their run that day was strictly defensive, opening an escape window that would allow as many evacuees to flee their home planet as could board the ships. Across the regions of Chaos, in the Gurans' system, hundreds of people were loading their ships in a misty morning and saying good-bye to their heritage. Many of them would not make it out despite their escort. But a few would, and the Threlks' dream of total genocide would not be realized. Such a small difference.

There was a step behind him. He shifted in his seat and turned. Nedar stood in the ward-room, a visitor's badge winking upon the frayed collar of his flight suit. He looked exhausted, battered, the whites too wide about his dark eyes. But he gave an arrogant smile.

"I heard you were flying from this station. I thought you had no taste for war."

"I take the contract I'm assigned to, the same as you do. I don't go looking for it." His voices sounded wary, taut, and he hated the way they betrayed his ambivalence toward a fellow *tezar*. He mellowed his tones. "Sit a while. I'm just looking over the day's flight charts."

"No." Nedar shifted weight. "I'm just off-contract and headed home." His eyes scanned the table in front of Palaton. "I've heard about your war."

"Have you?"

The Sky lifted his chin defiantly, his ebony hair tousled from the helmet he now carried by one strap. "Cutting your losses?"

"Not if I can help it."

Nedar paused. He put up his free hand and rubbed the base of his horn crown as if something pained him there. "You tried to warn me once, Palaton. Let me return the favor. It's easier to fulfill a contract when you stop trying to be a hero." He turned away abruptly and left the wardroom, the bulkhead hissing shut behind him.

He left a distinct vacuum in his wake, his missing presence a chill in the air. Palaton stared after in mild surprise, wondering what all that had been about. He turned his attention back to his charts, half-expecting Nedar to return and explain himself. He found himself staring without sight and rubbed his eyes again.

Palaton widened his eyes and refocused. The offensive sites marked seasons ago suddenly came into clear definition. The continent of Fimarl, where the Threlks were most strongly banded, was practically impregnable due to the shielding of their satellite nets and warning systems. But as Palaton looked at Fimarl now, his *bahdur* blazed within him as though he'd swallowed a hot pepper, and the netting showed transparent, then disappeared from his charts.

The system would fail. How or why he did not know, only that it *would*, leaving an opportunity for attack and the placement of offensive satellites within that window that would give the Gurans a much stronger position.

Palaton tapped his fingers upon the tabletop. If the netting did not fail, he and all his pilots would be annihilated if they attempted to go in. And his vessel was not meant for the intricacies of atmospheric warfare, being strictly outfitted for deep space.

But if the netting did go down, even for a handful of hours, it could turn defeat and retreat about. The Gurans would have the Threlks' complete attention. A grudging respect, even, perhaps, a respect that could lead to negotiation.

The charts wavered again under his vision and then they were as they had originally been with the defensive net of Fimarl firmly in place. To do as Nedar suggested would be to overlook this opportunity and he could not do that, no matter what the consequences.

Palaton spread his hand across the continent. One mother vessel detoured on a separate mission to Fimarl. What more losses could they incur? Would it be worth it? Whiffet, the Guran commandant-in-chief, would think him insane. But he would propose what he had to propose and then let the Guran mull it over.

He reached for his *bren* and took a sip. It had gone icy cold. The fugue state of intuition had left him sitting trancelike while his drink cooled. Palaton made a face, shoved his chair back, and went for fresh *bren*. When he returned, Whiffet was standing at the table, looking over the charts, a tired expression etched into his octagonal face. He touched the charts with his great arm. His Trade lingo held a charming accent.

"Working so early? And I would think you had these memorized by now?"

"I got the new weather charts in."

The commandant said, not unkindly, "There is no need to apologize to me."

"It was not an apology."

The Guran looked closely at him, then forced a facial grimace approximating a Choyan smile. "No, I see it was not. Well, *tezar*, your contract draws to an end."

"But not a desirable ending. Commandant, I have a change of action I'd like to discuss with you. Can you reach your sympathizers on Fimarl?"

"Possibly." The Guran's wide, amber eyes regarded him gloomily. "It matters little. We have our survival to think about, not an offensive."

"The Threlks' attention will be concentrated on taking out your evacuating wing."

The Guran shifted uncomfortably as if the Choya criticized him. "We're aware of that."

"Now is the time for your sympathizers to strike and take down the net over Fimarl. It can be done. It will be done, and I intend to be there to take advantage of it."

"What?" The sable pupils within those amber eyes grew huge in disbelief. "What are you thinking of?"

Palaton told him, swiftly and succinctly, omitting only his precognitive abilities. The little commandant sat down abruptly when he'd finished. He rested his great arm upon the table. His lesser arm he curled in his lap where his fingers twitched in agitation.

Whiffet sighed. "I'm loath to risk the sympathizers. I have some hopes they may yet persuade the rest of the Threlks to accept us. And these actions you propose will jeopardize the evacuees."

"Scarcely more than they are already in jeopardy." Palaton did not press. He could see the Guran mulling over the options he'd been presented with. Palaton could offer nothing further to persuade him.

Whiffet looked up. His furry brow wrinkled. "If the net does not go down, you will be destroyed. Your carrier and the wing you transport."

"It will have to be a volunteer mission, but I don't think I'll have a problem getting them." His pilots would not hesitate to go with him under the circumstances. The risk Whiffet anticipated was not the risk Palaton was preparing to take.

The Guran continued to weigh the matter. Palaton held his silence. The commandant placed both hands upon the table, great arm and lesser arm. Palaton knew the motion had cultural and religious significance, but he couldn't remember what it was. Whiffet's next words told him. "For the good of my people," the commandant said heavily, "I cannot order you to do such a thing. Nor can I order our sympathizers . . . however, this is our world. We will never be able to flourish as well elsewhere and we know that we are not guaranteed a homeland by the Compact." Whiffet looked up. The expression in his eyes was intense. "We do not want to leave. We will be forever grateful for whatever hope you can give us."

"Then, commandant, you have your first and foremost volunteer. Contact your sympathizers. Ask them to do what they can. I'll handle the rest. Only my carrier will go in. The others still have their primary function of evacuation."

Whiffet nodded briskly. "I understand." He hesitated. "And thank you, *tezar*."

Palaton's voices had carried well in the massive bay holding his carrier and the wing of attack crafts. He had the robotics halted and the other mechanics ceased their activities to listen. His pilots had gathered slowly, but all of them were in attendance by the end of his speech, and dead silence greeted it.

He had not guaranteed that the net would be down. But they knew if he felt it, if he had confidence, that the chances were great it would go down. If such a thing had been possible seasons ago, this war would have been over. There was no reason to think it possible now, except that Palaton felt it possible.

He scanned their faces and expressions. He could see them weighing their choices much as Whiffet had weighed them.

The oldest ace among them took his flight helmet from under an elbow and examined it as he held it in his hands. "I'm in," he said diffidently, as if he'd read an answer reflected in its battered surface.

The others did not even hesitate as long. Palaton felt exhilaration as they gathered close and decided how to refit the planes going in and began to re-matrix the robotic handlers accordingly.

Whiffet met him before he entered his carrier for launch. The other ships had been loaded into its belly and all was quiet in the massive bay. But this quiet was different from the earlier silence. This held anticipation, like that of a stalking predator before it strikes an unwary prey. This held readiness, not fear and consternation. Palaton halted for the Guran commandant, felt impatience, and curbed it.

Whiffet took the Choya's hand with his greater hand. "The sympathizers were reached. They, too, volunteered their aid."

Palaton wondered if it would be their efforts which would bring the net down. In all probability. He did not worry. "Thank you, commandant. If all goes well, I'll see you in about forty-eight hours."

"I pray," the Guran said. "For us all." He stepped back, a whimsical, lopsided looking creature, with all the worries of the world strapped upon his back.

Palaton carried that vision with him as he stepped onto the carrier deck and ordered the lift to take him to the con. His crew cleared the bridge as soon as he stepped onto it. *Tezars* pilot alone. He waited until the lock sealed behind them, then dropped into the control chair and, smiling, reached toward his instrument panel.

The launch was routine. As the carrier thrust into deep space, Palaton settled his shoulders against the padded chair, considering what he would do when they breached Chaos. Normally, they would emerge in-system, but a considerable flight outside the planet itself. He felt like cutting it closer. Much closer.

The carrier accelerated solidly and lights came on all over the panel, warning of FTL approach. Palaton did nothing. His pilots were ready. He was ready.

The moment of entering Chaos was always unique. Sound, sight, color washed past. Nothing was as it seemed. Palaton reached into his *bahdur* for the truth. The carrier seemed to hesitate for a moment, then steady on. He made his calculations swiftly, fought the controls to do as he ordered, rather than as the sensors indicated, and brought the carrier about on course.

Then he sat back and enjoyed the view, the view of a cosmos in complete and utter random movement, a view as soothing as the falling droplets of a fountain. A view as treacherous as it was lovely, if one got lost in it forever. He liked to think of it as the cutting edge of death itself.

When the time came, he brought the carrier out just beyond the planet's second moon, coming on-line to his pilots as they decelerated. Their speed would have them on approach within a matter of hours. The other carriers would be coming out behind them.

"No decoys to blunt any attack on us," Palaton reminded his pilots after he gave them their real space position so they could check their tracking systems. "Get ready for your drop."

His instrument panel lit up with the gridwork of the defensive and offensive systems down below. They'd emerged on the dark side, opposite Fimarl, but he'd no doubt that that continent was equally well protected. The small island chains and smaller continent that was the Gurans' beleagured home base showed under a different gridwork, one not as solid or impenetrable.

"I have blips, sir," one of his pilots called out.

Palaton blinked, then swiveled in his chair to view the screen. Incoming showed, but from the size and speed, they were the rest of the carriers coming out of subspace behind him. "On track," Palaton replied flatly. He signaled his intent to break away to the rest of the fleet. It was received with surprise but swift understanding. Palaton put his hands on the control board and communicated to his vessel what it was he wanted it to do.

They banked sharply right, cruising swiftly through the moon-shadowed darkness of night over the planet's surface, winging toward the dawn and Fimarl.

Automatic defenses began to go off. The instrument screens lit up as the defenses began to zero in on them, firing.

Palaton felt his intuition burn in the pit of his stomach. Or perhaps it was the result of too much *bren* in the early morning. He did not see the network falter over the Threlkian continents. What if he had misinterpreted what he had seen?

False *bahdur* was as deadly as no *bahdur* at all.

He sat, tension bunching in his shoulder muscles and the weight of his horn crown pressing upon his skull until his neck felt as though it could not hold his head in place. He stared, unblinking, at the control grids and various view screens. Something should give. If it did not, they were headed into deadly cross fire which he could not pilot through safely.

The gridwork glowed. He looked at the satellite mines, the configuration of their fire imprinting in his vision. If he closed his eyes, he would retain that webbing across the darkness. Death waited inside that grid.

He had known the network would go down. Not how or exactly when, but that it would. It was foolish to wait on the actions of others. He let his *bahdur* flare out over the screens, discerning points of maximum coverage and firepower and those areas where there would be weak spots of coverage. There had to be weak spots. All he had to do was find them.

A golden line flared out in the corner of his vision. He turned his head slightly and eyed it. Yes. There was a quadrant with minimal coverage at the edge of the field. They could possibly slip through there. It would be a tight and perilous squeeze and they would draw fire. No doubt about it. But the cross fire would be at a minimum. Palaton plotted the course and the carrier began to arc across the shadow, across the fading edge of night and into the dawn, over Fimarl. Somewhere below, the Threlkian war alarms would begin to sound.

The carrier did not respond well to the handling he required of it. It turned sluggishly and did not hold the coordinate line as precisely as he wished. He let out a string of Choyan curses and hastily tapped in course changes to right the vehicle. It plowed rather than soared into the stratosphere.

The carrier shuddered as a strafing line caught it. It shook like a trapped animal, then righted.

Palaton put himself on-line, prepared to stay there until he opened the doors to drop the wing out. "We're going in," he said by way of explanation. "Expect turbulence."

The network hadn't gone down. They were drawing fire and Palaton knew it would get heavier. The panels showed him laser fire streaking after them, missing, but barely, the crossovers getting closer and closer. They could expect worse.

Sweat trickled down his brow and alongside his nose. He didn't have a free hand to wipe it away.

They took a hit. He could almost hear the metal scream. The shield bucklers held but one of them disintegrated so badly he could see the glowing crumbs of it shedding into space behind them. Another hit would take his rear flank out. The carrier heeled hard but answered to him at the helm as he righted it.

Next time it would not.

On the open com, he could hear the pilots and robotics reporting damage assessments. One plane had come loose from all the jarring. Other than that, all was well in the hold.

Next time though it would be a different story.

Palaton swallowed, his mouth gone dust-dry. He shook his head vigorously. Droplets of sweat spattered across the cabin. An instrument keened, telling him they were being targeted.

He veered the carrier. It came about sluggishly, too heavy for the atmosphere and gravity that pulled at it, too vast for the split second timing he needed out of it. He was piloting it as though it was one of the needle nose planes down in the hold awaiting release.

Palaton eased back. He had to decide whether to go on or turn back.

The carrier shuddered again as a beam sheared across a fin, doing little damage but buffeting the whole ship, a warning of the death awaiting them.

Reluctantly, he put a hand out.

Suddenly, his grid lights went out. The instruments went dead. Palaton froze. Then his face cracked in a grin.

No. The circuitry was not dead. The network had gone *down*, just as he'd foreseen.

"Get ready for launch drop," Palaton ordered, and he steered the carrier down into the quadrant.

The Gurans made a ceremony out of contract's end. Their fortress was filled with decorated, celebrating aliens and the air was rich with the smell of food. Palaton wandered the hall, uncomfortable in his full dress uniform. Whiffet was as excited as he'd ever seen the Guran. Palaton contained his own humor as the commandant took him aside.

"A stand-off," the commandant said, "as you called it. Our satellites within their network. Brilliant. They must admit we exist. They have agreed to negotiate settlements with us. *Tezar* Palaton, there will be victory in this compromise yet."

"You have a lot to span."

The Guran nodded. "We know that." He paused. He put out his great hand. "I have never ended a contract with more satisfaction."

Nor I, thought Palaton. He took the Guran's hand. "Thank you," he said.

"And I have a message for you from your Householding. It asks that you report to your emperor's House as soon as possible." The Guran wrinkled his octagon face in an approximation of a smile. "It seems he has need of you, as well."

Chapter 9

He had not been in the imperial district since he had officially been commissioned as a *tezar*. The district was ancient, filled with the history and memories of the Choyan people. Neutral ground, it had never been under attack. It seemed God-in-all had even spared it from the vagaries of the weather and the acts of nature the rest of the planet was heir to. As Palaton gazed through the window of the skimcraft, he felt the pressure of ages upon him.

When the skimcraft came to the debarkation port, he hung back, getting a jacket against the chill of late fall, for the season here held a bitter bite to it. It had rained and the gray stonework about him had soaked it up in black, uneven fractal streaks. The streets were begrimed with black puddles.

Palaton shrugged into his jacket. His luggage had gone on ahead of him. He swung about, reading the portals, chose the one for the palace, and stepped inward. The glidewalk took him into the bowels of the inner district. His stomach churned with hunger and he wondered if he would simply have an audience with the emperor or if he would be required to check into the hostel there until Panshinea found some time to see him. Other than the directive bringing him to the district, he'd had no communication with the emperor.

He doubted that Panshinea had need of a hero, if he even filled that qualification. Or for a *tezar*, for that matter. And though he couldn't deny the prickle of unease at the back of his head, nothing had hinted at the emperor's purposes.

But Palaton felt a need to be wary. An emperor under siege, an emperor's House under siege, provoked nothing less.

The House of Star had taken the Choyan people far. Though it was the technology-oriented House of Sky which had given them spaceflight, it was the House of Star which had given them standing among other races who had also reached beyond the galaxies. It was the House of Star which had foreseen that their abilities to pilot FTL would keep them afloat in an interstellar stew of rivalries. The Choyan was one of the few races never to have colonized beyond their home planet. One of the few not to have billions of members to use for fodder in warfare. One of the few to be able to stand on equal footing with any other alien and not have to back down.

The House of Star had done this, and now it was collapsing under its own entropy as Houses did, and the Choyan people could only wonder what would happen next. The House of Earth was next on the Wheel, but it had become an uneven Wheel ever since the level of technology offset paranormal advantage, and no one knew for sure that Sky would not try to usurp Earth's place.

Or even if Earth had among its members anyone bold and canny enough to try for the emperor's throne. Hat was typical of an Earthan. Palaton himself did not know of any Earthan strong enough to come forward and wrest the elections away from either Star or Sky. But unlike other Choyan, he did not ask himself if Star was descendant on its Wheel. He *knew*, as did Panshinea. The mighty powers wielded by the House of Star had begun a fiery fall from the heavens.

He only wondered if civil war would take the rest of the Choyan with it.

He did not air his opinion among his brethren. Politics was a chancy topic these days. All feared the consequences of the future, for they had not only fellow Choyan to dread, but the Abdreliks and the Ronin and the other predators of the Compact.

The topic was as forbidden as talk of marriage outside Houses, the kind of genetic matings which had once produced erratic and dangerous talents, and had left thousands of Choyan dead as a result. Perhaps that was why he had felt duty-bound to assist the Gurans. Genocide was a terrible thing.

The glidewalk bumped as it entered the tunnels leading into the palace access. He could hear the faint buzz of scanners moving over him. He turned and peered into one surface which was certain to be a two-way viewport and stared solemnly at his reflection. He looked as though he'd come in out of a storm. He made a wry face and glanced away, anticipating the glidewalk's end.

An armed escort awaited him. They snapped to as he stepped off the walk.

"Your luggage has been picked up, sir," the lieutenant said, her voices carrying just the

right blend of authority and respect. She had
not shaved down her crown in vanity and its
proud Star scalloped edges bordered her mass
of bronze hair. She wore the emperor's sapphire
and gold, with the Star badge of her House
clipped to her shoulders. Her cheek was mosa-
icked with fine traceries of gold and silver under
its translucent skin. The jewelry cleverly
enhanced an already beautiful face.

The second with her seemed drab by comparison. His stocky body was also clothed in sapphire and gold, but he wore the badge of the
Prelate instead of a House emblem. He did not
need to proclaim himself as an Earthan, his
squat form did that. His hair was fringed with
silver, its natural color a mousy nothing that
the silver merely drew attention to. He seemed
resigned that other, younger, and more ambitious officers would always outrank him.

Palaton wondered why the Prelate had guards
among the emperor's security. He stepped into
their brace formation without hesitation. "Where
to?"

"Himself is waiting for you. We'll take you in
the atrium entrance, less fuss that way."

Palaton hid his reaction to being secreted in.
He lengthened his stride to keep in step with
the lieutenant, and the Earthan guard puffed
alongside beside, then behind them. As they
passed beyond the tunnels and into the open, a
light rain began pattering down. His guards put
their chins down and quickened their steps.
Palaton kept up with them, blinking against the
droplets lining his eyelashes. He could see the
throngs of administrators break into a run
across the palace steps. Many wore the peculiar
helmet thought to protect the wearer against

having his mind read. Palaton smiled grimly. Scant protection against the House of Star, whose *bahdur* in telepathy flamed brightly.

The palace looked much as it had once been, a fortress, a vault of mighty wealth, rather than an architecture of lofty inspirations and rule. When and if the throne passed from the House of Star, this bastion would remain in Star's hands. The bureaucracy would pull out, following the administrators to the new Householding, wherever it might be. Palaton looked at the Charolon, as it was named, and tried to envision a different capitol complex. He could not. This had been the hub of Choyan rule and politics for over four hundred years, and it had been ancient even before that.

His guards ducked down a side path, and through a garden gate of clever stonework, and under twisted, knobby vines bared for the winter, their stick fingers holding them in place along a trellis. As he dipped his head under, a last, dried brown leaf drifted past, slid off his cheek and wafted to the ground. The leaf was star-shaped.

The rain began to pelt them. The Earthan guard let out a grunt of distaste and began to run heavily, his boots thudding in the garden mud. The lieutenant led them through the winter garden, into the atrium where a lofty roof protected them, and there they waited. Palaton paused next to a fountain, which was still, its waters drained away, and he heard the faint strains of *lindar* music drifting toward them. The interior of the palace was lit against the gloom of the rain and it glowed warmly. He looked down at his boots, saw mud splatters along his cuffs, and made a face.

There was a straining, grinding noise, and then the fountain base moved aside, revealing an arched door. The lieutenant went ahead and the second came at Palaton's heels as they took him through it.

The *lindar* music swelled louder as they stepped into the study fronting the atrium, and he saw Panshinea seated at the stringed keyboard. The emperor's large hands roamed freely yet precisely over the instrument and the melody grew stronger.

The room was filled with the color and warmth of the hearth and the abundant glowing lanterns. Heavy pelted rugs littered the tiled floor and small tables encouraged one to sit or lie upon the pelts near the hearth. Volumes cluttered the built-in shelves of one massive wall and a library ladder hung from its tracks in the corner. Potted plants and hanging baskets from the atrium had also invaded here and their cool scent brought the rain in with them.

The lieutenant and her second came to a halt, listening solemnly as the emperor finished playing the *lindar*. The hammered strings swelled forth a final note and then faded.

Panshinea was dressed for winter, though it was the dead of fall outside. His sable coat was fur cuffed at the sleeves and collar, his boots were heavy, and his trousers thick. Palaton thought of an elder Choya, bundled against the cold of age, and held that thought as the emperor rose from the *lindar*.

Panshinea wrung his hands as he approached and their gazes met, and Palaton was instantly aware that the emperor knew what he thought. Telepathy or no, the Choya had read his mind as easily as he'd read the scroll of music he'd just played.

"Winter seeps into Charolon earlier every year," Panshinea said, and held out his hand to Palaton.

"Emperor," Palaton said, bowing over their gripped hands.

"I trust my lieutenant and her second treated you well." Panshinea stepped back. He eyed Palaton. "They brought you tromping through the garden loam."

The lieutenant flushed, her skin darkening to a rosy color. "My apologies, your majesty—"

He waved. "Think nothing of it, Jorana. It's good for a *tezar* to come down to earth now and then." Panshinea reached forward again and drew Palaton out from the brace of his escort. Jorana and the Earthan guard stepped back to the hidden doorway and fell into a stance they could hold for days, if need be.

Panshinea was the epitome of a Choya of the House of Star. They tended to be lighter in complexion, their skin more translucent, their crowns fuller and heavier, though blunter, their locks of hair tending to hold the reds and yellows of the sunlight in their hues, their eyes lighter as well, blue or green or hazel. His double-elbowed grace in playing the *lindar* was what could be expected of a Star, his body sinewy and well-corded but tall and wiry in its strength. He was not quite Palaton's height, and a little heavier, and there were humor lines about his luminous eyes. His hair was light brown with a red shine to it, and a tiny spattering of gray right where his horn crown held the mane back. His eyes were pale green, with a darker rim of forest green like a faint aurora. His nose flared well

and his jaws had not yet gone to the jowls of
a prosperous merchant, the only disagreeable
feature of the House of Star.

The emperor drew him across the wide study
and sat him down on a well-padded couch near
the hearth. He lowered himself to a large, flared
chair at its corner. The jade eyes considered
Palaton. "I remember you from your commis-
sioning," Panshinea said.

Palaton was flattered. "Thank you, sire."

"You're surprised? Don't be. We graduate
some five hundred *tezars* a year, and the number
of Stars among them steadily dwindles. I see
the fierce faces of Skies growing in your ranks,
and I worry."

The emperor's frank words startled Palaton
more than the recognition. It was true that the
number of Sky pilots grew at an astronomical
rate in comparison to the other Houses—more
proof, if one looked for it, that the House of Star
was in its descendancy, though the overall number of pilots was steadily decreasing. But there
were more than ten thousand on the current
rolls of pilots and that he should be known
among them did surprise Palaton.

The emperor twisted in his great chair. Flames
from the fireplace illuminated his profile. He
seemed on the verge of saying something else
when there was a noise at the proper entrance
to the study, and a Choya entered, with a com
at his side.

"I beg your pardon, Panshinea," the Choya
said, his dark eyes creased with years and wisdom, his black ebony hair streaked with yellow
white. "Trouble," he added, handing over the
com unit. He looked at Palaton and assessed the

situation. "If you'd care to come with me, *tezar*, I can make you comfortable while—"

"No," interrupted Panshinea. "He can stay. This news will be old before too much longer anyway." He adjusted the unit to his forehead and brought the microphone down for speaking.

The elder Choya gave Palaton a look, and in that look, Palaton saw himself as trespasser and unwanted, a look he had not seen since he'd become a *tezar*. He also recognized the elder as the emperor's chief adviser, Gathon, Minister of Resource. Gathon's lips pursed, but he held his silence, dark eyes boring into Palaton.

"What's wrong?" the emperor asked softly, his voices quiet with menace. He listened intently. "How many rioters and where did you hold them? All right . . . all right. Send me a briefing. But you convene a meeting and inform them once again that there is no choice in this. It's time for Relocation and what needs to be done will be done."

Relocation. Palaton tried not to listen and yet he heard, and he knew what had happened. The resources of their planet were thin, delicately balanced, the population of two hundred million Choyan kept in check so that the planet might bear their presence without too much strain. But after thousands upon thousands of years of civilization, there would inevitably be strain. Pollution. Soils too depleted for further agriculture. Whole counties had to be uprooted periodically and forced to relocate, to migrate to another section of the continent which had lain bare, resting, awaiting its turn in the cycle.

Householdings were stripped bare and left behind. Centuries of family graves and history forcibly abandoned. Charolon itself might be emptied someday. Protests and riots seemed inevitable. Sometimes bloody.

Palaton, lost in his thoughts, looked up and saw that the call had been finished. Panshinea had removed the com and was watching him with a neutral expression.

"Relocation," the emperor said, "is only desirable for the other Choyan."

Palaton smiled wryly. The homily seemed apt. Gathon stood, the com unit dangling from one broad-palmed hand. "May I be of further service, majesty?"

"No. But have cook send in afternoon *bren* and some sandwiches, if you would." Panshinea sat back with a heavy sigh as the minister left. "Tell me," he ventured, "about the Gurans and the Threlks."

Palaton told him what he could without breaching the security dictates of his contract. The emperor listened keenly and asked discerning questions, his mind quick and his knowledge already fairly complete. When the *bren* and food arrived, Palaton gulped what he could between the rapid-fire interrogation as Panshinea moved to fill in what he did not know of the story.

Panshinea sat back in his chair. "Evacuation had been decided upon before you came to contract, however," he said, finally.

"Yes. With great reluctance."

"Do you know where the Compact had agreed to resettle them?"

"No." G-flesh planets were not particularly abundant and most of them already held a population which could not be supplanted. Not legally or morally, anyway.

"If I asked you to, Palaton, if your emperor commanded you to, could you determine where?"

Palaton grasped for an answer, his mind whirling away with the why of it. Why would the emperor want to know? What good would it do for him to know? "I . . . could try," he got out.

"Then do it. I will not send you into this blindly," Panshinea said. He stood up. "We've resisted the inevitable for centuries, but if it is the last act of the House of Star, I intend to see us begin colonization. Cho's resources are too thin for us to continue our balancing act. We must expand. We must grow. We must allow our population to rejuvenate. We've no choice but to emigrate."

Despite the hearth's reflected heat, Palaton went cold. The Choyan belonged on Cho where the God-in-all could be learned and perceived by all of them. To leave was to leave the God-in-all, to search for Him anew . . . and possibly find false gods on false worlds. The Choya'i would bear differently, if they could bear at all. The children would mutate to adapt to the new planet however compatible it might be. They would change beyond knowing. They had been temperate for centuries, fighting to preserve the balance of their homelands. The House of Sky would fight him claw and horn about this. Did Panshinea want to bring down his House before its time?

He looked up and saw the jade eyes locked onto his face and knew that the emperor had read every thought tumbling in his mind.

Chapter 10

" 'Oh, but thou would wrest this heavy crown from mine brow before my eyes are closed in sleep,' " Panshinea quoted in irony. He reached out for a poker and stoked the fire as the sudden beat of rain drummed loudly on the roof, sounding as if the heavens had opened up. Outside the windows everything darkened to premature night. "No, *tezar*, I did not read your mind, but I did not need to. Your shocked expression is an open book."

"There must be other options." Palaton felt as though the couch he sat upon rested on unstable ground, on a treacherous bog. He listened to the rain thundering down on the ancient roof and wondered what rain on another world would sound like on another Householding. It was ridiculous to think such thoughts—as a pilot he'd spent most of his adult life on other worlds. He already knew that rain sounded differently, depending upon the building material of the roof and the weather pattern of the world.

"There are. To continue as we have always done is one. But it is not one I feel is in our best interest. Do birds always nest in the same nest generation after generation, despite the crowding and the lack of forage? No, they spread their wings and fly, unafraid, to the next tree and the next and the next. But we Choyan do not fly, because we are afraid of becoming less Choyan than we are now and we do not consider that we might become *more*." Panshinea kept his grip on the poker but waved it slightly as though he kept beat to a melody Palaton could not hear. "Before you think me seditious, understand that I have spent most of my years upon this throne considering the conclusion I've come to. Ask yourself why, among all thinking people, we alone can master Chaos. Were we not intended to fly beyond our nests? *Were we not?*"

Palaton looked up. "I can't say." He paused. "But if you wish me to inquire whether there was a planet set aside for the Gurans, there are others who are more discreet and experienced at this sort of inquiry than I."

"You refuse me?"

"I suggest that there are others more adept. I am a pilot, Emperor, not a diplomat."

"Your present demeanor suggests otherwise." Panshinea drew his feet under him. His wiry body tensed.

"We serve Cho and the Choyan as best we can," stated Palaton calmly, but his heart kept pace with the thundering rain still pelting the rooftops. His throat closed as he sensed the sudden swelling of *bahdur* toward him, emanating from the emperor like a lightning strike. The air stank of power.

But nothing touched him. Panshinea sank back in his chair, shrunken with pain, and Palaton watched, his throat muscles relaxing slowly, as the emperor writhed.

He knew then, as few in the world must know, that the emperor was dying of neuropathy, like a *tezar*, the degenerative disease burning away his nerve paths. The question was not whether Panshinea would die on the throne. It was when . . . if the Skies or the disease would bring him down first. Palaton reached forward instinctively to soothe the pain. "Sire. . . ."

The emperor took a shuddering breath. "You are honest," he said as he gathered his composure. "I must ask myself if I can trust an honest being. Have Jorana take you to your quarters. We'll talk again in the morning."

Palaton stood. Jorana was already striding across the library, her bronze hair flowing back with the swiftness of her movement, as if she had been listening for the emperor's faint voices. She stopped just short of securing his arm and Palaton knew he had been dismissed and that she would see he left.

They took a step away.

"And Jorana."

She swung around to the emperor.

"Hurry back to me," Panshinea said, a glitter deep in his eyes.

She flushed slightly. "Yes, Majesty," she answered. She would not meet Palaton's eyes as she turned back to him.

Gathon was waiting outside the study doors, his lips still pursed in that expression of his. Jorana halted, allowing Palaton to exchange words with the minister.

"Anything said within Charolon is confidential," the minister said.

"I understand."

"See that you do." Gathon jerked his chin and Jorana marched forward again. Palaton moved past, but he felt the minister's dark glare upon his back until the hallway turned, bearing them out of view.

Palaton wondered what a Sky was doing as a minister to the House of Star. He wondered if the Choya's innate abilities and devotion to Cho mired him in a job he hated.

The intricacies of Charolon were vast. Without a guide, Palaton would never have found the apartments he had been given unless he consulted his *bahdur*. Jorana led him there and left him. He entered the rooms, found he'd been given an exterior view, and that the rain had dwindled to a thin drizzle once more. The darkness had lightened to a foglike gray that hung over the park and grounds. Palaton threw open the windows and took a deep breath. He began to feel the fatigue of the journey that had brought him here and sat down on the edge of a bed. There was an aura about Charolon he had never seen before and he could not define it.

He had not asked to be in the emperor's confidence, but now he bore the burden of it. The emperor would not release him unscathed. The only question was what would be required of him, and was it an act he could perform and still live with himself?

With a taste in his mouth like ashes from the burning fire below, Palaton lay back on the bed and drifted into sleep.

He awoke to a soft knock on the door. He blinked, forgetting his dream as it drifted away from him, sat up and looked out the still open window. The room was icy, the sky outside the pitch of deepest night. The knock sounded again and he rolled to his feet.

Jorana stood inside the doorway as he opened

it, framed by the softest of lighting from the corridor. It set her mane into a golden aura.

"I thought it would be easier for me to find you than for you to find me," she said gently. She put an open hand out tentatively.

He took it and drew her in. She filled his arms nicely. "I thought the emperor waited for you."

"Panshinea has other amusements," she said, her voices low and warm. She fit her curves neatly to his leanness and did not complain about the chill in the room.

Soon he did not feel it either as her heat thawed him.

She left his bed in early dawn. He lay with one eye open, watching her dress, his nostrils filled with her scent, musky and perfumed and hinting of the sex they had shared. She stood and fastened her collar, one hand going to her House badges to make sure they were in place. Then she leaned down to give him a swift, fleeting caress.

"Trust no one," she said. She closed his eyes with a touch of her fingertip.

He waited until the door closed before snuggling into the warm hollow in the bedcovers. Her words sealed him back into an uneasy sleep. When he awoke again, the bleak sunlight was streaming through clouds and the birds were chortling in noisy clamor.

Breakfast was a public affair, buffet lines for those doing business with the throne that day. He found credit chits upon the bureau in his quarters and cashed those in for a breakfast of *bren*, weak and watery looking, fresh baked rolls, stewed *aprins* with nectar sprinkled upon them, and braised eggs. The food was good and hot, the *aprins* sweet and juicy though their season was summer and Charolon stood on the brink of winter. He savored the tastes of home.

He listened obliquely to the conversations going on around him, not endeavoring to pick up talk, but doing it anyway. There was a lot of concern about the relocation riots—Panshinea had been right in saying that it would soon be old news. Troops were being sent in force to evacuate the county of Danbe and bloodshed was expected.

Palaton knew about the Danbeans. Superstitious folk, as rooted in their river valley as the stone mountains surrounding them were rooted in the earth. He also knew the river waters were strained greatly by the population and that Panshinea had probably waited as long as he could before ordering Relocation. Strange that a population would stay and completely destroy the ecological balance before moving voluntarily, he thought as he ate his braised eggs.

Even stranger that they would add to their own destruction by warfare.

He found the Earthan second waiting for him when he cleared his dishes. The Choya stood with a resigned look etched into his heavy face.

"*Tezar* Palaton, please accompany me."

The summons did not surprise Palaton. What did startle him was the view across the massive dining hall, crowded with Choyan and alien visitors, of a *tezar* moving with an arrogance he thought he recognized. He froze in place and felt his gaze narrow.

The Choya was in one-quarter profile and Palaton stared a moment longer until he identified the aura as Nedar's. He wondered what purpose Nedar had at Charolon, and then wondered if it was the same as his own. Had Panshinea summoned him as well? And if so, why?

The Earthan guard touched his sleeve. *"Tezar,"* he repeated patiently.

"Coming," Palaton answered absently and followed the guard, pondering the paradox of Nedar's presence. What need had Panshinea of the best of the current pilots off contract?

Panshinea stood in his formal offices. He smiled widely as Palaton entered. "Brethren. Minister Gathon has convinced me that your instinctive reticence is invariably correct, and that you will be most unsuited to the task I suggested last night. However, I'm hoping you'll attend me for a season or two. I'm in need of a personal pilot and an honest Choya."

Palaton decided he must remember to thank the disapproving minister. He gave a correct smile. "My leisure time as a pilot is not always available."

"I'm the emperor," Panshinea said brusquely. "Something can and will be arranged." His eyes went hard. He turned sideways. "May I introduce you to the Prelate of the House of Star, Magi Rindalan."

In the rear of the oval office, ensconced amid upholstered pillows and rich, antique carved woods, the head Prelate of the God-in-all rested, his eyes gleaming like pale lights in the corner of the room. Palaton felt a pulsing at the base of his throat. Of the three Prelates of the three Houses, Rindalan was without dispute the most powerful.

The Prelate stood, large hand held out in greeting, his robes rustling about his gaunt body. His horn crown was the largest Palaton had ever seen, and his sparse fringe of chestnut hair barely covered his domed skull. He had pale blue eyes of the first water and his grip engulfed Palaton's own.

"*Tezar* Palaton," the magi enthused. "I am pleased to be meeting you. Your fame proceeds you and does Cho proud."

There was a glow beyond the warmth of flesh touching flesh as their hands met. Palaton had never encountered anyone with such a forceful aura. Their meeting practically sparked, and there was an answering flash in the Prelate's light blue eyes. An expression of satisfaction passed over the holy one's face before he turned away and Palaton wondered what he had done to please the Prelate.

"I am proud to be one with Cho," Palaton answered. "But I'm afraid whatever reputation I have has been greatly exaggerated."

"Nonsense," countered Panshinea. "You carried out your contract with the Gurans brilliantly."

"I took advantage of Choyan talents," Palaton murmured. He felt ill-at-ease. "And I did nothing but drop the wing. It was my pilots who delivered the payload."

"As modest as an Earthan," said the Prelate heartily. He stalked about the edges of the room, his robes rustling noisily about his ankles. "Are you sure this fellow is one of ours?"

A long, slow second passed. Palaton found himself holding his breath, unsure of what the emperor's Householding knew about him. Did Rindalan know of his dubious parentage—and if he did, was he challenging the emperor with it? Palaton hesitated, uncertain of what to answer. Panshinea filled the silence with laughter.

"Rindalan has a ribald sense of humor, does he not?" the emperor said, before sitting down with a thump. He added, "We'll be needing a sense of humor. The Danbeans have vowed to fill their river with blood before they can be forced to leave."

The Prelate raised a lanky finger in warning, a digit as thin and knobby as his entire body, and looked toward Palaton, who suddenly felt extremely uncomfortable. "*Tezars* are divorced from Choyan politics, Highness," Rindalan said mildly.

"It matters not," said Panshinea. "He'll be flying me over tomorrow."

Palaton felt his eyebrow raise before he could control it. He turned slightly away from both the Prelate and the emperor to hide his expression, embarrassed at his lack of restraint.

"And do you think," said Rindalan dryly, "that taking a hero with you will protect you from public opinion?"

"It couldn't hurt. Besides, I'll need the best piloting skills. Intelligence says they'll have their shields up in case we send in drones to dislodge them. They're an agro-community and their shielding won't hold against someone like Palaton here."

"You're defying them," Rindalan warned. "Even an emperor hasn't the right to mock his people."

"By the fading aura, someone has to knock some sense into their thick, horned skulls! The Danbe is dying. They're not thriving there, the population is doing little more than surviving. The laws of relocation were set up with a purpose in mind and must be obeyed. There is no right or wrong here, there is only *necessity*."

Rindalan examined a bit of fluff on his sleeve, but his voices filtered up strongly from his bent face. "I'm told there are those who say Charolon itself is overdue for relocation, and that those who must move and those who can stay are decided . . . politically."

Heat blazed up on Panshinea's face. The grimace of anger accompanying his words distorted his handsomeness. "They'll flee Charolon like plague-ridden rodents when I die. That'll be soon enough for my critics. Relocate carrying my ashes with you!"

Rindalan had not looked up, but he responded soothingly, "Now, now, my emperor. You are a Choya in your prime. Thoughts of death are beyond you. We can't afford to be melancholy. There's work to be done and you alone can do it."

"Do you hear that, *tezar*? The High Prelate has conceded a realm of Cho is under my rule rather than his."

Palaton, standing to one side, ignored till that moment, felt keenly that he had no right to be there, nor did he understand why the two of them tolerated his presence. He did not want to know the workings of the throne. He did not want to be privy to Panshinea's flaws or the Prelate's ambitions. "With your permission," he got out, "if I'm to fly, I'd like to oversee the plane's preparation."

Panshinea's gaze flew to his face. The emperor stared, while his color paled to normal and his distorted features reverted to normal. Palaton had the distinct feeling that the Choya had forgotten who he was and why he was there. The Prelate, too, looked at him, and though his face was half-hidden by the line of Panshinea's hunched shoulder, there was a wariness about his stance.

"Of course you wish to fly," the emperor said, his voices vibrating with patronization. "Like birds on the wing, let loose your *tezars* to the sky!"

"Another play, majesty? Or is it poetry this time? Your reference eludes me," Rindalan remarked smoothly, as if aware Palaton was suddenly floundering.

The emperor hunched, as if in pain. His walk crabbed. He crossed the room to the Prelate. He put out his hand. Rindalan countered. There was a flare of auras as they touched, a burst that made Palaton's eyes water with its brightness.

Panshinea took a deep, shuddering breath. His *bahdur* shone thinly. "Well," he responded. "If you need a plane, Gathon will order you one. And what would you recommend?"

"Nothing less than a stinger if you intend to make a fly-over through shielding." Palaton could hardly talk, but the warning remained on Rindalan's face to say nothing untoward. He had just witnessed a parasitism of talent, but the Prelate acted as if nothing unusual had happened, as if Panshinea had not stolen from him. Palaton thought of the parasitic pilot who'd died the last time he'd been to Blue Ridge. It had been a just fate for that Choya. What, then, should he think of his own emperor?

Palaton had no idea. The Prelate stayed half-hidden, his purposes his own.

"Do you know why I intend to go to Danbe personally?" asked Panshinea keenly.

"I suppose," Palaton answered slowly, "I would do it to show them their vulnerability. I would show them that I was willing to risk my blood first to save them the bloodshed that might follow if rioting continued and force had to be brought in. But I wouldn't settle for a fly-over. I'd land and tell them face-to-face."

"Let them know that no one is safe or above the law, not even their emperor?" Triumph colored the emperor's voices. His eyes looked brighter.

"That approximates it."

Panshinea smiled gently. "Then we're of a mind. I will not place my life in the hands of someone I suspect. I'll have Jorana take you to the airstrip. Gathon will send a commission ahead of you. Take whatever plane you see fit. I want to leave this afternoon, after my luncheon conferences." He turned to Rindalan.

Palaton was halfway out the door when the emperor said, "GNask has a most interesting proposition. He has offered to lend me mercenaries to save me the agony of sending Choyan after Choyan. What do you think, Prelate, of hiring the Abdreliks?"

"I think it absurd."

"As do I. The ambassador surprises me with his knowledge of the Danbe situation, but I won't let an Abdrelik set foot on Cho. Their intelligence is accurate enough." Mercifully, the closing door muffled the rest of the conversation.

Palaton stopped in the hallway, sickened by what he'd seen, and he took a deep breath to cleanse away the aroma of Panshinea's illness.

Chapter 11

His mouth had gone dry. He had felt both Panshinea's *bahdur* and his sanity flicker in and out, burn hotly and then gutter. Was he the only one who sensed it? He could not have been ... the Prelate Rindalan flamed with aura. By his very position which bespoke extreme closeness with the God-in-all, he could not fail to sense Panshinea's illness. Rindalan must know what Panshinea stole from him. As for Gathon ... the Sky minister might serve purposes of his own, but being taken down with Panshinea could hardly be one of them.

But Panshinea would fall. It was inevitable and the more erratic his behavior became, the quicker the downfall. Palaton guessed that Rindalan and Gathon must be praying for the time needed to consolidate their own futures. And when that time came, he would not give a gold piece for the length of Panshinea's life. The emperor would die.

He'd not seen such a thing in his lifetime. The old emperor, Panshinea's uncle Clibern, had died in his sleep, at an advanced age, a steady if unspectacular ruler. His boyhood memories of the funeral processions in each city's streets and the feasts of farewell were dim, as was his memory of Panshinea's ascension.

The palms of his hands itched as though he should be gripping something and could not. The only destiny he could control was that of the plane he'd be taking out as soon as it was serviced and the emperor was ready to leave. But the consequences of that flight would either serve Panshinea well ... or aid his enemies. Palaton would be riding treacherous winds and thermals which could downdraft or shear off without warning, bringing him tumbling down. With a feeling in his gut vaguely like hungriness, Palaton turned to the corridor that would take him to his rooms where he'd await Jorana's escort to the airstrip.

Two floors up, the Earthan second met him coming off the lift. He wore his winter uniform buckled against the outside weather. The guardsman's smile was tight.

"*Tezar* Palaton," he said in welcome. "My lieutenant is delayed. May I convey you to the airstrip?"

Disappointment pricked him, but he had no right to expect Jorana's personal attention. He inclined his head. "Let me get a coat against the wind and I'll be right with you, Second."

"Call me Darb," the Earthan told him, and took up position outside the door as Palaton entered.

Palaton scouted through his gear quickly. He took an all-weather coat and his flight suit as well, thinking that he might not come back to his rooms. He changed into flight boots, packed a small duffel, and stepped out of the room, his *bahdur* flickering about him, raising the hair on the back of his neck, his horn crown throbbing briefly. This suite was not his home—he had not stayed here for more than a day's span, yet he

had to resist the urge to look it over with a
sweeping glance of farewell as if he might never
return. He shut the door firmly on his superstition and stepped out to join Darb.

They left the palatial estate by way of a circuitous route and Palaton thought of times far
back in Choyan history when barons fled rival
armies through such back routes. Charolon was
old enough to have stood through warfare like
that. Its stained rock walls held flickering auras
that he might have read, if he'd had the talent
for it. It occurred to him, as he echoed Darb's
footfalls, that no one other than the emperor's
staff and Nedar knew he was there. He could
disappear from the face of Cho and no one
would know what had happened, unless they
stopped to read yet another anguished aura
splashed like blood upon the walls of this cavernous tunnel. A chill worked its way down the
collar of his flight jacket.

The tunnel mouth opened up and a stray beam
of light arced down from splitting clouds to illuminate the conveyance waiting for them. Darb
settled in the driver's seat, stating, "The emperor
does not always like a public departure."

"I guessed as much," Palaton answered dryly,
seating himself. "How far are we from the
hangar?"

"Another twenty minutes or so." Darb punched
in coordinates and started the vehicle. It
hummed into power and lurched away.

They drove through a newer section of the
city, its lines cleaner, straighter, its direction
driving upward, stacking inhabitants efficiently,
if not as grandly. Darb piloted the vehicle
through the passways, shadow lines of the

buildings dappling them and Palaton thought of his cadet days when he raced planes down blind canyon walls, his *bahdur* pinging like a fire alarm.

The Houseless lived in these areas, the Choyan who had no extrasensory talents, or at least none that were reliable and measurable. They were God-blind, this massive part of the population, dependent upon the guidance of the Houses. Palaton looked out of the window and wondered, for the hundredth time, what it would be like when his *bahdur* burned out. How would it be not to know the living from the dead, not to feel the vibrations of the God-in-all which ran through every organic part of Cho, not to feel connected to the balance of nature of his own world?

Palaton stared at the faces of the Choyan they passed, those walking in the streets, those glimpsed through storefronts, those whose faces were mirrored in the windows of other vehicles— none seemed particularly anguished. They did not seem bereft. It was not true that you did not miss what you had never had—there were yearly riots between the Housed and the Houseless. He wondered if the settlement at Danbe was Housed or if it was generally a God-blind population. A settlement which had a Householding had enough talent running through its gene pool to be sensitive, if not totally aware. If otherwise populated, then their resistance to Relocation might be easier to understand. Other than through scientific testing, they could not see or feel the damage they inflicted upon their surroundings. Without that inner sight, they could not truly believe.

Darb did not need to keep his full attention

on driving. Letting the vehicle do its automated work, he turned full-face when Palaton spoke.

"What's Danbe like? Is it God-blind?"

"It's not Householded, if that's what you're driving at." Darb's thin lips tightened further. Palaton saw the distaste on his face, his frown distorting the facial tracing under the fine layer of his left cheek. Plain onyx lines, rather than more expensive jewelry, and Palaton speculated as to what the second's background was.

"I was wondering," Palaton said mildly, "why the Danbeans refused to move."

"You don't have to be Housed to have a love for your home." Darb returned his attention to his driving and his expression settled into sullenness.

Palaton could see that the Earthan would not be pressed into further conversation. There were ripples here he could sense, but he had no way of discovering all the ramifications and he knew better than to stir such waters. He sat back and formulated flight plans while watching the canyons of apartments give way to service factories and manufacturers and then to reclaimed fields.

A breakwind stand of trees stood stark and bare along the line of a runway that had seen better times, but was still more than sufficient for their needs, with a hulk of bays and hangars hugging the far end of it. The vehicle turned in and came to a halt inside the wide flung doors of the foremost bay.

Palaton got out and stretched before reaching back in for his bag. Darb remained seated, keyboarding in an entry to his duty journal, and Palaton left him in the vehicle, anxious to see the plane. He moved deeper into the hangar, alert for the noises of the robotic crew serving the stinger, but a great, empty building greeted him. Palaton cast about, thinking the small, sleek plane might be hidden in the shadowy recesses of the hangar, but he saw nothing. He heard Darb shuffle up behind him and turned, saying with mild irritation and disappointment, "The stinger's not been brought in yet."

"Nor will it be, not to this location," Darb answered quietly. "This field's been abandoned for several years." His voices echoed in the cavernous building.

Palaton dropped his bag to show his empty hands, but Darb had pulled his enforcer and stood steady, barrel trained on the *tezar*. There was a quaver to the Earthan's voices which screamed out the second's instability, and Palaton fought to hold himself still and calm.

"What is this? Have I offended the emperor?"

"Panshinea? No. Him you have not offended." Darb looked old and tired. The enforcer wavered slightly in his hand and he wrapped his second hand about his first to steady it. "Turn around, *tezar*, so that I don't have to see my disgrace reflected in your eyes."

"You're not disgraced yet. Turn back from this."

Darb's nostrils flared as he gave a cynical snort. "My House orders this. I have no choice." He took a side step. "Surprised? You have a short memory for a *tezar*. You've faced assassins before."

He could not keep his amazement inside, but he masked it with sarcasm. "Calling yourself an assassin is rank flattery." Palaton gathered his *bahdur* as he spoke, readying to move before Darb could shoot. He fought to hold his aura even, before he could flare it out and leave it burning behind him creating the illusion of himself frozen in immobility while he moved out of harm's way. He'd never done it before and was not even sure it was within his talents' range, but it was the only chance he had with Darb facing him at point-blank range. His thoughts raced ahead of his words and he could feel his aura gaining strength.

"I don't deserve the attention."

"My House disagrees."

"The Earthans are not killers. Leave that to the Skies."

"We do what we have to for the greater good. The Wheel turns—you'd deny us our ascendancy, all of you! We are not adequate, they say, to the challenges that face us." Darb's lip curled back. "We'll take what should be freely given."

"I don't stand in your way."

"If you think that, then you're more of a fool than I thought you." Darb's voices hardened and Palaton could empathize with the squeeze of muscles that accompanied it. His finger would be contracting along the trigger.

Now, and only now. Palaton let his aura blaze, flaring with a heat that scorched as it left his body, and he threw himself to the left, skidding across the dusty, broken concrete flooring of the hangar as Darb fired at the illusion left in his wake. The weapon discharged, blinding them both, leaping in Darb's shaking hands.

Palaton got to his hands and knees. He bolted upward, racing across the building even as Darb let out a cry of dismay.

Palaton had never faced an enforcer before. He had no idea what kind of charge they carried but knew it had to be considerable. He took a running leap to catch a machinery crane, snagged the hook, and let it carry him swooping into the shadows. The enforcer spat again. Its heat seared across the back of his head and Darb cried out a second time.

Fear settled in Palaton's gut, cold and greasy. He kicked out with his heels and caught the high catwalk stretching across the hangar's eaves. He hung upside down by his knees for a second as he let go of the crane's hook. He had a blurred view of Darb searching wildly, then he righted himself with a grunt and perched overhead on the catwalk. He watched Darb flounder about below.

The second had called him a fool, and a fool he was. The world, he thought, was far bigger and more devious than he'd given it credit for being. He was a baron, and a rival's army had come to wipe him out. The reasoning behind it could be figured out once he had survived.

Palaton stood up cautiously. The catwalk gave no metallic moan beneath his weight to betray him. He did not think he could walk along it silently and if noise did not reveal him then dust surely would. He looked up into the darkened eaves of the building and saw utility cables which had come loose from their mooring and hung downward like vines.

They might loosen further . . . or not. Secure, they would take him to the rooftop and out the ventilation gratings. He might even make it back to the vehicle before Darb.

Palaton flexed his hands to work his nerve up. Then, with a short bound, he leapt up and caught the cable. He hung, dangling in the air for a moment, before the cable came loose with a tremendous whine and he plunged groundward.

Darb looked up and shouted. The barrel of the enforcer pointed upward, discharging magma-like into the dim recesses of the hangar, as Palaton swung downward. The flare missed. Palaton knew he was a target and that Darb could not possibly miss again. His *bahdur* smoldered, but for what purpose, he did not know. He only knew that he wished the Earthan motionless. Palaton lost his sight briefly and felt, before his eyes cleared, the impact of their two bodies colliding.

The impact jarred him to his teeth. He let go, the cable snaking about him like netting, and Darb rolling away with a loud grunt and an audible snap. Palaton slid to a halt on the flooring, trying to catch his breath, fighting to get back on his feet before the second could come after him again.

Gasping, Palaton rolled to his knees. Darb never moved. He lay stretched out on the broken pavement, his hand curled tightly about the enforcer, his uniform besmirched with dust and filth. His neck was twisted at an impossible angle. Palaton sucked in a breath as he realized that the impact had broken the Earthan's neck.

Choyan had incredibly strong necks because of the weight of their crowns, yet that same strength was treacherous just below the skull case at the apex of the neck itself, where the crown weight rested. There was that one small area of neck where the crown overwhelmed it, where a solid chop would snap the vertebrae despite the musculature.

There was the imprint of a heel in the flesh of Darb's neck at the nape. Palaton could not have hit him more solidly if he had planned to come swinging down from the eaves.

Gorge rose at the back of his throat, hot and burning. He got shakily to his feet and spat it out. He had done Darb a favor. His House would have treated the second much worse for his failure. He told himself that and knew it was true, and regretted the death anyway, and not simply because Darb could give him no answers now.

Quiet voices said, "Palaton."

He looked up and hesitated. Jorana stood in the hangar door. Her face creased in distress. "I saw," she said. "I would never have believed it if I had not seen it. I couldn't get a clean shot. I couldn't save you. . . ."

"He's dead," Palaton said lamely.

She strode across the hangar floor and knelt by the body. She touched him and shrank back. It astonished Palaton that she would react so to death. Surely she'd seen more of it more intimately than he had. "He's stone cold," she said. "But I saw him die. What did you do to him?"

"Nothing. I gave him an illusion aura to get out of range. His neck broke when we collided—"

Jorana swung about on her heels. She stayed kneeling at Darb's side. "He wasn't capable of this. Even for an Earthan, he wasn't capable."

"But he did."

Her expressive eyes watched him closely. "Who are you, what are you?"

"A *tezar*, nothing more."

She turned away from him, ran her hand over the body again. She shook her head, baffled. "The why and how of his death tells me that, even if you don't know it, there is more." She stood, slowly. "A Choyan who does not know himself is a mystery in itself."

Palaton's mouth felt like dust. He could not

know himself, not without knowing his parentage. But he knew himself well enough to predict his behavior and reactions, and no one outside his House had ever come this close to unmasking him.

"I did nothing." He shook his head for emphasis. "He brought me here. He turned the enforcer on me. I ran for my life. What would you have done differently?"

"Nothing." Jorana tilted her head in consideration. "He probably would have killed me. I thought I knew Darb well." She halted abruptly. "I'll take care of the body. Can you go on without me?"

"If I have to."

"You have to. The emperor is making preparations for the flight you've promised him. You'd better hurry." She turned her back on him and he left the hangar to let her mourn in private and then do whatever she had to do.

He picked up his duffel near the doors and headed back to the vehicle he'd arrived in. Jorana's skimcar stood off to the side. The on-screen readout showed him that Darb had doctored the vehicle destination and driver. According to the information, Palaton had driven it alone.

He climbed in the driver's seat. He sat for a moment, door open, listening to the wind keen, thinking about what to do.

Palaton reached out and closed the conveyance's door. He found the emperor's airfield in its stored memory and keyed it in. Let them think he'd gotten lost and wandered. Darb had doctored the destination journal and it would never lead to this location.

Jorana came out of the hangar. She paused

by the window. "I've erased the auras. If and when his body is found, they'll think salvagers did it. This area is due for demolition and redevelopment soon. The pickers will be swarming over it. From the condition of his body . . . the time of death will be dubious anyway. I've changed my duty log to show that I sent him on perimeter patrol."

This could not be free. "What do you want from me?"

She was close enough to caress him. But she did not. Her lips curved slightly. "I have a career," she said softly. "I worked hard to become Housed. I wanted to pilot the skies and the Chaos beyond, but I wasn't that good. But my child. . . ."

What she suggested lanced through him, piercing the shock of Darb's attack and death. "I'm a stranger here. I was told not to trust anyone but I've made the mistake of doing it three times." Rindalan, he thought, and the emperor and the Earthan second. No more.

"And you'll trust no more. You're learning," she said, and her voices trembled with regret. She moved away from the vehicle.

Palaton eased the brake off and the conveyance jolted forward. He had a flight ahead of him and now he let its importance overwhelm everything else. It seemed the one rock solid event in a swiftly changing world.

Chapter 12

"No flight plans," Panshinea said, rocking back on his heels.

"Your highness, I must. It's regulation and with good reason. If we should go down, it's the fastest way to trace us—"

"If we go down, *tezar*, the House of Sky will start a generation-long celebration and there'll be no one out looking for us." The emperor looked out the plane window with a melancholy air. "And I don't want the communicators knowing where we're going. I'm having enough damn trouble with the media."

Tezars did not need flight plans, they were for the lesser talented and instrument tracked, but Palaton had been well-instructed and Panshinea's whims went against the grain. Rindalan looked away as Palaton glanced at him and he knew that no help was forthcoming from the Prelate. "Very well, your highness," he answered. "Then we're ready."

The emperor looked back at him. "Have you ever, Palaton, not been ready?"

He did not need much time to think about it. "Not for flying," he answered briefly, went up front, shut the door between them, and sat down at his console.

The windshield revealed a flying lane cleared

for their exclusive use. The crew walked away from the plane, ducking temporarily out of his line of sight and reappearing near the hangar. Only the flagman remained, red banners filling his hands. He directed Palaton out onto the lane. The sky had gone bleaker, and it looked as though it might begin to empty out its tears soon. He thought briefly of Darb lying undiscovered, unmourned, where he and Jorana had left him in an abandoned building under that bleak sky. He brushed the thought from his head and ignited the engines for warm-up.

The plane thrilled under his touch. Its instruments were honed for lightning reflexes. He dried the palms of his hands on his pant legs. Then he began to key in targets, coordinates, thermals, and a destination that he simply *knew* lay where he said it did, because that was what he was. The console cued him when the plane was ready, and he eased it out onto the flight lane. When the flagman signaled, he pushed the throttle forward, the plane rushing to take off.

Then he was airborne, free, balancing between gravity and wind lift, the machine answering his wish, his hope. He leaned over the console, feeling like an aircraft himself, balancing between instrumentation and *bahdur*. The geographical and meteorological patterns of the world could be read by instrumentation, but there were other patterns affecting flight and those he searched after now. There was a topography of spiritualism that surrounded Cho, a topography that constantly changed, was being carved out and rebuilt, sculpted and let fall, nurtured and destroyed, and it affected the physical world in ways which only the talented could perceive.

He had not flown Cho in over two years, and

as he did so now, he grasped for its essence, held it ribboning in his fingers, silken, then harsh, fresh, then corrupt, and he wondered.

There was a rattle behind him and Panshinea leaned into the control room.

"How long before arrival?"

Palaton brought himself back to the instrumentation. "Two hours," he gauged.

"Time for a nap," the emperor grunted, and stumbled back to the lounge of the plane. Like the plane itself, the passenger area was sleek and dynamic. Panshinea would have to lie lengthwise if he wished to nap. Palaton smiled to himself.

He felt himself slowly losing that expression as Cho reared up at him, demanding to be perceived and understood. He caught a sense like that he felt when skimming Sorrow, that here was a mystery he must divine, that his own personal mystery depended upon its revelation. Flying into the low ceiling and a late autumn storm front made the plane buck and pitch, and yet below this reality was another layer just as storm-tossed and demanding.

Palaton's sense of well-being disintegrated into anxious watchfulness as the war plane skimmed over the continental divide, chasing the shadow of the sun, barely seen through clouds boiling in the sky.

He'd been wrapped in silence for a considerable while when the cabin pressure changed subtly, incense whiffed inward, and he knew the Prelate had entered. There was a creak in the gunner's chair behind him. Palaton checked to make sure the firing console was inactive before swiveling his head toward his companion.

Rindalan folded his hands over his robed lap.

"Do you ever think of the God-in-all as your copilot, *tezar*?"

"No. More like the wind beneath my wings."

"Ah." Rindalan looked out the windshield. "Perhaps that is more suitable."

"And desirable," added Palaton without thinking. Rindalan gave him a dry laugh.

"There were auditions for this position," he informed Palaton. "And I'm still not sure His Highness made the best choice."

"I'm not political."

"No. I can see that. Nedar is, but he's far too aggressive. Actually, I favored a pilot who is not a *tezar*, but Panshinea likes to bask in the adulation the commons give you."

That settled the unanswered question in Palaton's mind about why Nedar had been at Charolon. It had been buried behind all the other questions needing answers, but it had been niggling at him.

Palaton did not ask why the emperor didn't pilot himself: they both knew why. His *bahdur* could not possibly be reliable enough any longer. He did not divert much of his attention from the panorama before him, busy avoiding thermal drops which would waken the emperor if they hit a pocket, but he said, "If your eminence would enlighten me, perhaps I could adjust my attitude."

Rindalan leaned forward. Palaton could only glimpse the Choya's profile from the edge of his vision, but the Prelate looked almost predatory. "If you did," Rindalan said, "I'd not trust you the way I do now."

"Then," and the corner of Palaton's mouth quirked slightly, "I'll settle for being second best and first chosen."

"You may pray we had not," reflected the Prelate. "Your instruments show shielding."

"We're nearing the Danbe. Is the emperor awake?"

"Not yet. I'll take care of it." Rindalan rose from the gunner's chair. "And thank you, my child. You may not be political, but you are astute."

The cabin wheezed with slight pressure again as Rindalan left. Palaton splayed his fingers over his console, wondering what the Prelate would have said if told of Darb's attempted assassination. And hadn't the holy one just given him a vote of confidence? *Or had he?*

He turned on the main cabin comlink and display so that Panshinea would have full access to what Palaton was doing. He did not wish the gunner's seat reoccupied. He scanned the console.

"Coming into the Danbe River basin, Your Highness. Full shielding is up and instruments show that return fire is being readied."

"Identify us," Panshinea answered. Palaton imagined the emperor sitting on the edge of his seat by the side viewing window, the sunlight setting his hair ablaze.

"Doing so." Palaton keyed out their id, and his own as well. Recognition came back so quickly he half-wondered if they had a precog among their commons. The response denied access. He told the emperor even as he sculpted out a point of entry despite their crude shielding.

"Take us in anyway," Panshinea snapped.

It wouldn't be easy. The shielding had blinds for those with *bahdur*, diversions of aura and instinct. And he couldn't know that they wouldn't fire, so he built in evasive action, and sat back to look at the webbing they'd strung and what he needed to do to pierce it without being caught. As aura blazed into his vision, he knew that few *tezars* would attempt what he was going to try. But he thought he could do it, and knew he had to, if the Danbeans were to survive Relocation.

He made his choices and keyed them in quickly. The plane trembled in answer, surging forward. He took the controls manually, with the computer backup for assistance. "Gentlemen," Palaton said grimly. "I hope you're wearing your restraints." He banked the plane sharply and took it down.

It was like unweaving a delicate tapestry. The shield was built in layers, and he peeled them away, slicing through them, never coming in directly because that was how shields defended. The plane skimmed delicately under his handling and it bucked twice as ground to air fire erupted near them.

"Those are automatic shots from the system," Palaton said. Some shields were fully automated, while some relied on partial automation and self-determination, and the remainder were manually called shots.

He could hear Panshinea muttering, "And is that supposed to calm me?" He was too busy to answer.

The seventh pass brought them under the shielding, clear of all but ground to air fire, a deliberate act to bring them down.

Palaton called for a landing lane. The response came back reluctantly, giving him the west to east lane.

"I have landing clearance," he informed the emperor.

"Get it down before they change their minds."

Palaton nodded absently, banked a turn and brought the plane in, knowing there would be no other air traffic to bother him, and hoping that they would not now be fired upon. He waggled the wings on the pass and came into line with the runway.

The Danbean air was acrid, dry despite the river, warm and windy. He had taken crosswinds into account, but as he stepped out onto the airfield, Palaton thought that he hadn't done so enough. Part of the turbulence had to be accounted for by high winds. He looked across the ground and saw crews on the run, conveyances pulling up behind the security fencing, and general havoc awaiting them.

He remarked to Panshinea, who was right behind him, "I believe we surprised them."

"We by God-in-all had better have impressed them."

Rindalan muffled a sound behind the emperor. It was made inaudible by the growing noise behind the security gates as Choyan poured out of buildings and onto the airfield. They were shouting something.

"What is that?" Panshinea asked.

Palaton didn't answer, but the High Prelate did. "It sounds, Your Highness, as if they're shouting '*tezar.*' "

The luminary of Danbe sat across from Panshinea at the conference table. He was a massive Choya, broad across the shoulders, with an elaborate horn crown, and dark, ebony hair streaking down his head and back. He was not one Palaton would have liked to lock horns with, and even Panshinea spoke with a circumspect look on his face. The luminary was a commons, but he radiated confidence and charisma, and knew his city-state backed him.

A timid Choya'i entered, as if knowing she interrupted matters of import, and scurried across the tiled flooring. The luminary's aide took her whispered request and frowned. He looked across the table.

Malahki paused, even as his finger stabbed out a point to Panshinea. "What is it?"

"I'm sorry, your honor. The Secondary Education Level has come in with busloads of children. They want to greet *tezar* Palaton. I can't disperse the crowds until they do."

Rindalan muttered an aside to Palaton. "That's your third bow."

Palaton did not answer. He was used to welcomes, although never one this tumultuous. He stood. Panshinea said, without looking up, "I give you leave to go."

He had not thought of asking leave. "The God-blind ask for me."

Panshinea waved him off.

The luminary watched him, weighing him with eyes of brilliant gold and brown. Some commons chose not to be tested after a disappointing childhood. Palaton wondered just how much talent was buried behind that shrewd gaze. Rindalan stood up between them, smoothing down his robes. "I think I could use a breath of fresh air, Palaton. May I accompany you?"

Palaton let him by. By the time the holy one had passed, Malahki's gaze had already dropped to the tabletop where the Choya studied the notes he had been taking.

The Choya'i aide waited for him, her hands

tucked nervously inside the sleeves of her jacket. She smiled as he drew near. "The children," she explained, "have been driven a long way to see you."

"I won't disappoint them," Palaton said. "Do you test often in this area?"

"No," she answered abruptly, with no further explanation, and he followed her out the door to the balcony of the civic hall.

Choyan filled the courtyard. He could see the smaller figures being led to the front, and the adults stepping back. Eyes brilliant, flashing in the late afternoon sun as they looked up at him, the young of his world crowded under the balcony. They could not sense his aura, but they devoured the sight of him as hungrily as if they could. Palaton raised a hand to them.

"Tezar." Spoken in a roar. The sound of it sent a chill down the back of his neck. He could do what they could not yet there was no spite or jealousy in their voices. They adored him for his talents.

The aide handed him an amplifier. It was country-standard, technologically modest, and as he took it, he wondered if those to the rear of the massive courtyard would even be able to hear him. "Thank you," he said, his voices modulated. The crowd hushed to listen.

"The Choyan of Danbe have shown great courage, and there are even more days of courage ahead. It was my pleasure to bring your emperor here. He made a request of me because he is concerned about your welfare and your future. But my pleasure is also my pain because I had to cross your shielding to do so. Still, it was done because I am a *tezar* and have the ability to do it. There are others who can follow.

Remember that. There is courage in compromise as well."

Palaton looked down to the eager faces of the young. He smiled. "I hope to see some of you after the next Choosing. Thank you." He handed the amplifier back, suddenly becoming aware Rindalan stood at his elbow, so close he might almost have shared the amplifier with him. But the Prelate hadn't spoken.

The crowd roared again, their voices filling the air, until their words became indistinct thunder. He stood until he could stand no longer because the Choya'i tugged on his cuff, taking him away. He answered her insistent demand.

The balcony door shut behind them, dimming the sounds of adulation. Rindalan smoothed his hair back from his crown and very quietly said, "Listen to that. A *tezar* garners more shouts than even an emperor—yet even an emperor cannot bear to lose that noise. That is something for you to remember, *tezar*."

Chapter 13

Panshinea retreated with a sunken look to his eyes, Rindalan murmured a few vague apologies, and the talks broke off abruptly in mid-evening with the emperor leaving for the secured rooms prepared for him. Palaton hesitated as Malahki called him back. He looked to Rindalan for guidance. The Prelate smiled. "Remember," was all he said before disappearing after Panshinea.

Malahki smiled. "Don't worry," he said. "I've been told that you're merely the pilot. A drink in the rear courtyard? It's been a long day."

Palaton followed in curiosity. The luminary strode out of doors, where a fog could be seen rolling in from the river as the dry night air coaxed it upward. A small table had already been set with cups and a carafe of wine, and a hand-*lindar* against the balcony wall. Malahki grabbed it up before sitting.

"Do you play?" he asked.

"No. But I enjoy its music. Shall I pour?"

"You honor me," said Malahki by way of permission and leaned over the instrument, cradling it in his arms. He began to stroke its strings vigorously, as if releasing pent up energy. The melody was a commons folk dance, lively and strong, and sweat dappled the luminary's brow before he finished.

He drained his wineglass in one gulp. He held the empty glass to the light and looked through it at the wine stained walls. They were a pale yellow in the night.

"Do I convince you of my appetites?" asked Malahki abruptly.

If Palaton hadn't cadeted with a few commons, he would have been startled. The commons hated the stereotype of coarse, gutter mentality even as they embraced it for its shock value. But he merely smiled.

"Each Choya to his own," he answered and saluted with his half-empty glass. He would not drink any more for the rest of this meeting, not knowing when he would be called upon to fly. He watched Malahki.

"What was our flaw?"

"Ah, now. That would be telling."

Malahki leaned over his hand-*lindar* to pour himself another glass of wine. "And the flaw was nothing the God-blind could see anyway."

"Partially. Partially it was skill. And partially it was because, no matter how challenged, none of you had made your minds up yet to fire at your own emperor."

"No guts, eh?" Malahki took a deep drink. If the pale amber wine affected him, he didn't show it. He brushed back a stray lock of his deep black hair. "Was the fly-in your idea or Panshinea's?"

"Does it matter?"

"It does. If I knew that Panshinea had suggested it, I might develop some respect for the Fallen Star." Malahki ran a quick bridge across the *lindar* strings. He looked up, catching a flash

of something in Palaton's eyes. "Now that surprises you. You've been away, *tezar*, doing heroic
things for other worlds. While you've been gone,
our emperor has lost a considerable amount of
esteem."

Palaton kept his voices smooth. "The Wheel
turns. We all know that. Sometimes it seems to
creep, at other times to spin."

"Shall I pour you another cup?"

Palaton quickly covered the mouth of his
glass. "No, thank you. I've had enough."

"Yes," said Malahki sitting back so quickly
the strings of his instrument pinged, "I suppose
you think you have." He looked out across the
night-darkened courtyard, a much smaller one
than where an audience had greeted Palaton
earlier. "But we haven't had enough. This is our
river, our valley, our land, our homes. We
haven't had enough."

"Tell the emperor."

"I have been. All day. I may be just a common, but I sense that Panshinea isn't listening.
Relocation is as much a political maneuver as
it is an ecological one. We're to be made an
example of, to show that he still has his authori-
tarian grip. Well, *tezar*, that remains to be
seen." And Malahki launched into another vigorous musical rendition, punctuating the melody with boot stomps and slaps of his hand
against the belly of the instrument.

Palaton listened, hearing the power and the
dream and the frustration in the song. He did
not dare excuse himself until it was finished lest
he miss a nuance or anger the luminary. The
wine lingered until only a last, shimmering
drop, like a yellow diamond, gleamed at the
bottom of his glass.

* * *

Rindalan woke him in the morning. The elder Choya gave him a critical look, peered at the whites of his eyes, then said, "You look fit enough to fly."

"Of course I am." He swung his feet off the bed, dressing automatically. "When do we leave?"

"As soon as possible. His Highness and Malahki have been at it since dawn. Panshinea has issued an ultimatum. Now we leave and then we wait."

Palaton paused with one flight boot on and the other dangling from his hand. He heard disapproval in the holy one's voices. "Trouble?"

"Not for you, no. Unless, of course," and Rindalan cleared his throat, "you drank too much last night."

"And you've already given me my preflight clearance on that one." Palaton tugged his boot on. He hefted his flight bag. "I'm ready."

The Prelate led the way, swaying within his robes with the stride of a stately yet careful walker, wary in case his body should suddenly fail him. Palaton followed, shortening his own steps, trying not to overtake the older Choya.

They had no farewell committee. Panshinea waited impatiently with only two of the luminary's aides to protect him, his cheeks flushed with the chill of the morning. The wind had tousled his brilliant hair, nearly obscuring his horn crown. His eyes fixed on Palaton.

"Fit to fly?"

"Always," Rindalan answered for him. "Why such an early start? Are we being kicked out of town?" He held his robes with two fisted hands, a beanpole in the wind, his only belonging the humplike pack on his back.

"In a manner of speaking. Malahki asked for seventy-two hours, I wanted twenty-four, but I gave him forty-eight." Panshinea's gleam brightened, with his awareness that the aides listened to them despite the biting wind. Palaton gave him half his attention, the other half watching as the crew fueled and readied the plane. "Forty-eight hours," the emperor repeated, "or I'll declare martial law and Relocation will be forced."

Palaton never took his eyes from the maintenance crew. "We'll be ready in moments," he said.

"Good." Panshinea turned, eyeing the panoramic foothills of the river basin valley, ignoring the quiet leave taking of the two aides. In seconds, they were alone on the airfield. Palaton waved the crew off. He went over the plane himself for a last check.

Then he pulled down the small stair and helped Rindalan mount it. Panshinea sprinted up the steps as if in a hurry to leave Danbe, and Palaton followed.

The holy one took his seat, breathing heavily. Palaton looked toward him and raised a brow at his emperor.

"Don't worry," Panshinea said. "Age affects us all." He followed Palaton into the control pit but did not speak until he'd ignited the engines for warm-up.

"Can you land this anywhere?"

Palaton looked curiously at his ruler. "It's a war vehicle," he said. "It requires quite a length of lane. But if it were flat enough and long enough. . . ."

"Good. Circle around when you get up. The shields are off for the moment. I'm betting Malahki will put them up as soon as our exhaust trail shows. But I want you to come back. There's a site I want you to put down by, if you can."

The shield went up almost before they were clear of it. Palaton climbed, then banked, leaving the vapor trail Panshinea had requested. Then he set up jamming frequencies and took the plane down, hopefully out of range of the facilities and instruments of Danbe.

The emperor leaned over his shoulder. "Down there. See."

Palaton brought his targeting grid up for a closer look. "It's an industrial complex. Possibly even a crematorium. It appears deserted."

"Can you get us down there? The abandonment, I'm sure, is temporary."

Gone was the erratic, paranoid emperor. In his stead was a decisive leader. Palaton did not hesitate as the lane swept close. There was a grassy length along the river, possibly muddy, long enough for the plane to land and turn about again for takeoff. He could do the maneuver, though he wasn't entirely sure he wanted to.

"I can do it if it's necessary."

"It's necessary," answered Panshinea. He left the control room for his seat, whistling a classical air, as Palaton took the stinger firmly in hand.

The plane and the river nearly betrayed him. The grassy strip was boggier than he'd anticipated and as the hard brakes came into play, the stinger struggled to spin sideways and down into the river. Palaton fought and kept the plane straight, but his arms were trembling with the effort when it finally stopped. He could hear Panshinea and the Prelate get to their feet, but he called out, "Wait till I've turned about."

"Good idea," Panshinea returned. "We may have to leave in a hurry."

Palaton had enough fuel to leave the engines idling, so he did, but he blocked the wheels before trailing after the emperor and Rindalan. Panshinea bounded across the yard like a child. He headed, not for the complex, but for the crematorium Palaton had targeted earlier. He squatted down, rooting among the ashes and incomplete waste with a river stick.

Rindalan said mildly, "What are you doing, Highness?" His pale blue eyes watered slightly in the chill wind.

"Gathon gathered this bit of intelligence for me." Panshinea looked up from his squat. "This crematorium is illegal and, sadly, inadequate for industrial waste. But we asked ourselves, why did they have it? Why did they want it? What were they attempting to destroy so completely we would never know of it?" The emperor dug up an empty vial which hung to the tip of the stick. "Whatever it was, they shut this down quickly when we flew in. They didn't finish burning. Have we anything for samples?"

The two of them stood there at a loss. Palaton could see even more waste beyond the emperor.

"Rindy, toss out your pills and give me that massive vial you carry about with you. I can get soil and ash samples, at least."

"Majesty, my medicine—I'm at risk without it."

"Palaton will have you back to Charolon in a twitch. Take one now, just in case, and we'll get you more. Come on, Magi. Where's your trust in the God-in-all?"

Rindalan looked sour as he pulled a good-sized bottle from his inner vestment. "The God-in-all helps those who assist themselves," he muttered. He put a tablet under his tongue and then emptied the bottle in a muddy hole before Palaton could offer to keep some of the pills for him. He toed the ash and silt over the tablets before handing the bottle to Panshinea, who promptly filled it.

Palaton pulled his transcripts out of his inner breast pocket and took the protective pouch off them. He returned his private transcriptions to the pocket, took the pouch, and filled it with vials, sediment, and what looked like half-charred computer memory bits. He zippered the pouch shut and pushed it into Panshinea's hand. "This should do it. I suggest we leave, Majesty, before we risk contamination."

Rindalan said heartily, "And I second the suggestion." His lips were pale.

Panshinea took it and stood up. "You don't question me?"

They stood silently. He tilted his head. "Perhaps you do. Ask yourselves why they do not come to the Choosing yet show a *tezar* as much adulation as any Householding. Perhaps they haven't given up on being talented—perhaps they've chosen other methods of achieving it."

"Remnants of the Lost House," Palaton murmured.

"No. Nothing so simple. Genetic experimentation, if Gathon's theory is correct." He lifted the bottle and pouch. "If this shows waste tissue or

serum, we'll know why they refuse to abandon
Danbe. They're conducting experiments here they
cannot leave and cannot reveal."

Rindalan sneezed.

The emperor lost his obsessed expression
then, the lines of his face softening. "Come on,
Rindy. Let's get you out of the wind." He took
the Prelate's arm and led him to the plane.

Palaton trailed after thoughtfully. Genetic
experimentation had been outlawed centuries
ago, long after the Lost House had destroyed
itself with aberrations too horrible to contem-
plate. Even commons could not be so fearless
of the consequences . . . could they? He thought
of Malahki's fierce gold eyes and wondered. And
then he considered the method within Panshinea's madness and wondered some more.

Chapter 14

Nedar was waiting for them at the airfield.

Palaton instantly spotted him among the maintenance crew, just from the arrogant stance, before any other difference set him off. He throttled down for his landing, found his jaw clenched, and forced himself to calmness even as his plane touched the air lane, wheels burning.

The weather at Charolon had taken another turn toward winter. There had been ice on the runway, but the crew had sanded it, and he controlled the minor skid, bringing the stinger in just where he wanted it. He finessed the taxi, shut the plane down, and barreled into the main fuselage. The windows had been curtained and the lounge darkened.

Rindalan lay prone, Panshinea leaning over him, reading a bound text of classic plays, his voices rolling with timber and emotion. The gaunt Prelate looked past the emperor. "Home?"

"At last," Panshinea answered, setting aside his book. "Now you go partake of your medicine and rest in peace."

"God forbid," the holy one said. "I've indigestion from that dose you made me take. Never fix what isn't broken. Still," and his bleared eyes focused on Palaton, "it's good to be home."

Palaton opened the lock and put the stairway

down. He waited until the two had gone ahead, did a quick sweep about the cabin to make sure no belongings were left behind, and trotted down.

Nedar had greeted the emperor and the priest and moved on, his palm hovering over the skin of the stinger, just about to stroke it when Palaton grabbed his wrist. The two paused, almost in a dance move, animosity more chill than the dropping air temperature.

"No one," Palaton said, "touches my plane but me."

Nedar smiled widely. "A careful Choya. Still, one wonders why." He twisted his arm quickly, breaking Palaton's hold, and dropped his hand to his side. "A stinger," he commented, looking over the plane. "Nice. The emperor called me out and asked me to be waiting for him."

Palaton didn't answer. He knew what Nedar was doing, using *discernment* to determine where they'd been, and he didn't like it.

Nedar's smile grew more brittle. "There are other ways," he said, and turned away. He quick-marched to catch up with Panshinea, offering to carry his pack and the specimen pouch. If his skills were great enough, that alone would tell him they'd been to Danbe—but not how Palaton had broken the barrier. It was important to Palaton, for a reason he could not explain, that Nedar not know that much about their flight.

A shuttle took them back to Charolon. The two pilots did not talk. Rindalan sagged, his spare figure within his robes looking as if it could fly into pieces at any moment, and Panshinea wore an odd little smile of triumph on his face.

Jorana met them at the side entrance, saying the media communicators had been hounding the palace since late evening and that Gathon advised a statement be made, whether Panshinea wanted to or not.

The emperor said, "Open the conference room, then, and I'll be there as soon as I've talked with Gathon." The lieutenant nodded. Her gaze lingered on Palaton's face as she turned away.

Panshinea dismissed Nedar, then said to Palaton, "The rest of the day is your own. Talk to no one, please, even if the opportunity should arise."

"I understand."

"I wonder," Panshinea returned, tapping a finger against his elegant lips, "if you do." He offered an arm to Rindalan and escorted the Prelate up the public walkway into the palace, leaving Palaton at the mouth of the hidden ingress.

It was cold at the tunnel entrance. The streaked stonework sparkled with the bite of frost here and there, where the morning sun had not touched it. Winter had the capitol building in its ever firming grip. Palaton shrugged into his jacket and went up the secret passageway. Jorana's and Nedar's auras still tarried, marking the trail for him.

He retired to his rooms, found a new pouch for his transcriptions, and made his latest additions. He did not describe Malahki well and did not wonder that it wasn't within his skill to do so. He made a visit to the palace chapel and took a perfunctory seven-step cleansing, but did not feel absolved.

He took dinner alone, watching the rebroad-

cast of Panshinea's statement. Little was said
beyond the fact that representatives of the
emperor had met with representatives of Danbe
and that a forty-eight hour ultimatum had eventually been declared. Palaton turned the broadcast off, mulling over the ultimatum.

If Malahki's city-state had done the unthinkable, would forty-eight hours be long enough in
which to destroy all the evidence before Relocation? Or would they want total destruction?
What had they to hide and what might they
have accomplished? Younglings who no longer
had to attend the Choosing to measure their talents and see if they could be aligned with a
House was a matter which could change the
entire society of Cho as he knew it. Commons
who were no longer God-blind, yet totally unin-
structed and unprincipled in their use of their
bahdur. . . Palaton contemplated chaos. There
was no foreseeable way to navigate this future.

What did Malahki see when he looked into it?

Palaton stood restlessly. He went to his windows and saw that the capital city had quieted,
stunned by winter's first real blow—snowflakes
skirled past the window, muffling all sound and
light. Streetlights illumined the clouds of snow
drifting into the city. It hadn't been snowing
long—the dirty black stonework shone through
its cloaking. Palaton watched the storm. It
should snow most of the night. He felt its chill
and shrugged into a fleecy pullover.

He did not feel like sleeping. Palaton consulted the palace directory and found what he
was looking for. He left his apartment to begin
what looked to be a long convoluted walk. He
found his thoughts haunted by children—those
of Danbe, and those of the humankind who'd

once asked for his help, and the one which Jorana said she'd wanted from him.

Children were the future. Children without heritage or knowledge of their potential and without the training to help them achieve that potential . . . His own issue would not know its destiny, and he could not conceive with Jorana without revealing his own lost past. Sexual liaisons were one sweetness, bonding to reproduce another, and one which he'd denied himself. It hadn't been difficult earlier but now he was in his prime and others about him were making that commitment. He owed it to his House and to the *tezars*, for his line bred strongly, and fresh talent for his stenuous profession was always needed. Always.

But even though Jorana spoke of releasing her fertility, he didn't think he could release his. He did not have the love and trust in her that he needed before he could reveal himself. Her beauty did not hide her ambition. Her advice to trust no one, he feared, applied to herself as well.

With Darb's death between them, he didn't know how long he could deny her. The more hidden the second's death remained, the more doubt there would be to cloud the issue. He had done something which he couldn't undo and which shrouded his own future. Perhaps today it was still not too late. Perhaps.

Palaton stumbled within his thoughts, looked up, and found himself at the private exhibition galleries of Charolon, the end of his journey. Inside the palace security system, the gallery remained unlocked, though the doors were closed. Security scans did not track his progress.

He asked admittance and it was given him.

The artwork was incredible. He stood inside the threshold, the night suddenly given light and depth by the works displayed for his viewing. After long moments, he wove his way through the sculptures and mobiles, past the pictures and projections, until he reached the tapestries and wall hangings. There, the tapestry his mother had woven drew him inexorably.

He marveled at the detail, at the threadings, woven and then embroidered over. The panorama drew him in until he found himself examining it minutely—and then knew what it was he searched for.

He had dreamed, or been sent, that moment. A single drop of blood glistening on her slender fingers. Would Tresa allow it to mar the work, signifying an artist's pain and struggle, or would she not? In his dream, she had put her finger to her lips ... but now, as he drew close and looked, he saw the rusty-brown stain, as transparent as a teardrop, marring the threads.

In the years since her death, he'd thought his dream was only memory reawakened, surfacing out of his grief. Now he was riveted to the spot, unaware of where he stood or what he knew. The incident had to have been a sending and in it the artist had changed her mind and not allowed her work to be stained. A second chance. Palaton put a fingertip to it in wonder.

That portion of the embroidery showed the Great Wheel in Chaos above Cho, balanced upon its threaded turning the three Houses of Sky, Star, and Earth, depicted both in ethereal terms and with the more concrete symbols of each stitched in. The Wheel hung above Cho, rising.

Or, as he looked at it, perhaps crashing, diving into the flames of Cho which had birthed it.

Palaton stared for a long time. What had flames to do with the Houses of his people? This was not a classical representation of the birth of the Houses and he was not of a mind to understand his mother's artistic interpretation. And yet that tiny bloodstain upon the Wheel had captured his attention. Was there a message written here that only he might see and understand? Had she yet things to tell to him, to reveal?

"I'm incomplete, Mother," he whispered to the hanging. "You left me that way and because of it, I can't hear what you're trying to tell me." He dropped his hand to his side.

The staccato of bootheels upon the flooring outside the gallery caught his attention. Palaton turned, made his way to the open door, and slid it nearly shut, unwilling to be seen. His horn crown prickled with intuition.

The gallery lights dimmed. He watched through his narrow avenue of sight as the walkers came his way, one brisk, the other stumbling, slurred or reluctant. They came into view and Palaton caught his breath.

Jorana, and a young Choya, barely out of his childhood, eyes glazed, hanging upon her escort. Palaton felt his nose flare slightly, but he could detect no drug or alcohol upon the youth. From the coarseness of his horn crown, Palaton guessed him to be a common.

The Choya gave a convulsive jerk, pulling out of the lieutenant's hold, and he fell, taking her with him. Drool splattered the floor beneath his head and he stayed down, mumbling into the tiles. Jorana cursed, got to her knees and tried

to shoulder lift him up. His weight was too
much for her.

Palaton stepped out of the gallery. "Can I help
you?"

Startled, her eyes went wide, then narrowed.
"Of all wrong places for you to be in. Get out
of here, Palaton."

He bent to bring the youth to his feet anyway.
The Choya appeared stupefied. His mouth stayed
slack and he had no idea where he was, or with
whom. "What happened?"

"No questions. None." Jorana shouldered the
limp form. "Please."

He knew then, for he could suddenly feel the
aura taint. This youth had none of his own,
sucked out of him like a dried fruit, but an oily
overcoating slicked him and Palaton knew whose
it was.

Panshinea.

The emperor has his own diversions, she'd told
him. Like stealing the *bahdur* from the innocent
and defenseless? The rape of a soul unable to
defend itself? She saw his eyes and said, "God-
in-all. You *know*. How could you?"

"How could I not? Where are we going?"

"I'm getting him out of here and you're going
back to your apartment. It's your life. Get out
of here while you can."

He hesitated a moment longer. He lifted a
stray tress of hair from her eyes, so that she
could see better. It was soft beneath his fingers.
"How could you let him do this?"

Her lips tightened. "It keeps him going," she
said. "A small evil weighed against many . . . I
don't know. Now get out of here before you're
found. I'll come to you later." Struggling to balance the youth's weight she brushed past him.

Palaton looked up. He'd noticed the corridors had no immediate scans. Now he knew why.

It was more important to protect the emperor's secrecy than hundreds of years of artwork.

He took a deep breath and left.

True to her word, she came to him in those last, still hours before dawn, when all Choyan slept deeply and the souls of the weak often slipped quietly away.

But he was not weak, and he did not sleep, and he was on his feet the moment the door began to open.

The gold and silver traceries under the translucence of her face underscored bruises of fatigue. Her gray-blue eyes held the traces of tears recently shed. She carried a carafe of freshbrewed *bren* in one hand and two mugs in the other.

He drew her in and shut the door firmly.

"For your information," she whispered, "the security recording of this sector has been temporarily disabled."

She trembled with weariness as she sat down at the small round table by the window. She drew the curtaining back. "It's finally stopped snowing," she said.

Her hands were chill when she handed him his drink. She'd obviously been out in it.

Palaton mulled over the various things he could say to her, but before he could voice them, she said, "Darb's body was found earlier tonight. It's been established that salvagers killed him. The cold snap froze his body down and exact time of death couldn't be established." She sipped at her *bren*. "You're lucky."

"And I shouldn't press the fates."

"No. I don't think you should."

"Then I won't ask what you did with the Choya."

"Good." She looked back out the window. There were damp streaks in her bronze hair where snow had melted. "I couldn't tell you anyway, except that he'll be all right. His talents . . . what there were of them . . . have been bled. He was, and still is, a common."

"But talented enough to infuse our emperor. How close to being Housed was he? Were any of them?"

Her gaze flickered. "Close," she said. "It was Gathon's idea. I think if Rindalan found out, he'd break all ties with Panshinea. That, in itself, might bring the throne down. We can't afford that now. We can't afford for the failings of one Star to be intrepreted as the failing of the entire House." She rested her mug on the table.

He reached across and cupped her hand. "How long has your family been Housed?"

"I'm the first." A certain fierceness and pride underlined her voices.

He should have been surprised, but wasn't. Some of the new converts fought more fiercely to preserve their birthright than the old, established lines. He could sympathize with her, but not with the emperor. "Panshinea has to be stopped."

"No! He has to be cured."

"There's no cure for the neuropathy. It can be slowed or even remitted, but there's no going back."

"He doesn't think so—" Jorana stopped abruptly. She drew her hands out of his reach.

"The more I tell you, the more danger I put you in."

"All right." Palaton rocked back in his chair. The *bren* felt good in his throat, warming as it sank to his stomach. "I've enough for balance."

"Balance? Oh ... Darb." Jorana half-smiled. "How quickly you fit into palace politics."

"No," he said. "How quickly a pilot learns about updrafts and downdrafts."

"How to stay aloft."

He shook his head slightly. "Not quite." He watched her shiver despite her warm drink. He put his cup down and extended his hand once again. "I've a better way to warm you."

Sudden hope arrowed through her expression, then dimmed as she read the look in his eyes. "No promises," she said for him.

"No promises."

Jorana rose, taking his hand and pressing it to her throat. Her pulse drummed wildly under his touch. "For the moment, that's good enough." She came to him a second time.

Chapter 15

Sun streaming in the window woke him. Palaton blinked at its brightness, then realized that it was near noonday, and the light reflected from the snowfields about Charolon. He rubbed a watering eye and sat up, sheets tangling about his hips.

Jorana murmured and moved away from him, settling into the warm hollow he'd left behind. Her face had gone soft with sleep, peaceful and content. He put out the back of his hand to caress her cheek, then froze in mid-movement.

She shouldn't still be in his bed.

Palaton paused, thinking. She slept with abandonment, without worry over duty or work. Either she was off-duty . . . or part of her duty was to be with him.

He didn't think she would have revealed seeing him last night before meeting him. No, she'd been too genuinely worried about that. Therefore, that incident did not affect her coming to him. If it had, if she'd worried about implications, she would not have seen him last night.

Palaton pulled his hand back. He got out of bed carefully so as not to disturb her and went in to bathe quickly. He dressed in his high altitude flights, warm even in this winter aftermath, and pulled on his boots. The image of Nedar meeting him at the airfield, attempting to discern their whereabouts, and the knowledge that the emperor had called him out, nagged at Palaton.

There was no need for Nedar if Palaton had been chosen as Panshinea's pilot. Unless there were jobs that Nedar would do that Palaton would not.

Such as leading in a military force through Danbe's shields before the forty-eight hour ultimatum had expired.

Palaton snatched his jacket off its hook. He left his apartment at a run. He'd known he wouldn't be privy to whatever the labs had found in the samples they'd brought back, any more than he'd be privy to Panshinea's economic councils. He was a pilot, nothing more.

But if he'd been used to thread the needle, to find the fatal flaw in Danbe's shielding so that Nedar could later destroy it, that was his business. It was his skill which was being perverted, skill that Nedar couldn't quite match. Not only was Panshinea making a mistake, he was compounding it by using the ambitious Sky to do it. Whatever public opinion would later review these actions, Nedar would twist to his advantage.

He left through the public entrance, wide steps sanded so that the snow and ice would not prove a danger. Media communicators littered the vast staircase, muttering about the emperor canceling public meetings again. Where was Panshinea this noon?

At the airfield, watching his police enforcers take off. Palaton snagged an empty conveyance, programmed it, and skimmed off with no one noticing him.

The abandoned airfield was abandoned no longer, a hub of activity, the winter day streaked with vapor trails from the planes taking off, the air whining with their propulsion. Nedar must already have been gone, spearheading the flights.

He found Panshinea alone at the edge of the air lane, his furred coat flapping about him. He left the conveyance and approached the emperor.

Panshinea's green eyes widened at his approach. The emperor smiled wryly.

"Gathon told me you would know."

"I should have known sooner." Palaton breathed deeply in regret.

"And you would have stopped me?"

"Yes."

The emperor hummed to himself. He shoved his hands deep into pockets. "You can't save me from myself, *tezar*."

"Somebody should."

Their attention was drawn by a stinger screaming to become airborne overhead and winging away. Palaton's horn crown still rang with the noise when Panshinea said, "We found genetic waste. All we feared was in those samples we took. I won't use that as an excuse, of course. Too much panic if we revealed it. We'll call it toxic industrial contamination, necessitating immediate removal and Relocation. It's for their own good. Malahki will fight at first, and when he's lost, he'll have saved face. He won't reveal it either. And he'll have to bury his experiments even deeper underground next time.

We'll add years to his schedule, perhaps even discourage him altogether."

"Should he be discouraged?"

Panshinea looked away from the sky, meeting his gaze face to face. "Let me tell you something you won't have learned as a child from your history books. Let me tell you something most Choyan don't admit under any circumstances. There is no Lost House. We destroyed it, we Stars, Skies, and Earthans. The House of Flame, it was thought to have birthed all of us, but we destroyed it. Why? For doing much as Malahki was doing for the commons. We gave back the talents of healing, because a Flame could poison as well as heal. They meddled where no one, not even the God-in-all, should meddle. And there's not an emperor along the way who regretted the decision. Not even me. Not even if a Flame could have healed me." Panshinea shrugged defiantly into the wind.

It tasted of afterburn. Palaton looked around, then back at the emperor. He thought of his mother's artwork. The Great Wheel . . . descending or ascending . . . from a bed of flames on Cho. Had she known of the annihilation? "How . . . long ago?"

"Centuries. Before modern civilization. Oh, I don't doubt there's a stray or two out there—even the commons have talents there's no accounting for—but they'll not come back. We scourge them if we find one. We don't miss them much. Science makes up for miracles. But we've strict ethics for our technological community, rules which Malahki has chosen to ignore. He'll pay for that. Maybe enough that he'll hesitate to do it again. If not, he'll go the way of the Lost House. You've my word on that."

Panshinea looked up sharply. He must have felt Palaton's slight wince. The emperor showed his teeth in a half-smile. "My word not good enough for you?"

"I said nothing."

"An honest Choya doesn't need to. It's etched all over you, my Palaton. I can't keep you, now. You refuse too steadfastly to be corrupted by me. You would destroy yourself trying to save me. Not physically, as the others are doing, but morally. I'm not worth it. An incorruptible *tezar* is worth far more than a corrupted emperor. We've contacted Moameb at Blue Ridge. He's got a contract for you. You'll take it, of course."

"And if I don't?"

Panshinea studied him. "You would give up flying."

"Not voluntarily."

"That doesn't matter to me. The *bahdur* flickers in every *tezar* sooner or later. No one would dispute our word that you're done for, burned out, dying."

"Blue Ridge would."

The chill of the winter morn had brought a harsh flush to the emperor's handsome face. He half-turned from Palaton. "You cannot fight me." His breath fogged in the air. "There is always some secret, some price too high to pay. Don't make me search for yours, Palaton."

But as yet his secret remained hidden, or Panshinea would have revealed it to him. Given the choice of flying or not, he would fly. At least he was being given that option. He did not show the relief he felt. "All right, Highness. If you wish it."

"I wish it." Something gleamed deep in his

green eyes. "Or do you wish to stay and save me?"

"I'd save you . . . if I could."

"Then look and listen, *tezar*. Not even Gathon knows this, nor my devoted Rindy. Somewhere out there, someone knows how to renew *bahdur*. Not my poor, perverted way, but someone who knows what they do. The last emperor had begun to track them down, but they've grown canny. Find them for me, Palaton. Find them for me and save us all. Even yourself," and the emperor put a hand out and grasped his wrist, a chill band of iron. "It flickers in you as well. I know it. I've seen it in your eyes. Save yourself as well as me. Find out how they do it. Promise me."

His touch chilled Palaton to the bone, and he was struck speechless, unable to answer. Finally, he was able to force a single nod.

Jorana never suggested she should go with him. She watched him pack, his luggage as spare as always.

"I'll try to get him to bring you back."

"I don't want to come back." Palaton fastened a strap. He paused. "I want to fly Chaos."

"He's given you a garbage run!"

"For now. He could have had me killed for what I know. It wouldn't be the first time someone has tried."

Jorana blushed faintly. She put a hand on her hip. "It may be seasons before we meet again . . ."

"And maybe then I'll be ready to give what I can't today." He offered her that slim hope.

"Crumbs?" she said, her voices light.

"No. Not for you." Palaton hoisted his duffel. "Perhaps Nedar—"

She struck him. Not hard, but his cheek stung. His eyes blurred with sympathetic pain, then cleared.

Jorana hissed, "If the emperor's not good enough for me, why would you offer Nedar?"

Slowly, he said, "You've got high standards."

Jorana collected herself. She opened the door and paused in the threshold. "You could lose yourself, if you tried."

"Should I try?"

Her eyes sparkled too brightly. "No. Please."

"Then I won't. I'll come back to Cho, to my home at Blue Ridge. You'll be able to find me if you want to." He passed by her.

She whispered, "Thank you."

Palaton was waiting for shuttle assignment to Blue Ridge, looking forward to seeing Moameb, when he noticed a security crowd forming. At the end of the port, he saw diplomatic signs being flashed and then a large conveyance pulled up. Through the scanwalls, an Abdrelik could be seen moving with that odd, lumbering grace that defied gravity.

Palaton thought wryly that GNask had fallen from Panshinea's grace at about the same time he had. He ignored the furor in the Charolon port and turned back to what he had in hand, reading.

GNask cast a large shadow over him. He smelled boggy and his symbiont made a litany of slurping noises before lapsing into sudden silence as if the Abdrelik had somehow hushed a noisy watch animal. His guards, Choyan and Abdrelik alike, remained a discreet distance away.

"Well. Shipping out, *tezar*?"

Palaton looked up. The Abdrelik showed his tusky smile. "Ambassador. It appears so. But I'm going cross-country while you're out-bound."

"Too bad we can't share accommodations, eh?" GNask laughed. His bulk jellied in response. "I hear you turned down Panshinea's generous offer of employment."

"I prefer deep space. Most *tezars* do."

"That's what you're bred and trained for. Or so I hear." GNask lowered himself onto a table instead of a chair, his weight being more suited for it. "Myself, I abhor the travel. I am thankful my job rarely calls for it."

"Going home?"

"Back to Sorrow. Regrettably, not home. And you?"

"I've a new assignment." Palaton watched the ambassador mildly, feeling the probes in his questions.

"Nasty business in Danbe."

"So I hear."

GNask scratched his whiskery, rubbery under-chin. "Colonization would ease the strain of such incidences. You Choyan manage your population admirably, but the land does wear out. A new planet, new lands—the future could be vast."

Palaton made no comment. He knew the Abdrelik was aware of the Choyan position on colonization. He said, "I wish you a comfortable trip."

"And I wish you a fulfilled destiny," GNask replied ironically in passable Choyan. "You saved my life once. I am disposed to thank you for it. My security force has given me a small parcel. It would be ... awkward ... to try to remove it through outbound customs. However, I think it might be appropriate to leave it to you. I am done with the material." He took a pouch and gave it to Palaton before rising and making his way down the terminal, security force in tow like some nebulous train of fabric trailing behind him. Palaton watched him go.

The ambassador knew, or shrewdly guessed, of the dissent over Danbe. Perhaps Gathon, Rindalan, and even Jorana did best to keep Panshinea in power. A civil war on Cho would bring the Abdreliks swooping in like carrion scavengers, eager to pick the Choyan apart for their secrets.

He went to a privacy cubicle before opening the pouch. It was diplomatically sealed and Palaton knew that probably the Abdrelik would not have been challenged on its contents. Whatever awkwardness there would be in carrying it through was in GNask's imagination.

The first item in his hand froze his heart in mid-beat. Palaton stood and looked at the missive. It had been reconstructed from partially burned paper and Palaton knew why the Abdrelik hadn't kept it—it was not admissible as evidence in any court. Reconstructions were too dubious, to subject to forgery. But this was Choyan in a way the Abdrelik probably wouldn't even be able to recognize and so Palaton didn't doubt its authenticity.

It was the Earthan directive to Darb to have him killed. It was from his House and his Householding, brief and simple and without explanation other than that it was work which had to be done for the greater good of all Cho. Palaton's heart stumbled back into a normal rhythm. He steeled himself to empty the rest of the pouch's contents onto the viewing vestibule.

There was a tiny, crystal vial of poison, a single injection. The tag on it was in Abdrelikan, but the label was in Choyan. It was, he saw, addressed to him. With it was a small note, bearing the crest of his Householding. It said: "Save yourself. Deal with Panshinea."

Palaton handled the fragile vial gingerly. If it had been sent to him, he'd never gotten it. He fingered the note with his grandfather's embossed seal. The aura was too faint, too corrupted by Abdrelik stink, to read. How, by the God-in-all, had the Abdreliks gotten it? And what did it mean? Had it been meant for him, or merely been rigged to appear as though it had been meant for him?

The last item was another bottle, small and intricate. He curled his fingers around it, caught by the perfumed memory, the aura too powerful for even the Abdreliks to muddy it. *Jorana*. Runes were etched into the glass, naming it, with instructions on how to employ it. He placed it on the vestibule tabletop next to the poison, for it was as insidious. He'd heard about such concoctions, had often wondered if they existed, and now he had the proof before him.

It was an aphrodisiac. If he had not left, if he had still insisted on not releasing his fertility, she would have stolen it from him.

He didn't know if such drugs worked, but Jorana had evidently been willing to take the chance. He put a fingertip to the bottle, rolling it along its side. The faintly purple liquid inside foamed a little as it stirred. He wondered only if the Abdreliks had retrieved this from its hiding place in her room—or in his.

The dual fertility of Choyan partners made accidental pregnancies and sexual politics damn near impossible. Had his mother been so compromised or had she planned what she had done to give birth to him? Was he crossed outside his House or perhaps even with commons blood . . . or had he been stolen from her body, though she never gave him up to the thief who had conceived him with her?

Trust no one. Palaton activated the incinerator in the vestibule and, one by one, he destroyed the three items with all their implications. What motive the Abdrelik had in giving them to him, he couldn't be sure. He was only certain it hadn't been gratitude. He also knew that when he left Cho this time, he couldn't look back. The emperor had given him temporary exile. Palaton would be wise to flee as far as he could.

A call for boarding his shuttle flashed, repeated in audio. Palaton hoisted his duffel and crossed the terminal in answer. He looked forward to the peace of Chaos.

PART II

BURNOUT

Chapter 16

"We're being tracked," the Ivrian said, hovering about his sling in agitation, wings blurring, his eyes all pupil, iris a bright ring about a well of darkness.

"I've got it," Palaton answered smoothly. He watched his screen. "Ronin or maybe even Abdrelik. They're waiting." He sat back in his chair. The control room illumination cut sharp planes into his face. "This is a strange region to be playing these games in."

Both knew the tracker was attempting to plot the workings of the *tezarian* drive, even if on a very limited basis. Palaton had not had a tracker in years. His palms itched now, before he placed them over the control board. It would do no good for the tracker to trail them into Chaos, but they never learned. Even the Ivrian navigator/copilot at his side would be banished from the control room before he pulsed the engines into FTL, and once into Chaos, only another *tezar* would have the remotest chance of finding them.

Palaton licked dry lips. "They're anxious to lose another ship."

Rainbow left his hammock chair and advanced to Palaton's flank. "He wishes secrets," the Ivrian hissed.

"And you don't," Palaton answered wryly. He looked over his shoulder in amusement.

Rainbow stretched his back in discomfort. His pupils pinpointed. "Nevertheless," the alien said.

The Ivrians had achieved a limited short run success in Chaos piloting, the best of any of the other races. Rainbow had been the thorn in his side as well as his copilot for the duration of this contract, spying as much as aiding, and both knew the Ivrian's purposes. If there were a secret to be found here, Rainbow undoubtedly felt he'd earned it, and he resented the usurper plotting their present course.

"It doesn't matter."

"To you, perhaps," Rainbow said sulkily. He withdrew to his acceleration sling over his control board and moodily watched the screens.

Palaton laid in his final course before he reached the sector where he would complete acceleration into Chaos. When that moment came, the Ivrian would be banished from the room as well. It did not matter how trivial, how unimportant the run—and this one was just to release several barges of toxic waste into the sun of the nearby system—he would not ignore his procedures.

The tracker grew bold, came close, and knew it must surely have been picked up by their instruments. Palaton watched it, knowing he would lead the vehicle to its death, and wondering how to discourage it.

Rainbow continued to pout. "Tell them to go away," the alien muttered.

The idea had merit. Palaton opened a comline, searched around for a suitable frequency, then hailed the vehicle.

The answer came back swiftly and smoothly. "*Tezar* Nedar, it is our pleasure to meet again."

Palaton paused carefully. Chaos patterns did not often intersect, but Nedar must be in the region somewhere. He hadn't had a meeting with his fellow pilot for years. Nedar had been in the emperor's graces little longer than Palaton. He looked to Rainbow. "Is there a war nearby?"

The Ivrian shrugged. A few gauzy feathers drifted down from the gesture. "Always. Somewhere."

Palaton put himself on-line again. "I beg your pardon, but you are not communicating with *Tezar* Nedar. This is *Tezar* Palaton. Please keep your distance. I'm on a waste run and contamination is possible."

A static of confusion followed his information. The link cut off sharply. He watched his grid, saw the ship rapidly gaining ground, all coyness gone. Were they approaching to confirm contact . . . or to eliminate an awkward witness? Or worse, were they on a covert capture mission, an attempt to take apart a ship with *tezarian* drive just to find out what made it tick? Such subterfuges were usually done in wartime runs, where lost ships could be explained more easily. If so, that also explained why they thought they were contacting Nedar. These were games no Choyan could afford to play.

"Rainbow, go secure in the secondary cabin."

"But Palaton—"

"Get out of here. We're going into FTL now."

The Ivrian flew from the control room, leaving a trail of dust motes and fine feathers swirling in his wake. Palaton swung about only long enough to determine that the Ivrian had indeed left.

The ship vibrated in answer to his abrupt demands on it. The barges in tow pulled dully in response, dragging them down.

The Ivrian's shrill voice came over the intercom. "Palaton, they're arming."

"I see it."

"We're well within range."

"I see that, too." His eyes, his hands were busy, playing the ship for all it was worth. The instrument augmentation had only one real advantage over conventional FTL drives—it was incredibly responsive. He set it up now and then waited for the final kick into FTL.

It came with a blur of color and a ringing of noise. He sat back in his chair and watched the aura-light of relativity go momentarily haywire, then collect itself again. Before he blacked the view screen down, he stared out a moment and let the sight of Chaos make his senses reel like the most heady of wines. Then the shield went dark, protecting him.

Rainbow's voice jarred. "We've lost them."

"No," murmured Palaton quietly, too low for the intercom to pick up. "They've lost themselves."

If they'd enough sense, they could pull back and drop out of Chaos, emerging in a region of space they could not chart for, but most likely emerging clear. They would probably even emerge in known space, although at some distance from where Chaos had been entered. But the longer they remained in Chaos, the more likelihood there was of destruction. Palaton felt sadness but not remorse. They had known what they were doing, though why they had hailed him as Nedar. . . .

The run through this brew of Chaos would be short. Palaton set a timer, pulled out a book of poetry and began to read, ignoring the Ivrian's attempt to plot random motion, voicing frustration over the intercom.

He had nearly finished the volume when his timer sounded. His panel surged back into life, flashing with color. The instruments gave him a confusion of readings, unable to cope with what they attempted to measure by normal methods. He looked instead at the Choyan panel, saw a few more coherent readings, and took a deep breath. Instead, he looked for the diffuseness within Chaos, the pattern that was not a pattern called the Butterfly, and one he likened to the Singing Choya'i. His *bahdur* burned when he called on it, giving him the sight to see with, the hands to steer with. He sought the sun which would act as the attractor within this random shape, found it and, with reluctance, left the spaceway of the Singing Choya'i, her neck in a graceful stretch as she no doubt sang the praises of the God-in-all.

He decelled the ship rapidly, not wanting to lose his advantage, and as the normal instrumentation leapt into valid readings free of Chaos' confusion, he saw he'd done well. He pulled the ship into alignment with the sun and said to Rainbow, "Find me a trajectory to drop the barges off. I don't want to go in too far."

"Just drop them and run, eh?" Rainbow answered.

"I'm tired," said Palaton and suddenly knew he was. He closed his volume of poetry, returning it to the recessed bookcase in the cabin, and sat back in his chair. His brow ached just below his horn crown and he put a hand up, massaging it absently as he leaned over the large grid-panel control board. Rainbow read back a decaying orbit passage to him and he okayed it. There was nothing to endanger here, this was a barren solar system, and the sun would annihilate the cargo he delivered to it.

Rainbow confirmed the release of the barges and Palaton banked the ship out of their pathway. He felt, rather than saw, their journey past, large, shadowy, indeterminately evil things looming and then gone. He stretched his hands over his control board again. "Let's go home," he said.

He would be bored but for the danger. Chaos challenged him now. The more he piloted the more complicated it grew, gathering offenses from his past mistakes, it seemed, all minor and yet gathering momentum until the day he would make that miscalculation which he could not save or undo. Pilot paranoia, the *tezars* called it, and anyone who flew enough had it. Unfortunately, it was not an imaginary paranoia. Sooner or later Chaos would claim any without sufficient *bahdur* to traverse it . . . claim them or drive them out of its turmoil forever.

It was a bottomless grave into which he would someday sink.

Palaton blinked, found his hands shaking, and clenched them quickly. "FTL acceleration on my mark," he got out to the Ivrian in the secondary control room.

Rainbow acknowledged. Palaton signaled the engines, felt the swoop of response to acceleration and, just as his horn crown began to ache with the speed, they entered Chaos.

The moment his shield went dark, he knew they were not alone. He thought of the Ronin tracker, but the aura approaching him was entirely different. Palaton wavered in confusion, then steeled himself.

He'd caught the edge of it, a psychic backlash of confusion and pain and hopelessness. He wondered if perhaps it had bled out of Chaos into the barren solar system, for it mirrored the dark feelings he'd had just before acceleration. He was intersecting paths with another *tezar*, a Choyan in crisis.

Palaton made whatever course adjustments he could, then sat back and opened his mind, scanning, reaching out to the pilot in distress. His *bahdur* scattered sparks of hope into the darkness like a crown of fire radiating from his core. *Come to me . . . center on me . . . reach out. . .*

The miasma sucked it in, greedily, as though the darkness itself fed on his energy, but he knew it did not. But it was frenetic energy that diffused his own. He redoubled his efforts, throwing out a psychic lifeline. Behind his closed eyelids, he could see it, a golden rope that, caught by the maelstrom of Chaos, spiraled and then convoluted into patterns he could no longer watch.

The effort left him open to the backlash of despair from the lost one. Palaton caught his breath sharply as it lanced through him, leaving a yawning gap as though it had clawed his insides out. It left him panting in pain, sweat stippling his face as it ran down.

He thought, for a split-second, of saving him-

self and abandoning the Choya in trouble. He
rejected that thought as soon as it emerged,
knew a fleeting second of shame for having
birthed it, and then shoved that out as well.
He had no time for self-doubt. Still in pain, he
loosened another burst of *bahdur*, felt it staining
the universe as it washed out of him, and
prayed it would find the soul he searched for.

A willow wisp of a touch. Brazen, Palaton
extended himself again. It was like a fleeting
vision at the edge of his range. Smoky, indistinct. He wondered now if it were indeed
another Choya he endeavored to help. Could it
be the Ronin ship he'd misled earlier? But those
thoughts didn't matter even as Palaton thought
them. He would give whatever aid he could to
the lost. He unraveled his talent again and
tossed it forth, watching it disappear into Chaos
faster than a spider drops webbing strands. It
wove into a gossamer pattern, then disappeared
from sight.

His face and neck were now drenched in
sweat. Focused within himself as he was, he
could feel the warm stream running across the
planes of his cheekbones, his chin. His hands
trembled where they rested over his knees. His
heartbeat felt enlarged, vibrating his sternum
as it pulsed. He forced himself to breathe steadily before he looked back into the void.

Contact! The other grasped at him, gulping
down *bahdur* as though it were a hot cup of
bren, sucking it out of him so quickly Palaton
gasped. His fingers knuckled into his legs in
reaction. The other would strip him dry and
they'd both be lost! Palaton anchored himself.
He put up blocks the other hammered away,
desperately, a drowning Choya like some cadet

in a deprivation helmet. He fought to keep himself from being turned inside out.

The lost one slowed, weakening again, and then Palaton had it, his aura, knew who the Choya was. *Nedar.*

He realized he'd known it all along—that the Ronin had tipped him to Nedar's presence in the sector and that no one else could have been expected—but the shock chilled through him anyway. Nedar, burned out and adrift in Chaos.

Nedar. Follow me.

There was an angry strike of recognition as Nedar realized who his feeder was. Then Nedar pushed away, a rejection, as physical as a violent shove. But Palaton could no more leave the Choya adrift then he could have Moameb or Hat. He entreated, baiting the plea with *bahdur* aura, knowing the other would bolt toward it instinctively before he could think or react otherwise. Survival would draw him after.

And Nedar did come, reluctantly, taking the bait, the bright energy extended to him, hungrily, like a starving man, hating himself for doing it and unable to stop himself.

The Ivrian interrupted his silent struggle. "*Tezar* Palaton. Are you all right?"

A struggle to speak. The cords of his neck extended. The weight of his horn crown felt oppressive, as though he could not hold it. He mopped his slick face. "I'm fine, Rainbow. But I'm busy."

"Yes," the Ivrian answered, his affirmative sounding apologetic. "It's just that I thought—I thought it was time to emerge."

Palaton quickly spun out a second inquiry, of discernment, finding their location in Chaos.

The Ivrian was right—he'd overshot his exit
window, but that mattered little in Chaos. He
could repattern to double back and did so, panting again from the exertion, as though he ran
through the void instead of flew. He found a
new window and headed the plane toward it,
Nedar still in tow.

Suddenly Nedar blazed, his *bahdur* rekindled,
and Palaton felt him peel away in confidence,
surging deeper into Chaos and out of touch.

Palaton felt emptied, alone, abandoned, used.
He shook himself, knowing that it was the other's nature. He said to Rainbow, "Prepare for
decel," and found himself aching in every fiber,
as he came fully back to himself, and wondered
how close Nedar had come to draining him. He
should leave it alone but knew he would not.
He could not.

He found Nedar at base, sitting in one of the
quiet bars that only Choyan frequented, being
more like a chapel in its solemnity than a public
house. The Choya looked up as he entered. His
dark eyes smoldered.

Nedar wasn't quartered at this base, but he'd
had no choice about where to land. He probably
couldn't have flown much further. Palaton had
known that Nedar, for the moment, couldn't get
out of his reach. He approached the table.

Before Palaton could sit, his classmate said,
"I won't hear it from you."

"From Moameb? Would you hear it from
Moameb?"

Nedar stabbed a finger at him. His complexion had paled, setting off his facial jewelry in
harsh tracings. "I overflew my boundaries. It
happens." There were tiny lines about his eyes,

harsh ones at the corners of his mouth, etched in by age, making his expression severe as well as handsome.

"The pain. . . ."

"There is none. I haven't got it yet. I just overstepped my bounds." Nedar curled his hand back around his glass. He looked into the depths of his drink as if he could divine the future in it. Being a Choya, perhaps he could.

Palaton pulled a chair out and sat. "A visit home. A cleansing at Blue Ridge. . . ."

"Where you'd have Moameb waiting for me, waiting to counsel me, telling me being grounded isn't so difficult?" Nedar let out a single harsh laugh. "When's the last time you were home, Palaton? Have you seen the wasted rack you took flying lessons from?" Nedar leaned intently over the table. "For now, *flying is all I've got*. I won't let you or anyone take it away."

"Any time you contract, you represent all of Cho, all of the *tezars* who pilot."

"Any time I contract, I'm fulfilling my destiny. I move forward. You should try it." Nedar tossed back the rest of his drink. He signaled the automatic innkeep for a refill. His breath hazed in the air between them. "If you want thanks, I give them to you. Thanks, my Palaton, for coming to my rescue during a moment of extreme fatigue. Now go away and leave me. There is no cleansing for the likes of us." Nedar pinned him with his intense gaze. "For any of us."

Palaton blinked. The vague memory of Panshinea gripping him at the airfield, telling lies for absolution, held him. *Someone, somewhere, knows what they do. They know how to renew* bahdur. How many *tezars* had the emperor driven into exhaustion and into the void, looking for miracles that did not exist? He was amazed that Nedar would have listened.

He still felt the yawning emptiness feeding power to Nedar had given him, but unlike the other, he did not seek to numb it. He stood up.

"What did the emperor say to you?"

Nedar's gaze sharpened. "What did he say to you?"

"He told me to leave."

Nedar laughed again, bitterly. "He begged me to stay. He begged me to stay so that he could break me, see the look in my eyes as year after year I grew no closer to the throne I coveted." He threw his chin up. "Do you know what you are called at home? The 'hero in exile.' The word got around that you tried to stop the massacre at Danbe, that you stood up against the emperor himself. No one talks about the fact that you laid down a *bahdur* trail so that I could follow it in and annihilate their shields. No one murmurs that you were used by the emperor. No one knows the truth."

Palaton felt his jaws tighten. "And neither, it appears, do you."

"I know a lie when I hear one. Perhaps you haven't listened to enough lies. There is a mockery holding the throne at Charolon. If I find a cure, I won't be extending it to him."

"We do what we do because we are driven by our own desires. If Panshinea sent you out and you went, you're the fool. You keep saying boundaries to me, and I wonder what you know of limits. I intersected a Ronin ship which was lying in wait for you. If it had found you in this condition, we would have lost both the ship and a pilot. I don't need to tell you what the Ronin do to pilots if they can, do I?"

Nedar cupped his refilled glass. "The Ronin have been vivisecting Choyan for decades. They still don't know what we are or what we can do."

"All it takes is one, Nedar. One craven coward who talks instead. One coward who has already reached his limits and hasn't the strength to resist."

"I'm not a coward!" Nedar shoved himself to his feet.

"Neither are you a realist." Palaton held steady. "Get some rest. Go back to base. Abort your contract and go home. We can't stop the disease once it starts, but we do know excessive fatigue kicks it off. I look at you and I see a shadow of the Choya I beat for wing leader."

Nedar shoved his glass viciously across the tabletop. Amber drink spilled over Palaton in a spray. He took his hand and contemptuously wiped himself down, then left without another word. Behind him, he could hear Nedar fall back into his chair and order yet another drink. He did not see the shadowy Choya emerge from a secluded corner and approach the surly pilot who, after a few whispered words, sat up abruptly and listened closely.

Palaton returned to his quarters at base. The hall was on downtime, shadowed and still. He checked his chronometer and knew he would have a full night's sleep if he turned in now. His message light blinked, so he went to retrieve them first.

The first was from Jorana. He would acknowledge it later. She kept in touch with him,

briefly, from contract to contract. She was now
a captain of the guard and also one of Panshinea's cabinet members. The higher she rose, the
harder she would fall when Panshinea finally
stumbled once and for all. The thought filled
him with mixed emotions. He still did not know
how he felt about Jorana.

The second was from his grandfather. The
visual transmission was occluded by sunspot
interference, which was just as well, for the
spine straight elder facing the viewing screen
was no one Palaton recognized easily. But the
voices were the same, though there were qua-
very pauses for breath here and there.

"Palaton. I thought it my duty to inform you.
Our Householding is being Relocated. Not by
imperial order, but by financial decree. We are
bankrupted. You are our line's only current
tezar. Your cousin has been killed on contract
and your two nephews washed out of Salt
Towers. The expense of maintaining our home
here has become a burden I cannot shoulder on
your tithes alone. Your mother's grave . . ." and
here his grandfather's voices faded so he was
almost inaudible. The visual showed him visibly getting a hold of himself. "Your mother's
grave will remain with the Householding. I'm
sorry, Palaton. You still have your home at Blue
Ridge." The transmission recording ended.

He sat in stunned silence. Not that he had
ever had much of a home in his grandfather's
Householding—Blue Ridge had been his, in his
heart and in his destiny from the moment he'd
crossed its threshold.

But that his line should have suddenly grown
so weak. And why had his nephews, half-neph-
ews, actually, been sent to the Salt Towers

instead of Blue Ridge? He found himself unaccepting of the transmission and wondered if Panshinea had not now, years later, found a way to vent his spleen. Only death washed members of Palaton's Householding out of *tezar* school once accepted. Only death. Yet no deaths had been mentioned for his nephews. They had proved unacceptable for one reason or another once under trial. He found it hard to believe.

As for his cousin, Palaton bowed his head and breathed a remembrance to God-in-all for her passing. Dying on contract meant she'd suffered a work accident . . . or been lost in Chaos. He hardly knew her, she'd been older and already a *tezar* at his birth, but it was in her footsteps he'd first followed.

His mind in turmoil, he lay down to sleep. Thinking of Blue Ridge and Hat and arrogant Nedar, he closed his eyes. The cadets used a meditation ritual to purify their thoughts and discipline their fears. Mechanically he fell into it now, for it was the only way sleep would come. Sometime during that drill, he slept.

The intercom woke him. "*Tezar* Palaton."

He was on his feet before he spoke. "I'm here." His mind cleared, thoughts separating into distinct images of reality from dreams. He cleared his throat. "I'm here," he repeated.

"We have an emergency and desperate need for a pilot. Are you available?"

Besides Nedar, he knew of no one in downtime at the base presently, although someone could have come in while he slept. But he knew that if they had, or if there had been a fresh pilot available, he wouldn't be getting the call. And Nedar was in no shape to fly, whether using the patterns or on straight duty. He rubbed his eyes awake. To fly and to serve, the motto of Blue Ridge. "I'm available," he said, and moved forward to answer the call.

Chapter 17

He took no secondary navigator or copilot on the run. He watched silently in the bays as the hospital ships were tractor linked to the main ship he was to pilot. The crews and troops of the hospital ships loaded with a quick efficiency that surprised him. Order out of cacophony and disaster. He was to tow in three of the immense medical facilities. It was important work, far from the garbage runs he'd been doing, for various contracts over the years. As he watched the preparations, he pondered Nedar's accusation.

Only those who know their destiny fully can charge forward into it, achieving it or failing. Only those who know what their bloodlines have prepared them for—Palaton knew he was meant to be a *tezar*. That, at least, would not escape him. For him, it was enough.

Moameb seriously ill now, the neuropathy advanced enough to waste him . . . that was an image he could not erase from his mind. It was time, he thought, to return to Blue Ridge in spite of the emperor's wrath. After this contract, it was time to go home for a little while and catch his breath. Perhaps make a last visit to his mother's grave before the Householding lost all rights to the land. Time to say good-bye.

And time to greet Jorana again, perhaps. He felt a tightening in his throat.

Slender fingers trailed across his flank and went to the small of his back, kneading gently. "You're too tense," Faba said, her voices soft and low, for his hearing alone.

Palaton turned his head. The Choya'i mechanic gave him a smile. She'd gotten out of bed to ready the vessel, her dark mass of curly hair still uncombed within her scalloped crown. She knew where his body knotted up, and when to leave him alone. He welcomed her presence for the moment though their liaisons had never been intended to entangle either of them in anything permanent. Her fingers continued to roam his back, seeking out the knots.

"Are you flying this morning?"

There were no real mornings on base, simply uptime and downtime, thanks to the deep space shielding surrounding the facility, but old habits made the artificial environment homier. He looked out across the deep velvet. "Yes."

"They're lucky you were logged in." Her fingers left his back. They brushed his jawline briefly. "I'll make sure you have a safe flight." Smelling of perfume and machinery, she sidled past him and went down into the bays to work.

He watched her tiny-waisted, full-bodied form go down into the berthing pits. Her voices echoed back up to him as she began to check the fitness of the vessel he would pilot. Palaton smiled slightly in response. First she'd checked him out, now she was checking the ship out.

The medical emergency which had precipitated the activity had sounded severe. The Compact had just voted to send in the hospital ships and supplies to a system ravaged by natural disaster and plague, a system just out of Class Zed status, like an infant learning to walk, unprepared for the havoc its own internal strife would engender. There was also some rumor of alien contamination, that the plague would destroy the majority of the population of this twin-planet system, that the viruses had been introduced by the intrusion of the Compact itself. The natives could not combat the ravaging which had begun. The Terran system, he thought briefly, had been more deserving of reclassification. But he had no say in Compact politics unless Blue Ridge sent him there, and certainly not in the councils which decided matters such as these. At least a decision had been made and would be carried out swiftly.

Cargo holds filled, the medical personnel entered the hospital ships, troops at their heels. The ships would stay in orbit and temporary hospitals would be prefabbed dirtside, the troops to provide manpower for construction as well as security. Palaton waited until the "all clear" sounded. Even Faba left the bays.

He walked through all four ships and then his own vessel, as Choyan did, knowing that all five were in his hands alone. He would be the final authority on whether they would space or not. He found a leaking fuel cap, gasket rings twisted, ordered a replacement, and went on. Nothing else seemed amiss.

He rubbed sleep out of the corner of one eye and walked the ramp of the Compact escort which would be his vessel for this run, the *tezarian* black box drive in his free hand. It took him three minutes to install it and then he felt the berth cradles begin to shift the vessels into position for launch. He sat down and secured himself.

The tiny hairs at the nape of his neck prickled in anticipation. Palaton looked about his cabin, searching with a vague uneasiness, saw nothing, discerned nothing, then turned to his job as the base launched him and then the four hospital ships in his wake. He reached under the control console and found a Compact tracer, stretched his lips wryly at the feeble attempt to track him, destroyed it and knew that, even if there were others, they would do no good. Only he could betray himself and his methods.

He spent his free hours until FTL acceleration could be reached plotting their pathway, keeping in mind the size difference between the sleek escort and the massive hospital ships following. Their course had already been set, but Palaton liked to manipulate the numbers. He monitored their sector to see if he drew any Ronin, but if there was other traffic it kept clear.

As they neared FTL acceleration, he notified the hospital ships to prepare for Chaos flight. Because reality bent in Chaos, it was disconcerting, even terrifying, to the senses of the uninitiated. Tranquilizers and confinement combated the effects. The Choyan were not particularly susceptible to it, although he'd seen a few cases of stark, raving terror of colors that bled, time that bubbled, solid material that appeared to become nonexistent.

"Thank you, *tezar*."

Palaton looked to his rear screens. The cable that stretched between them, like an umbilical cord, was just as necessary to preserve their lives. It stretched lazily across the expanse, waiting to be dropped when he launched them on their own. The pilot of the transports was doing a good job, keeping the cable stretched but not taut. He wondered who it was—a Quinonan perhaps, or an Ivrian, or perhaps a Norton. Someone who burned, no doubt, to know his secrets.

He took them into Chaos with a majestic sweep, grinning at the sheer power of it, at the wonder of it, feeling like a dark sorcerer. He bypassed the Singing Choya'i and searched for the Falling Tree instead, going deep into the patterns, making haste with caution as Moameb would say. The escort responded with hair-trigger quickness, but the four transports lagged behind, sluggishly, and the cable drew tight. He adjusted the escort to match the transports' ability.

Chaos took away the hull of his ship. He felt as though he rode a chair suspended in space, its currents whirling with light and sound and fury, the console a keyboard in front of him to strike and coax celestial music from. Palaton liked this effect although it did not strike him often and made most pilots uneasy, especially those with a fear of falling, for it seemed he sat on the brink of eternity, about to plunge into it as the starship hurled forward.

After a few heady moments, the hull and shielding reformed, and he was once more inside their protection. He mourned the loss of sensation, then scouted for the peaks that were so like those beyond Blue Ridge. Nothing met his search.

Palaton rubbed his eyes and sent his discernment arching out, looking for the Mountains of Sunrise. The configuration eluded him, as though he'd gone blind, and then he realized his *bahdur* guttered like a candle burning out.

Panic closed his throat. He'd been sitting back in his chair, at ease. He slammed forward on its edge, the console digging into the flat of his stomach as he leaned over it, peering into the shielding which mirrored only his anguished face back at him. Chaos was right there, patterns laid open for him to read—and he saw none of it.

He took a gasping breath and knew keen empathy with what Nedar must have felt. He did a quick meditation pattern to open himself, letting the *bahdur* well up, like a fountain.

Emptiness met him. There was nothing secreted inside him, no wellspring of reserve, nothing. His soul was dead, empty, as quiet as stone. He clawed at it as if he could scrape enough power together to save himself—to save the four hospital ships he took with him to certain death—and found not even scrapings.

Then it blazed briefly, illuminating his world, filling it with a sky bowl of fireworks, showing him they were about to plunge over the rim of the pattern called the Waterfall ... a plunge as mystical and dangerous as a real life drop over an immense falls. His comlines came on, all four ships, and he knew they were taking a rough ride.

He forced his voices steady. "A mild disrupton. Keep everybody buckled in. I'm taking shortcuts and hitting a few rough spots."

The escort dropped, plunged, his stomach going with it, the four ships following as the cable jerked taut and drew them down. It was like hitting a ten-thousand-foot air pocket drop.

He clenched his teeth, wondering when they were going to hit bottom.

Darkness came when the descent ended. Palaton chewed on his lips, found them flaking and chapped as he did so, his mouth gone unutterably dry. Where had he taken them? How mired in Chaos were they?

He found one trembling hand laid over the black box of the *tezarian* drive. He looked at his instrumentation. He abandoned *bahdur* and grabbed the keypad he'd been doing calculations on. He knew where they'd been heading—he knew they'd just left the Waterfall. He wasn't completely adrift. Yet. . . .

From the feel of the ride, he could tell the swirls and eddies which took them. He let Chaos control them, keeping track of the journey, making corrections to keep them on course. Then, Palaton sat back and looked at what he had done.

They were close enough so that he could bring them out—if he could *discern*. If he cut loose the cable, he could slingshot them away from the escort, giving them the impetus to make that exit window—even though it meant he himself could not go. It was possible.

If he had any *bahdur* left at all.

If he was willing to sacrifice himself to deliver them.

There was no question about that last. He licked his lips. "Transport One, I'm going to cut you loose and slingshot you through. You'll have to send for another pilot when your mission is done."

A silence. Then, "Are you having trouble, *tezar*?"

There was no easy way to answer it. All pilots

knew the danger, even those who did not face Chaos. He fought denial. This couldn't be happening to him. He'd had very few episodes. But it could be happening. It *was* happening. He smelled his own fear, rank in the control cabin. He forced himself to respond. "Yes," answered Palaton. "But I can get you through safely."

There was a muffled exclamation at the other end, cut off, and the voice resumed, "I'm with you. Ready to slingshot at your mark."

"I want you to accelerate for . . . six clics only. Then decel to leave Chaos. Do you have that?"

"Six clics. I have it."

Palaton took a deep breath. His lungs ached, as if he had not been breathing, or had drowned and had the water squeezed from them, bruising him. He felt a certain headiness as new air flooded into him. He closed his eyes and searched for any tiny spark of talent he might have left.

It answered him feebly. Pain shot through his right arm, arcing over his collarbone and into his sternum. *Neuropathy*. The beginning of his end. If he had ever thought otherwise, the disease lanced certainty into him. A nerve at a time would burn its agonizing way to death. He had seen *tezars* beg for their end. He bit his lip against the stabbing, burning sharpness of it and looked through Chaos, willing the curtains to open and reveal his destination.

He found it. He aimed the escort toward it, bucking across random currents wishing to carry him otherwhere. Then he steered into the currents, readying for the slingshot that would bring the transport out safely.

"*Tezar* . . ." The voice of doubt.

"Stay with me, Pilot One. On my mark."

"There is disagreement here. Four hundred lives, highly trained physicians and technicians—"

"Pilot One! On my mark! I'll lose you otherwise." Rear screens showed him the cable vibrating. They sought to cast themselves without his guidance.

"A Choya in burnout ..." Another voice, overriding the pilot. An administrator? A general of Compact troops? Whatever the title, he heard authority and skepticism in the other's voice. The cable bounced. The escort slewed in response as the heavier transports dragged slightly on it.

He drew on his talents and threw back his own voices of command. "Stay with me!" He had no idea whether the comline transmitted him faithfully, but there was momentary silence in response. Alternating between sight and blindness, he calculated wildly. Then, "Mark!" And he freed the cable as he sheared the escort off violently, accelerating rapidly.

But the escort did not respond properly, and he knew that quite possibly the transports had released the cable before he did—slinging them into nowhere.

The transports arced away into Chaos. His *bahdur* arrowed a golden blaze across their pathway and charred into the nothingness of the God-blind. His breath sobbed to a halt in his throat. Had he done it? He could not see! He looked to the black box and saw their fate being calculated, their courses set in numbers too awful to read. Palaton slammed his fist across the screen in fear and loathing. "No! No! *No!*"

Darkness descended like a blinding blow to the back of his head.

Chapter 18

GNask enjoyed the company of the Chinese junior ambassador. He smacked his lips as the rotund humankind prepared a freshly caught fish and presented it in a skillet redolent with exotic herbs and spices, the fish still gasping with life, its body seared by the cooking.

"My dear ambassador," the Abdrelik said, picking up an eating utensil. "Diplomatic skills and a chef, as well. Does Thomas appreciate you?"

"Perhaps," the moon-faced man said. "And perhaps not. We should discuss it sometime, Ambassador GNask."

GNask smiled as he cut away a portion. He and Thomas had arrangements that the junior ambassador could not breach no matter what he tried, but his efforts were occasionally rewarding. GNask decided to lead him on.

"I had not known your planet to be so . . . fragmented," he commented.

The Chinese humankind's skill at the Trade dialect was slightly limited. He frowned over the observation, then smiled. "Not fragmented. Just independent. And self-concerned to some extent. We have hopes in the area of computerization that the Class Zed act might be applied to our advantage—"

GNask's com chimed. The Abdrelik paused in irritation. His secretary knew better than to interrupt him at mealtimes.

He opened the comlink. "What is it?"

"An urgent communiqué."

GNask thought. Then he said, "I'll be in in a moment." To the junior ambassador, he apologized. "But you know how these things can be."

The round yellow eyelids shuttered. "Yes, Ambassador. I know." He reached for a portion of fish himself as GNask swayed his bulk past him.

His secretary had sealed the office when he arrived. "What is it?" His annoyance smacked with every syllable. His symbiont, which had been sleeping placidly, began to stir upon the side of his head.

"Ambassador Thomas, sir, on the private com."

"Ah." GNask seated himself, feeling more civil. He mopped his wet chin. The flat screen came to life.

The sticklike figure of the man had been moving in agitation. GNask watched it with the avid fascination of the hunter, attracted despite himself. Then Thomas saw that the flatscreen had been activated and came to a halt before it.

"Ambassador," GNask crooned. "How kind of you to call. I have your junior here, cooking me lunch."

"I don't have time for pleasantries, GNask. They've taken her."

"Really? So soon?" GNask put a hand up and tickled his *tursh*. The slug began an inaudible purring that vibrated comfortingly into the Abdrelik' hide. "We weren't expecting this. What happened?"

John Taylor Thomas had bleary, red-rimmed eyes. His hands trembled as he pulled out a linen cloth and touched at them. "Skimcraft accident. My wife was injured slightly, but they reported my daughter's death. The skimmer burned ... the remains were almost impossible to identify. We went through hell ... then I got a call. 'Don't worry,' they said. 'We've got your daughter. It's time.' "

"Interesting," GNask murmured. His eyes hooded slightly in pleasure. Ruthless of the Choyan, who would have thought it of them? But admirable. Yes, very admirable. And if not their subject, then who had died? Not his worry, of course, and the Choyan were absolute masters in genetics ... the replacement would match the original in almost every way perceptible. "Thomas, we prepared for this."

The symbiont culturing had been most successful. That was years ago, now, but GNask still slitted his eyes in thoughtful remembrance. He had wanted to reabsorb the symbiont so that he could experience the manchild in the ways she had undoubtedly experienced him, but the *tursh* offspring had not survived the induction. Something in humankind chemistry had made it weaken and die, though not before it had done its task. The child would be, what, fifteen years old as the humankind reckoned themselves. Yes. Old enough to have some power in the world. Able to reach and utilize tools. Able to manipulate, to think, to respond, to operate covertly.

"We'll find her soon, Thomas," GNask said. "They operated callously. We'll find her and stop them."

"They let me think she was dead!" John Taylor Thomas caught his breath, on the edge of a sob.

GNask leaned very close to the flatscreen. "Now," he said intensely, "we find her and we take our vengeance."

The man looked up. "Not until we have our children back."

"Naturally," GNask reassured. "They are our evidence. Now, if you'll excuse me, Ambassador, lunch is waiting. Like vengeance, it's better served hot." He terminated the call and hefted himself up.

The Choyan had overplayed their hand at last. He would have proof of species interference. He might even have insight as to the *tezarian* drive. At the very least, he would further disrupt the power of the erratic Panshinea. *Good news was always the best appetizer*, he thought, as he waddled back to the Chinese underambassador. He wondered what the Choyan did with all those children.

The streets of Sao Paulo teemed with life, life broken, dirty, struggling, filled with potential, yet seldom achieving it, drowning beneath the toxins of waste and poor air, poverty and the utter cheapness of its regard for human flesh. The church grounds overlooked a neighborhood which balanced between middle class and ghetto, neither fish nor fowl, its buildings squat and ugly. Father Lombardi looked out his begrimed window and issued a call for Bevan. His desk was cluttered, his equipment old and obsolete, his fax nearly four decades old, though Lombardi thought it worked better than the new instatrans machines. An apostle of Mother Theresa, who was on the brink of achieving sainthood, he felt that all he could do was be a small island of comfort and sanity in Sao Paulo. All he could offer was a modicum of healing and a lot of faith while the doomed met their fate. He could teach the dream of a better tomorrow, but it was his lot to struggle with the overwhelmingly undermet needs of today.

He pulled at his white plastic collar. The fabric scratched. Pools of sweat runneled down from his armpits staining the dark cloth coat of his Catholic uniform. He waited for Bevan.

From the moment Lombardi had reached down into the cholera-ridden gutters and pulled the child up, he had been different. The father knew it and most certainly Bevan had. He'd rarely been sick a day since being taken into sanctuary. He had seemed to know his lot among the Theresites was destined to be different and so, when the Choyan had come, neither Lombardi nor the child had hesitated to make a deal. Otherwise Bevan would languish here, too vibrant to be comforted about dying, too vital to be wasted.

A chancy hope for the future was preferable, no matter how shadowy it seemed. Lombardi had only given three or four of his children away to the aliens in the past. He had never heard from any of them again, but he didn't feel uneasy in his dealings. These were a deeply religious people, he knew, from having spoken with them. They offered quiet support of the massive financial strain of the sanctuary. They received promising children as students from time to time. Father Lombardi gave no one away who did not wish to go.

Quiet as his thoughts, Bevan had entered and stood waiting when Lombardi looked up a second time. The slender youth had snapping dark eyes, a nose overly large for a fine-boned face, luxurious hair that maned down to his shoulders, thin quick fingers. He perched now on the crowded corner of Lombardi's desk.

"You sent for me, Father?" he asked in the native tongue of Brazil, though he knew Compact Trade fairly well, and English fluently. Also he spoke a smattering of Japanese and Italian. He picked up a fax and read it idly.

"It is time," Father Lombardi said with dignity.

Bevan dropped the paper. His obsidian eyes reflected excitement, though his carefully schooled face did not. "Time?"

"It is time for you to leave us, Bevan, as you and I agreed."

The youth looked about the office as if expecting to see aliens in the corners. "Where are they?"

"You'll not see them here. I will have you sleep in solitary tonight. Their common procedure is to come while you're asleep. I don't know if . . ." Lombardi cleared his throat uneasily. "I don't know when you'll wake. Off-planet, most likely. Take nothing with you. Destroy all your personal belongings. Give nothing away."

They looked at one another, sagging Caucasian Catholic priest and dark-skinned, uncertain lineaged street child.

"You never lived here," Lombardi said gently. "You never existed. That is the only way I could give you a future."

"Then," said Bevan brightly, "that's the only way I can take it." He slid off the desk and snapped his fingers. "Don't worry about me, Father Lombardi." He slipped lithely out the office door before the priest had dismissed him, but Lombardi let him go.

He rocked back in his chair with a sigh. If there were only some way of knowing what he did was right.

The old fax began to hum, another missive coming in. It was an offer of black market medicine, if he had the monies available.

Thanks to the Choyan visitation that morning, he did. He wondered if prayers were being answered.

A man and a young man stalked the corridors of the space station, watching the cloud cover shift over the blue planet below. The father had the look of an impoverished businessman, a common class in the Americas of the day, but his son was dressed in a flight suit, the new material still sharply creased from its packaging. They paused at the view window.

"It doesn't look so bad from here," the boy murmured. He was already as tall as his father. He was fair, with wide turquoise eyes and a dark shock of hair that continually fell into his eyes, though nothing could hide his earnest expression. He would never be handsome, but he would always be honest and intense.

"No," answered his father. He was not so much looking at the view as searching for the invisible personnel of the way station, the aliens who came and went here so freely.

The boy's hands knuckled over the safety rail. "I want to pilot, Dad," he said suddenly. "So badly I can taste it."

The businessman looked aside at his son in surprise. "Do you?"

"Always." The boy looked up. "So don't feel bad about giving me away."

The man's jaw dropped. "Randall, I didn't— I didn't give you away—"

"Traded then. Me for new methods of waste removal and purification. It'll save your business. It'll help Earth, and I'll have a chance for what I want."

The trade had never been as concrete as that, but the father couldn't bear to disillusion his child. Still, he hesitated. "I don't know ... I don't know what they want of you. They spoke of college, but—"

Randall gave a slow, strong smile. It illuminated his entire body. The businessman thought of his wife when his son did so. For her, he would have moved the sun and earth itself. "It's not what they want of me," the youth said. "It's what I want of them. Nothing less than all the stars and suns and planets they can offer up. Nothing less." He went back to staring at his world below.

After a long moment, the father slipped an arm about his son's shoulders and they stood in quiet, unmentioned farewell.

Chapter 19

Sharp insistent sound pierced his unconsciousness. Palaton forced himself out of dreams as deep as dark water, drowning him, pulling him down. He struggled to surface and came awake in the escort control cabin. He lay for a moment, cheek upon the instrument panel, uncomprehending. Then the sound, the fuel alarm, registered.

He clawed his eyes open. The noise reverberated through his skull and he pawed at the panel, fumbling to shut it down. Then the significance of the signal brought him erect in his chair, and he stared at the controls.

He was alive, and happy for it, despite the searing pain that ran from his wrist into his shoulder and chest. He was alive, and ashamed of it, because of the four hundred he had led into death. By the God-in-all, he should not struggle to survive now, but he had to. If only to tell the Compact of the mission's failure, so that new crews could be sent out.

To do that, he had to leave Chaos. He had to pull out, regardless of what destiny lay ahead, and send his message out. Then he faced drifting until the escort's systems ran down, or he might emerge in solid rock, though it was more likely he would be in open space, completely at a loss as to where he was or whether any system was within reach of the escort. And if he were going to pull out, he had to do it now, while there was any fuel left for maneuvering at all.

His right hand crippled by pain, he fingered the black box, locked in decel commands and triggered them. The escort answered promptly, its surge pushing him deep into his chair, where he sat, panting for breath and wanting not to die.

It was funny, he thought, that flying had been foremost in his mind until it came to making a choice between flying and living.

The shields went up as the escort veered out of Chaos and came back into real-time space and he found himself staring into black velvet on the outer edges of a system with a G type star. His panels lit with a transmitted frequency.

Not only was he somewhere, he was somewhere which supported life—and which transmitted for incoming space flights. He had the luck of a child, as the Choyan said. Over Compact frequencies, he fumbled to send out a message of the disaster. He locked it in so that it would repeat, sealing his own fate. His failure would be broadcast for any with ears to hear. If he did survive, he would be grounded unless he could be recertified.

With neuropathy, that hope was gone, seared out, like the nerves which created and transmitted his *bahdur*. Palaton could be a *tezar* no longer. But at least he was alive.

The homing beacon came from the fourth planet out. Readings showed that it was inhabited, though it was more likely to be a colonized planet than a planet with its own native civilization. Palaton took a deep breath and, over a regular hailing frequency, broadcast his incapacity, detailing a low fuel emergency, and asked for permission to come in. He eyed the fuel gauge. The escort could make it in under its current momentum but not much farther. He sat back to wait for permission.

Side screens nagged for his attention. Palaton turned his head and saw, on the outer edge of the system, a ship coming in fast. The computer brought it up on grid and ID'd it for him.

Ronin.

Palaton knew it must be coincidence, unless he was approaching a Ronin colony. The ship could not have traced him through Chaos. But the quilled aliens were opportunists of the first water. They'd take him out if they knew he was nearly disabled. The fate he'd warned Nedar of was about to become his own.

Palaton slapped his hand down, heedless of the pain, cutting off both the Compact signal and the emergency broadcast. He swiveled in his chair, hit the console's arming controls and brought up his weapons systems. The power lights answered feebly. He didn't have much to fight with.

"Hailing Compact Escort One, we have received distress call and need confirmation."

The Ronin voice coming over his open line left no doubt in his mind. Palaton steadied his own voices in response. "Ronin answer back, I've had some trouble, but it's in hand now and I'm tracking a homing beacon." He wanted desperately to ask where he was and whether he encroached in their territory, but knew he dared not reveal any weakness before the Ronin. He waited for the Ronin comeback.

Silence met his statement. The target grid

showed the other ship bearing away. Palaton watched it warily.

It turned on him almost faster than his instruments could track it. Palaton bit off a curse as his hand failed him in his first attempt to lock in the targeting grid. He fired a warning shot. He had nothing to lose by engaging with them. Their actions declared their intentions.

The Ronin ship curved in evasive action, his shot going wild and destructing. Palaton smiled grimly. At least they knew he meant business. They must be frantically wondering just how disabled he was—and how much of a fight he could put up.

He was either in Ronin territory or so far out that no one would hear of the incident. There was nothing holding them back.

The ship rocked as the Ronin returned fire. Sensors told him that damage was slight—one of the rear conning towers—and Palaton reluctantly put the ship into defensive maneuvers. The fuel sensors dipped alarmingly. The Ronin fired again. The torpedo sped past harmlessly, exploding aft, and the craft cut through the wake of it, scattering debris.

He could not lead them on. Palaton made a decision and abruptly cut engines back. The ship coasted. He knew that Ronin sensors would pick up the abrupt cessation of the drive. He watched them bearing down. They would not blow him out of the sky—they wanted him.

That was the difference between him and them.

They loomed on his rear screens. Palaton shut his jaws firmly, took a reading, and fired everything he had. An orange burst answered.

The escort vessel rocked and shimmied violently when the aftershock of the blast reached him. Palaton brought the escort around and assessed the damage.

There was little more than wreckage left. It could have been called an act of war—if there had been anyone to know of it. With grim satisfaction, he plotted course into the system, hoping he could make it in before everything shut down. The cadets talked often about flying on a wing and a prayer, and that was exactly what he was doing now.

Shaking, he put a hand to his brow. Fever burned it. Pain so ravaged his right arm that both elbows bent in, muscles standing out in rigid cords. He curled it to his flank, cradling it. He stared at the tiny speck on the view screens calling him to safety. He hoped the colony had a decent spaceport, and he prayed that it wasn't a Ronin colony. The control room's lights flickered out, replaced by the dimmer glow of auxiliary lighting as systems started to fail. The ship fell into a spiraling descent toward the yellow sun.

He began to pray. He was not aware of it when he fell into a pain-racked stupor.

The God-in-all looked him over. His magnificent horn crown cupped a bowl of silver curls, and his eyes were dark and bright. "Well," he said, his voices full of the same laughter that creased lines about his eyes and mouth. "You've come a long way." His Choyan was oddly accented, as if grown rusty with disuse. He put a hand under Palaton's head, taking the weight of the *tezar's* too heavy skull into his palm, and bolstering him. "Have a drink of this now.

When you crash, you do it in style. Most of that escort can still be flown out of here."

Palaton struggled to speak, to tell him. Every bone in his body hurt and his eyes were almost too heavy to keep open. "I failed," he got out. "Lost in Chaos, four hundred. I . . . failed."

"We've heard enough of that," the God-in-all said. "Whatever tales you've got to tell, we can hear later." In Trade, he added, "Cleo, woman, bring those soaking rags over here."

And damp, cooling rags were laid over his limbs, relaxing his convulsive cramps bit by bit, until he could tell he lay on a crude cot stuffed with leaves and herbs, their scent being bruised out of the ticking by the pressure of his weight. Another figure came into his line of sight—it was a humankind, a woman, bulky and with laugh lines of her own around luminous blue eyes. Palaton put up a hand. "Those eyes," he said.

The woman smiled broadly. "My," she answered. "Compliments already. It's the fever. You'll come to your senses soon enough. A *Tezar* complimenting a human. What's the world coming to!" She laughed warmly, and he knew she teased him.

The hands supporting his head let go, easing him back onto a pillow that had been meant for a Choya. Palaton blinked.

"You're not . . . God-in-all."

"By the great wheel's turn, no! Nor did I ever claim to be. No, my child, I'm an old *tezar* and you're in good hands. Now rest, for that's all you need to know and all I'll be telling you." Dry, callused fingers closed his eyes firmly and held them so for a second.

That second was all it took to put Palaton
back into a deep, healing sleep.

"I should be dead," Palaton said, his voices
falling unnaturally loud into the silence. A cooling rag lay over his brow and he could not see
who he spoke to, so he spoke Trade, out of
courtesy.

"Wait a bit," the woman answered. He could
hear her now, rustling about the room. "You
can probably accomplish that yet." The rag was
whisked off his forehead and replaced, giving
him only a blur of sight, and she dominated
that vision. "Of course, I'd be wondering why I
was wasting all this time on a corpse."

He listened to her move about the room. She
hadn't the grace of a Choya'i, but few alien
races did. "How long have I been here?"

"Four days or so." A pause. "I've been listening to you rave most of that time, but you
sound fairly sane now."

"Only fairly," answered Palaton.

"Good. Then I'll get Daman. He's been waiting for you."

Palaton heard and felt the pressure change of
a recycler as she left. Bad air outside? Or just
an inadequate atmosphere? Where was he? And
into whose hands had he fallen? He turned his
cheek and found his own hands bound loosely
at his sides. He tossed his head and the compress slid into a soggy lump beside his forehead
as he stared upward, blinking, until he could
see.

The room was prefab and sterile, uninterest-
ing and unrevealing. Geodesic dome style, it
might almost have been a unit knocked together
just to house him. His bed was a matting laid

on the floor, and he'd been in it long enough
that the herbal fragrance had mostly dissipated.
He worked his wrists inside the trussing. Was
he guest or captive?

The recycler wheezed faintly again, and a
massive, burly Choya filled the room. It was he
Palaton had mistaken for the God-in-all—silver
curls and all. The elder had brought a stool with
him. He now dropped it in place and sat down.
"I'll speak in Trade, for the benefit of my
durah," the Choya said, confusing Palaton. A
durah was a lifemate, a bonded partner, and
Palaton had not seen or heard any Choya'i treat-
ing him.

The humankind came in behind Daman and
sat as well. He saw an unconscious imitated
grace in her posture, an echo of Daman's. She
wore her chestnut hair shoulder length, and
long silvery locks of gray streaked it along her
brow. Her smile was crooked, tight at one corner, as though she shared a confidence which
pleased her sense of irony. The Choya wore an
old flight suit, somewhat frayed at collar and
cuffs. She wore fuller clothes somewhat akin to
the robes of an Earthan priest. Something
native to her people, Palaton guessed, and his
attention flickered back to the elder Choya. A
tezar himself, Palaton remembered.

"Can you send a transmission?"

"No," the Choya said flatly. He held up a
broad, work-stained hand. "There is no longer
any need. What's done is done. What's lost
is . . . lost."

"No." His heart twisted.

Daman stared sternly at him. "You've been
here for days in the throes of first stage burn-
out fever, and you deny me? I've been away a

long, long time, but I've never missed the arrogance of a *tezar*."

"A failure cannot afford arrogance," said Palaton.

"Too true. Had you only thought it before this tragedy might have been averted."

He clenched a hand. "If I lived, they might have, too! If you can get word out—"

"Our facilities are primitive, and, at any rate, our outgoing broadcasts were shut down when you chose to duel the Ronin. We don't need that kind of trouble," the humankind said. Her eyes flashed.

"They'll not come here. . . ."

"They might," argued the Choya. "They've been known to do it before. However, they're not my immediate concern. You are. I am Daman, of the house of Sky from the Salt Towers, and you are, unless lineage mistakes me, a Star. This is Cleo. How turns the Great Wheel on Cho?"

The woman laughed. "He would refer to me as his *durah*, but you already look stunned. What we are is not what you suspect, but there's no word to describe our bonding."

Fever began to build in his body again. He felt the ripples of involuntary chills shake him. He clenched his teeth. "Your matters are private," he said in answer. "But tell me, where are we, and why would the Ronin haunt you—and why won't you help me?"

"The Ronin haunt us because they want me for the same reason they wanted you—a lone, forgotten *tezar* is fair game. I won't help you because I can't help you. What's done is done. I can't give you back your transports just as I can't regenerate the nerve damage. And as for where we are—we are so far out on the frontier even the Compact has no inkling of where you've fallen. So if you want to hide, *tezar*, you've come to the right place."

Palaton's frame began to thump helplessly on the cot. Cleo rose quickly. "The fever's hit him again."

Daman got to his feet. "Take care of him as best you can." He vanished from Palaton's blurring vision.

He saw the woman raising a hand to his brow. With great effort, he asked, "What are you to him? Why does he call you *durah*?"

The crooked smile drew tighter. "As if you could ever understand. He's a *tezar*," she said, "because I gave him back his *bahdur*." A compress descended on his brow, curtaining away his vision.

Palaton awoke, feeling weak and drained. The pain in his right arm had numbed, but he felt like a newborn, and though he swung his legs over the side of the cot, he didn't think he could stand. He got to his feet though, driven by the need to void his bladder, and stayed up, bolstered by the framework of the room. He found the conveniences, primitive as they were, and used them. Then he staggered back to the cot and sat down heavily, his head reeling.

He could remember Moameb dealing with burn-out fever like a massive hangover. It came and went, leaving disaster in its wake, and pilots coping as best they could. He had hoped he would lose his talent spark by spark, quietly, almost unknowingly, instead of by this massive blow. He was still alive, but was it worth it?

"Is that arrogance boiling down to self-pity I hear?"

Palaton turned around achingly, slowly, to see Daman in the far corner, rocking back and balancing his chair. He had evidently spoken aloud. "Probably," he admitted.

"Ah. I wondered. Is this a common trait at Blue Ridge?"

"Actually," Palaton said slowly, "I think it began as a tradition at Salt Towers."

"Hmmm." Daman brought the legs of his chair to earth. "You can't be so close to death with that sense of humor."

"Truly?"

"Truly." The Choya stood. "Now we must decide what to do with you."

"I haven't *bahdur* enough to get back to base, even if we could launch the escort—and I don't remember you telling me how badly it was damaged."

"I doubt that. You practically aura-blinded me at the peak of your fever. But you've lost control, the ability to access what remains." The silver-haired Choya paced beside his cot, dark eyes smoldering with thought. "As far as the ship goes, it's serviceable enough."

"You could take me in."

"No." Daman stopped in his tracks, an unreadable expression on his broad, creased face. "No, that's not a possibility."

"Why?"

"Because I don't touch Compact lands anymore. I've reason for it, and the less you know, the better." Daman rubbed his hands together. "Do you feel well enough for a hike after dinner?"

His knees felt like rubber. "I could . . . try."

"Then I'll take you out to see the escort yourself. And you can make a decision there. You can go back, or you can bury yourself alive here."

Palaton looked at him. "Like you did?"

Daman's head jerked back as if Palaton had clipped his jaw. His eyes narrowed slightly. "I stay for Cleo's sake. If we left, they would take her away from me. I don't think either of us would survive that. Again, you seek to know that which would jeopardize you. Don't ask me again."

He wouldn't ask. Like his own failure, they must seek to hide secrets of their own. His guts clenched, out of both self-hatred and hunger. Hunger he could deal with. Palaton stood up, locking his limbs and staying up from sheer determination. "Which way is the kitchen?"

Chapter 20

The escort was more than serviceable. It was, reflected Palaton, in far better shape than he was after hiking out to take a look at the crash site. He'd brought it in over a saltwater lake and back bay flats, then let it skid to solid ground. They would have to build a launch cradle for any kind of a lift-off, but Daman was confident there was enough fuel left to get to the trading port which serviced the planet and would have off-planet launching berths.

"Then," he said, with a broad grin, "they'll take your back teeth for payment if you let 'em."

"I'd prefer to keep my teeth a little longer. Will they take Compact credit?"

"It's possible. Always possible. Are you that eager, my friend, to face disgrace?"

An emotion butterflied around inside of him. It took Palaton a moment to identify it as fear. He sat down on a deadwood stump and looked at the escort vehicle, its side tiles scraped with salt and weed. "No," he said finally. "But I can't stay here."

Daman crossed his arms over his broad chest. "Rumors are the Great Wheel is descending for the House of Star. Who's up next . . . refresh my exile's memory."

"The Earthans, supposedly, but everyone knows they can't handle the intricacies of the Compact and its policies. Star feels it doesn't have to let go, and Sky is waiting to wrest the throne away."

"Then little has changed since I left, except that Panshinea has come to the throne and grown old."

"Old?" Palaton found it difficult to reconcile his impressions of the emperor with becoming an elder. Rindalan, now, must be almost rickety, but Panshinea would still be holding to the edge of his prime and maturity. Unless his illness had bested him, he would still be vigorous and as erratically brilliant as ever. "Not him."

"You think not?" Daman's brow arched. He wore no facial jewelry . . . in fact there were no tracings or tattoos anywhere on his exposed skin that Palaton could see. Only the faint tubings of the oxygen mask they both wore to augment the thin air of this poor world. "Well, you've seen the ship. It's best we get back before dark."

Palaton stood. He hesitated. "I want . . . to transmit."

A sharp glance from the other. "It will do no good, and it may well bring the Ronin on our necks."

"I have a duty."

Daman sighed. He uncrossed his broad arms and gestured. "And I a conscience. To fly and to serve, eh, *tezar*? We have a quarter hour. Set it on a pulse trans, and we'll shut it down before we leave. Otherwise, you'll have a power drain as well."

Palaton smiled wryly. "You're a good com-

promiser. Maybe you should go home and vie
for the throne."

Daman's face became stone. "Cho is no home
of mine." And he stood impassively as Palaton
brushed past him to enter the ship's emergency
lock.

Cleo met them at the stead's front locks, wiping her large capable hands on a lab apron. "It's
after dark. I was worried," she said. The top of
her head barely reached Daman's shoulder. He
put an arm about her comfortingly. Palaton
turned his head away quickly, unnerved by the
show of affection between the two. As he looked
away, the walls and ceilings of the buildings
swapped gravity, and he hit the floor.

Cleo knelt beside him, putting the back of her
smooth hand to his forehead. "Relapse," she
said to Daman. "It's going to hit him hard."

"Ummmm. My fault. I should have known a
pilot never walks when he can fly. Hold his head
up, I'll get him."

Palaton, weak as a wrung out rag, lay on the
floor and listened to the two discuss him. He
could not even protest when Daman hefted him
up like a child and carried him over his broad
yet bony shoulder. Cleo swam, upside down, in
and out of his view. Palaton was just about to
retch despite his empty stomach when Daman
dropped him onto the cot.

Palaton clenched his jaws and thought better
of the idea for a moment. Cleo leaned over
him. The cup of broth in her hands smelled
delicious. She hesitated, spoon in hand, looking to Daman. "Perhaps I could do for him
what I do for you . . ."

A private thing. Daman gave her a look with

a thousand expressions and not one of them did Palaton understand. But the answer was clear. "No."

She nodded and knelt by him, offering the soup. It seemed to keep the worst of the fever at bay for a while, but eventually Palaton succumbed to the joint-rattling shakes and lapsed into dark dreams of Sorrow where a thousand young stared accusingly at him from their crystal coffin.

He ran from the look in their eyes and found himself at the Householding of his youth, his grandfather's estates, the House of Volan, but the buildings were empty, old papers rattling along with his footsteps like dry leaves on a barren riverbed. Gone, all his people, all his kin, all his past. He walked his mother's wing, saw the dust marks on the walls where her embroideries had hung and been taken down. He traced the designs left behind in cobweb, faded stone, and hanging pegs. He walked through the wing, with its studio and atrium additions, to a back door which led to the gardens and, inevitably, to her tomb.

He'd never seen it, but still knew where he stood. One of her few sculptures, a broken pitcher fountain, adorned it, and water still ran from the pitcher's spout into a pool of reflections at the monument's base. It mirrored a serenity he thought his mother had never known in real life. He thought it basest irony that death would give her what had been needed most and now could never be appreciated. The broken pitcher seemed to represent the view Tresa had held of herself. He put a hand out and let the cooling water run over it.

The actual engraving on the tomb held her

House, her Householding, her birth and death
dates, and a sentiment which she must have
constructed herself. "DO YOU REMEMBER
ME."

Both command and question, a charge and
a plea, the duality of her voices, and her life.
Appropriate, he thought. I do remember you,
and I do not . . . because you would not lend me
your secrets, and I've no place else to go. He
had not been brave enough to ask the questions
of himself that had been placed before him.
Now he had no recourse, the Householding he'd
been raised in taken from him as well.

And as he stood, time changed, and he remembered the garden without the fountain,
himself hanging on to his mother's tunic, quiet,
triumphant, and afraid, his grandfather towering over the two of them, his voices trumpeting.

*"He will be a tezar," his grandfather Volan
shouted, "and you will let him go."*

*"No," Tresa said. He could feel her trembling
within his hold. "I saw the test results just as you
did. They must be buried, destroyed! Or they will
destroy him."*

*"My name, my money, is good for something,"
his grandfather returned. "I've hidden him as well
as I can. But you . . . you betrayed me, your destiny, and this Householding. I thought you dallied
with a common. . . . I hoped our blood would run
true. But his bahdur burns the way no one in our
line has ever burned. What House did you sleep
with? What fates have you knotted and tangled?"
And Volan bore down on them, his face dark with
anger.*

*Palaton remembered his mother shrinking back,
turning her cheek, saying, "I don't remember!"*

Not that she would not tell, but that she did not remember.

He broke into a cold sweat at the revelation of dream memory, shaking. Who was he that the House of Earth would send assassins? Who was he that the children of Sorrow and Earth haunted him? Who was he that *bahdur* could burn so brightly and then so suddenly abandon him?

He woke in the night, and saw Daman bowed by the cot, chin on his chest, snoring, voices rumbling deeply. It was a wonder Palaton or Cleo or anything else could sleep with that thunder. He thought of his grandfather for an odd moment, then knew the head of his Householding would never have sat up with him. Tresa had, doing her quiet embroidery. He eyed the Choya. He did not understand the relationship with the woman. It was not sexual, exactly, nor was it equality—but there was something undefinable between them which both attracted and repelled Palaton. He felt as though he were a voyeur, viewing an unspeakable act which was both profane and holy. He knew without being told that it was because of this relationship that Daman had forsaken Cho and would never return.

It had to be. Humankind was not a member of the Compact yet, and any close contact of this kind was strictly forbidden. Therefore, Daman had removed himself from his race and Cleo from hers. Even those who knew of burnout associated it with the regimen of maintaining the mechanics of the FTL drive. What was their relationship that Daman would have betrayed himself to her?

"Slept enough and thought enough?" asked Daman quietly. It took Palaton aback for a second until he realized that, at some point during his musing, Daman had stopped snoring. The Choya put his callused hand out and caressed the air around Palaton. He was, Palaton knew instinctively, outlining his aura.

"You look well tonight."

"I feel better. Have you ever had burn-out fever?"

"No. I know what it's like to have the talent leave you, tease you, like waves rushing in and then retreating from the shoreline. I know what it's like to be yawning empty one second and then bursting the next. But I never got the disease like you have. I had it treated at the onset."

"Treated?" Palaton sat up on his cot. It molded with his movement and he bolstered it behind his shoulders against the wall.

Daman hesitated. "Cleo thinks I should tell you," he offered. "She has no children and never will. But she has maternal feelings which well out of her. I sometimes forget she's not Choya'i."

"I don't want to know your secrets," Palaton said hastily, suddenly feeling as if he could bear no more burdens.

Daman's eyes crinkled. " 'Twould be a help to you, I think. But I'll abide by your wishes—" The two suddenly froze.

Daman undoubtedly felt it more clearly, but even Palaton could sense the sudden change in atmosphere. The massive Choya lurched to his feet. "Damn it all."

Then Palaton heard what they'd sensed. Starship, coming in, like a comet streaming into the atmosphere, sizzling with its heat and speed. His heart sank as he realized what he'd done.

"I've drawn them here."

The big Choya shook his head. Moonlight glinted amid his silver curls. "Take Cleo. Tell her I said to get underground. I've a single rider jet sled. My best weapons are aboard that ship." He bolted from the room.

Palaton got up unsteadily. He cast about. Used to senses beyond his ordinary ones, he wavered across the room. By the time he was through the lock, Cleo had the lights on and was joining him in the main room, pulling on her oddly styled clothing.

"What is it?"

"Incoming," Palaton answered reluctantly. "Daman said for us to go underground."

He was not used to her reactions. Her face grayed suddenly and she swayed. He put a hand out to catch her. Her luminous eyes brimmed with unshed water. "Oh God," she muttered. "They've come after us."

"After me." His mouth went dry. "What did Daman mean by underground?"

"This way." Cleo hesitated. "Can't you go with him?"

"I'm useless this way. If they're Ronin, well, the Ronin are not brave. A good defense will change their minds fairly quickly. He's gone to the ship to use the on-board weaponry."

The woman put a hand to her mouth, her gesture stilted because of her lack of Choyan joints. Her gray-streaked hair looked disheveled. She hesitated.

"He said to go underground," Palaton repeated mildly.

She yielded. "Follow me."

The steading had been cleverly built for just such a siege. Palaton joined her in a lift that went down at least sixty feet before it opened onto a solidly lined tunnel. There were cots, privies, a water course, and an older recycler generator to keep the oxygen level up and pure. The shelter had been made for air strikes. She sealed off the shaft and led him into the tunnel.

Cleo lay down on one of the cots. She rolled into a crescent, her face blank, as if she could follow Daman in her thoughts. Palaton did not interrupt her trance, if that was what it was, although he thought it odd. He'd had no inkling that humankind had any kind of talent whatsoever.

After long moments, it was not necessary to depend on talent. The very land surrounding them shook, reverberating with bomb attacks. Cleo looked up wildly, water streaming down her face. Palaton could feel the tension in his hands as though he played the console board, keying on the weaponry, and he knew that his *bahdur*, faintly as it had returned, transient as it might prove to be, gave him this empathy.

Then, darkness.

Cleo let out a shriek and collapsed sobbing upon the cot. Palaton went to her instantly, smoothed her hair back from her forehead, talking constantly, small nonsenses, to quiet her.

The sobbing stilled to a moan. Then Cleo lifted her face from the cradle of her hands.

"He's dead," she said. "It's over."

Palaton agreed, but he said, "He's a Choya and a *tezar*. Don't underestimate him."

Cleo looked at him. Her chin dimpled and trembled. "In the morning," she asked, "will you take me to him?"

If there was a morning. If Daman had taken the Ronin to death with him. Palaton nodded. "In the morning."

Morning illuminated the charred and still burning wreckage. The wind from it stank of death and saltwater bog. Palaton stood in it as long as he could bear it. From a sandy knoll nearby, he had seen the scarring where the attacker had come down as well, a wide swath carved into the earth, and a fiery charred cavern at its end. Thin gray smoke curled into the air above it.

He watched the woman pacing the wreckage as though she wished to comb through it and yet knowing that nothing remained in that twisted ingot which had once been a proud starship and was now a slowly cooling molten coffin for a Choya. She kept her hand to her mouth, muffling her cries. At long last, she turned away from the wreck and came back to him.

"You'll take me to the spaceport."

"If you wish." He had brought this on her. He would undo it if he could. It did not seem possible Daman's vibrancy could be so suddenly wiped from the face of the world. "I'll help however I can."

"No," she said. "I'll help you. I'm going to take you to the only other place we could have called home. I'm going to take you to the College. No matter what it costs you."

Palaton stared at the crazed woman. He agreed because he had no choice. He could go no lower. He had murdered out of ignorance and denial and last night, he had murdered out of selfishness. He owed her his life and his soul.

A tiny spark of *badhur* had been rekindled within him. He had no inkling of what a humankind would do with it.

"I'll take you," he said, "wherever you want to go."

Chapter 21

They helped each other make the journey. They took the hover sledge, a slow, clumsy vehicle modified to transport supplies in bulk, to the spaceport. It was, by Palaton's standards, an extremely primitive facility. They had only three launching berths, two of which were serviceable and the third of which was being used as a dry dock repair bay. There was no distress homing beacon, which, though he had no memory of it, explained to Palaton why he had brought the escort in on a crash-landing basis—because there had been no other way to bring the vehicle in.

The primary occupants of this world were saurian, lazy at midday, scurrying about busily in the morning and evening hours when their body warmth found activity more conducive. Cleo told him they had been a servile race to the Quinonans; he did not remember any such, but knew the Compact had forced the Quinonans to divest themselves of imperialistic activities several centuries ago. This resettled planet might be the result of Compact action.

Cleo did not speak much of the saurian tongue. She had neither the physical attributes to do so nor the tutoring, but Palaton watched in bemusement as the saurians attempted Trade

along with a hand-sign language complicated
by how spindly their fingers were compared to
those of the humankind. Whatever communication needed to be made went through speedily,
however, for Daman had evidently been a respected member of the community and Cleo
had no trouble spending the credit of his estate.
Daman also had his own starship. She ordered
it fueled and berth-loaded. She backed up her
orders with no nonsense body language, unmis-
takable in any speech.

She turned around, her face pinked by a day
in the sun on the unshielded hover sledge, and
fanned herself with a reed-woven hat. "It will
take a while, and there'll be a noonday break,
but we should be able to board by dusk."

Palaton held himself very tall. He looked
down at the woman. His voices sounded faint
to him when he spoke, and he hated himself for
showing weakness. "I need to rest."

She put a hand out, catching him by the
wrist. "Of course you do. They've a center not
far from here. How about a cup of hot *bren*?"

"That sounds agreeable."

"Daman made the hotelier order a private
stock and keep it for him. Come with me," and
Cleo, who towered over these saurian people
much as he towered over her, led the way
through the bustle of the port.

The hotelier poured real *bren*, hot, dark, its
bittersweet aroma pungent in the private booth
he'd led them to. Palaton sagged gratefully onto
cushions and watched as the obsequious inn-
keeper, his girth well rounded for one of these
saurian folk, bowed and left them.

Momentarily, a look of amusement veiled the
expression of regret masking Cleo's face. She

circled her hands about the cup, her single elbows resting on the table. She looked awkward, Palaton thought. The amusement fled, her sorrow returned. "Will the Ronin return for them?"

"Probably not. They'll send in spies this time. Daman taught them caution, if nothing else. And, finding nothing, they'll leave." Every word was an effort. His chest ached when he finished speaking and he drowned his pain with the hot *bren*, draining his cup. Cleo refilled it automatically from the silvery urn the saurian had left for them.

"You've asked no questions about where I'm taking you."

"It would do me no good to."

She fanned herself again with her homemade hat. "The answers would do you good."

He sipped cautiously at his second cup, this time feeling the tongue-numbing heat, as the aroma wafted along his palate and curled into his senses, giving him the familiar, soothing taste and, with it, a sense of well-being. "Whatever I have to give is yours. I cannot possibly repay the debt I owe you." *Or the Compact.* He sat watching her, knowing again the yawning ache of his power fled, unreliable, smoldering into gray ashes from what had once been a bonfire of possibility.

"It's not what you have to give me, it's what we can give you." Cleo lifted her cup, but he had the impression it was to hide her face rather than to drink, as it remained motionless at her lips. "If you're not too proud to take it."

She knew little of the Choyan, for all the years she'd spent in companionship with Daman. He had no pride left. She sat and watched a shell

performing movements, struggling to maintain
a balance, a norm, without imploding under the
emptiness. "There's nothing you can do for me.
The *bahdur* goes with the neuropathy. The disease progresses at its own rate for each Choya.
I have no idea have much time I have left," he
answered slowly.

"How do your hand and arm feel?"

"A slight numbness here," and he pinched
two fingers together. "The telegraphing pain is
gone."

"Minor neuropathy then. You've hundreds of
nerves in your hands. You can afford to lose one
pathway."

She pricked his anger. "Woman, I'm familiar
with my own composition. I know what I face.
You do not. How can you know what *bahdur*,
or its loss, is?"

"You'd be surprised what I know," Cleo answered enigmatically. She stood up. "I'm going
to close the booth off for privacy. I suggest you
lie down and wait. We've a credit line here, too.
If you're hungry, order something. Just do it
before noonday break. And don't leave without
me."

He shot her a look. "I've nowhere to go."

Cleo laughed. "You'd be surprised about that,
too. If the general folk around here learn a
Choya is in their midst, you'll be pestered to
death. They think your touch is a talisman.
You'd spend the day blessing babies. The hotelier
is ensuring our privacy now, but if you wandered . . . you'd be theirs until they brought you
back." She set her hat on her gray-streaked
hair. And stood waiting for his response.

"I'll stay," he said grudgingly and settled
back on the booth cushions. The *bren* was

already warming his interior. Sleep sounded like a welcome alternative to arguing with this creature.

"I'll be back." Cleo turned and left the cubicle. It closed off and dimmed in her wake. Palaton shut his eyes wearily.

He awoke to the distinct feeling of being watched. The hotelier stood inside the booth, two young saurians hiding under the shadow of his girth. Palaton thought that Cleo had not left him as well guarded as she thought. He sat up.

"Master *Tezar*," the innkeep got out in acceptably spoken Trade. "My get. I implore you, for their well-being. . . ."

Palaton put a hand out and the younglings crowded in, each getting a blessing. They hissed with pleasure and scampered out of the booth.

The hotelier beamed through wide lizard jaws. "Thank you."

"It's nothing." He ordered food as Cleo had suggested, picking and choosing carefully, unaware of the differences between his diet and hers. "You can bring it after noonday break," he added, whereat the hotelier who had been looking distressed, relaxed again. He waddled out of the booth after his young.

The disturbance had allowed the heat of the day to penetrate and it lulled him back to sleep. When he woke again, Cleo sat across the table, picking through food the hotelier had quietly left.

He roused as she said, "Our ship's been berthloaded. Fueling's nearly done."

"Have you finished your business?"

"Yes." Her eyes brimmed suddenly. "I wanted to dispose of the homestead and our goods."

"You won't be coming back?"

"No." Cleo shook her head emphatically. "Not this way."

"Then we'll board as soon as we've eaten. I don't fly a ship I haven't inspected."

The brimming in her eyes intensified suddenly, and he knew without her answering that he'd said something that reminded her of Daman. He looked away, unable to bear the additional pain he'd inflicted.

Daman's ship was a standard class cruiser, old, but he'd flown older, and it had been modified with the black box *tezarian* drive, so it was more responsive than he expected. He brought it off-planet in an ungainly move, a sheer triumph of brute force over gravity. Cleo sat in the navigator sling, her face drawn by the strain as they broke free.

"I'd forgotten," she said. "How hard it can be."

He did not answer her, lost in his own thoughts about the job before him. He brought the engines up so that they might enter Chaos as soon as possible. He'd never entered Chaos before without an inkling of where he wanted to go.

Cleo put her hand out again, touching him. A peculiar habit of these humankind, he thought, but did not move away. "When you're ready," she murmured, "I will show you where to go. Daman left it with me."

He looked at her in surprise, then. "You've talent?"

"Oh, no. But I've memory. And Daman knew we would—that is, you could—retrieve it."

The thought of such an intimacy with an alien shocked him into silence. He sat looking at her, ignoring the flashes and beeps of the instrument console which warned him of the approach of the void.

Cleo whispered, "You must do it quickly. It's been a long time since I've faced Chaos. I'm not sure how well I'll be able to take it. It's been tougher than I thought."

He realized then that, like Daman, she was no longer young. Nor could she be expected to look into the face of Chaos like a Choya. He took her fingers off his arm gently and, extending his own hand, cradled the side of her face carefully.

"Look into my eyes."

She did. Beautiful eyes, he thought, before ripping aside the curtain of her thoughts and reaching inward.

Daman's sending burned crystal clear. He took it and left, so swiftly he might have been a lancet piercing a wound, pain induced and then removed. Cleo let out a gasp and her eyes fluttered as he left her. Then she sobbed and buried her face in her cupped hands.

He drew back in shock. "Have I hurt you?"

"No." More sobs. Then, "Oh, God. I thought you'd take it all. I thought . . . I thought I'd have nothing left of him with me." Cleo mopped her face on the back of her hands and sniffed. "Thank you."

Baffled, he returned, "Do not thank me until I have brought us to journey's end." And he prepared for Chaos to take them, praying to the God-in-all that the splinters of *bahdur* he held up to light their way would be bright enough.

PART III

ARIZAR

Chapter 22

Spring bells bloomed over the south wall of the lower campus. Cleo trained her eyes on them as they clung ivylike to the red brick administration building, the Arizarian sky a vibrant blue backdrop to the plateaus which held the college. She rubbed her arms against a chill she didn't remember from her youth, listening to the murmurs of the upset Choyan behind her, deliberately not looking back to the waiting room with its one-way viewing door which showed the haggard Palaton slouched upon a couch, eyes sunk in weary thought. Two Choyan stood guard over him. The welcome had been far from what she'd expected.

She spoke up, over the agitated muttering. "He brought us in on a mere flicker of *bahdur*, alone, without one of you to guide him, with only my human memory (she did not mention the final visions given her by Daman, nor would she ever). He was incredible. And he will be brilliant again, if you aid him. How can you think of turning him away?"

The Choyan in this room dominated her in a way Daman never had, not even in their first days as Brethren, and she reacted in spite of herself, biting her lip at her boldness of speech.

"You haven't come through our gates in

thirty years since we gave you away to be bonded. *Tezar* Daman broke our trust then. How do we know you haven't returned to break our trust again? Circumstances have changed."

"*You* haven't changed, Reeve Bryad." And the Choya who faced her with hair of ebony and eyes of rainwater blue had not. He had aged imperceptibly. Perhaps there was a new line in his face, perhaps not. He carried the weight of authority as easily as his horn crown, but he was still the tutor she remembered, though now he was the Reeve in charge of the entire campus. "I don't know why Daman left. I do know that we never set foot on Compact lands. He vowed he would never do that, and he didn't. No one knew who he was, what he did. He was a technician and a trader. If he broke a trust with the College, I don't know how he could have done it."

Provost Ferson said bluntly, "He left and took you with him." Ferson had had a stroke since the days when she had known him as secretary to the old Reeve. Perhaps that was why Bryad had taken up the succession instead. The Choya held himself cupped protectively, favoring his left side, the left side of his mouth slack, his eye drooping slightly, his arm in a cast. His white hair had that yellow sheen of age. He carried a wicked looking cane. She somehow imagined him slinging it at impetuous students.

Cleo blinked. She brought her mind back to the matter at hand. Were they telling her Choyan never left with their Brethren? "Was this never done?"

Bryad moved a pace nearer the one-way screen. He ignored her question. "He's one of the House of Star?"

"Daman said so. I've talked very little with him. He's recovering from a terrible round of burn-out fever." She would let Palaton speak for himself of the rest.

Provost Gracet had remained seated, saying very little in her soft voices. She wore her dark hair in short curls, beribboned among her horn scallops. She said now, "The greater the talent. . . ." Her eyes were quicksilver gray, like lies.

A thin, wiry Choya with dark hair and hazel eyes sat at the desk. He kept bringing up information on his data screen. He looked up briskly. "There's been no contact from here." He looked at the Reeve. He seemed nervous and his voices had been among the tenser tones she'd been listening to when they talked among themselves.

"He won't be in our data base, then," the Reeve mused. "It will take some time to access what we need to know, without being found out. Won't it, Ferson?"

The thin Choya nodded energetically.

"Give us the name again, Cleo."

"Palaton," she said slowly, and spelled it.

The Reeve abruptly put his hand up. "I know the name." He swung about and stared intently now at the failed pilot in the waiting room. "Are you sure? That's him. . . . Four hundred went to their deaths because of him?"

Cleo answered reluctantly, knowing she could not protect Palaton's privacy any longer. "Yes."

"We picked up the emergency transmission he put out. It was almost a *sending*, it was so strong." The Reeve mused.

"Another Fallen Star," Gracet said, once again letting the full meaning of her sentence trail away, catching the Reeve's glance. They traded a look.

The Reeve seemed to make up his mind. "Ferson, get Dr. Ligo up here. Our guest will need some downtime before he's ready to talk about the College and what we can do for him. By then, we should have records accessed. As for you, Cleo," and the Choya looked at her down a long, thin nose. "What do you want of us?"

She spread her hands uncertainly. She knew what she'd intended to ask, but the Reeve was correct. Things had changed since she'd left. She wasn't at all sure what the changes were, or if she liked them. But she had nowhere else to go, and this was where she had found Daman. "I'd like to stay here. I can work with the new students."

The Reeve caught up one of her work-creased hands. "You know the greater portion of the lower campus is a biosphere. We can use a skillful gardener as well as a dorm mother." He smiled at her.

Cleo returned the expression hesitantly. She put her other hand in his, determined to use him just as she knew he was determined to use her.

The Reeve waited until he and Gracet were alone in his office. He looked at the data filling the screen which Ferson had left on for him. "Such a one," he said, "would never have come to us on his own."

"Only because we have to be very circumspect in our recruiting."

"No. Not this one."

Gracet stirred, her lips pursing much as they did when students gave her an argument. She did not like being crossed. Her stern expression was at odds with her beribboned hair, but Bryad knew which was the real Gracet. She had never been dainty or pliable and would not be now. "It's too risky. We expect Nedar of Sky. Our contact was sure of his response. That one is desperate. Our information shows them to be classmates and rivals, of a sort. One or the other, Bryad, you must choose."

"We can't afford to choose! We need all the new blood we can get. And Cleo, in her bonded way, senses what is most important to us. He has *talent*, all the bounty a *tezar* is subject to. We can't overlook him or turn him away. We have the advantage, he doesn't. We know the course of the disease. We know his talent will return nearly intact after this initial bout, he doesn't. We have him at his most vulnerable."

"And if he proves a liability?"

Bryad smiled. "According to the records, he's been presumed lost. We've no risk."

"Not unless he himself turns on us." Gracet got up to leave the Reeve's office. She paused at the doorway. "Remember that," she said.

"I didn't inherit this office on the merits of faulty judgment."

"Just remember." She opened the door and left.

Bryad returned to his chair. The information Ferson had accessed so far had been sketchy but intriguing. "So, my Choya," he murmured to himself as he stretched his fingers over the keyboard and made private records. "You think yourself responsible for disaster. I wonder how long I can keep you in the dark?"

* * *

It was dark in the ground shuttle. Most of the windows were shuttered against the violent squall which had hit them after leaving the port. Randall stubbornly kept his open as the shuttle rocked and bumped through dark swirling clouds. He saw a sheet of lightning flash, gone so quickly he could barely see it, except that when he closed his eyes, it was emblazoned on his inner sight.

Most of the others were quiet, shocked by the stormy weather and rough flight, still in the grip of the tranquilizer which had been given them for the first deep space leg of the trip. He had only taken half his medicine—he wanted to savor the experience. Now his stomach finally began to unclench and the sour taste at the back of his throat receded, and he could see without experiencing that terrible vertigo. He'd only had one look at one of the infamous Choyan pilots but it was a sight he wouldn't forget.

He kept his cheek to the window. The chill of the insulated pane helped his head clear. The darkness boiling about them made him wonder what kind of storm it was they flew into. Was the Choya who'd piloted them this far still at the controls? If so, he had no fear. If not . . . this was a storm that could bring all but the mightiest down.

The girl sitting next to him pressed her leg against his. He looked down uncomfortably, wondering whether she'd done it on purpose. She looked up at the same time. She smiled quickly. He had only a moment to see that the smile did not make her eyes happy when the shuttle pitched and the youth across the aisle fell from his seat, landing on their feet.

The fallen youth cursed softly. He sat up, a

broken strap of webbing hanging over his shoulder. His eyes were dark, his hair a luxurious mop, and he flashed a white-toothed smile that said he knew the worth of his roguish looks. Randall felt a twinge as the girl leaned down quickly to help him up. She squeezed him onto the seat between the two of them.

"Who are you?" she asked softly as he lashed himself in for a second time.

"Bevan," the young man answered. His voice was full of the rhythms of the South Americas even though they all spoke Trade. "And you?"

"Alexa. And this is. . . ."

"Randall," he said quickly.

"Ah," laughed Bevan. "Your name is too serious. It makes you serious, too. I'll call you Rand."

The shuttle lurched again. They were thrown together still more tightly. Even across Bevan's wiry body, Randall could smell Alexa's subtle aroma, the slightly musky-rose scent of a perfume that had been popular at home. His stomach gave a peculiar twist of homesickness. She looked at him as if she knew his thoughts. She wet her lips quickly and looked away.

The nine other students talked little. One girl shrieked every time the shuttle dropped or rolled until her voice went hoarse and then silent. Randall went to sleep thinking of her open mouth gasping to produce sound.

He woke with his ears popping, his body straining against the safety web. Bevan put a hand on his shoulder. The cabin air smelled very acrid.

"I think, my friend, this is it. I overheard some chatter up front. Our guardians are nervous."

As Randall understood it, a second leg of deep

space flight was not necessary. Once into Chaos, one could pilot anywhere with a Choya at the helm. But they'd been told they were being moved in stages. Two deep space legs. This shuttle was taking them to a second port. He wondered if they were being followed.

Alexa's face was very pale in the dim light of the cabin. "Are we landing?"

"No." Rand shook his head sharply. "This is no approach." His glance met Bevan's. "This feels like evasion action."

Bevan said, "They want no followers. In space or through Chaos. It's going to be a rough ride."

"Looks like it."

Alexa laughed harshly. "I'm dead already. What does it matter?"

"What?"

"Never mind. How do we survive this?"

Bevan answered. "I think we follow crash procedures."

They stood up, kicking the seats down into their recessed placements and relying strictly on their safety webbing. Hung in their stable yet resilient hammocks, they waited. In the orange-washed light, they could see others get to their feet, snap themselves into the hammocks and do the same.

Alexa wrinkled her nose. "I feel like a fly in a spider's web."

"If it keeps us in one piece, that's okay," said Bevan with his soft accent.

Randall tried to calculate the angle of descent. He swiveled his head about, looking out his window. Black mountain pierced gray cloud. He saw the vessel pacing them. "Oh, God," he said. "That's an Abdrelik ship." The aggressiveness of the Abdreliks scared him. The aliens were unpredictable. And he was off-world now, in territories where they could bend the rules.

Alexa kicked her feet, twirling lazily in the hammock, so she could look out. "Is that it? We're being followed?"

They all knew secrecy was of the utmost importance. They had been told that when they were recruited and it had been reiterated when they'd been collected. Now the revelation of their secret was about to obliterate the adventure they'd begun.

Then the shuttle hit, bounced, and hit again, and the force of the shock sent them spinning through air.

Chapter 23

Rand had been wrong about a landing approach. Light flooded the cabin and the crew entered quickly, disentangling the students from their slings.

"Come on, kids, let's move!"

He dug his toes into the floor for purchase and began unfastening himself as the crew wove their way through.

"Who told you to put the crash webs on?"

"We did," Rand and Bevan said simultaneously.

The crew chief paused. He was a beefy man of florid complexion whose chunky body made folds in a suit never designed to contain his kind of structure. "Good thinking," the man said softly, and worked his way past the three of them. "Get out of here as quick as you can and make for the launching berth."

Rand had to help Bevan down—the slender youth gave an impression of tallness, but although slightly older, was actually an inch or two shorter than Rand—and they both disentangled Alexa. Her form came into their hands, warm and supple, and Rand started, suddenly aware of how different she felt compared to Bevan's lean wiriness. Bevan flashed him a grin as if aware of the same difference. Randall swallowed.

"Let's get out of here."

Up front, the most sedated students were being awakened roughly, gotten on their feet, and force-marched. The hoarse screamer was carried out over a crewwoman's shoulder, slung upside down, her face contorted with the effort to scream.

The sharp, thin air of a desert plateau hit Rand as they moved out of the shuttle. A quick search of the sky showed a building storm front on the leading edge of a range. He could see the dull lights of the berthing cradle and began to move toward it instinctively.

"What's going on?" the girl behind him asked. Bevan made a noncommittal sound, but Rand answered, "They're trying to keep our movements hidden."

Bevan snapped his fingers. "That's why we're going on a two-leg jump."

"Probably."

Alexa stumbled in the dark and bent over to massage her ankle. Her curly hair bounced around her face as she did so. "I don't understand." Her posture muffled her voice.

"We're trying to shake off trackers. That's why they strip-searched us before we boarded the first ship in case we wore homers, and that's why we're pulling some of the tactics we're pulling now."

Alexa stood up. In the desert night, her face seemed pale. She met Randall's gaze squarely. "Wasn't that an Abdrelik ship?"

"Looked like one. We either lost it in the cloud cover coming in or—" Rand's glance flickered to Bevan. He had a suspicion they'd traded shots.

Bevan shrugged fluidly. "He thinks, my lady," the young man said with his accented words, "we shot them down."

"What?"

Rand took a breath. "We lost 'em somehow. Come on. I have a feeling they're not going to wait for us—they're in a hurry." He took Alexa's elbow and coaxed her toward the berthing cradle. They had exited first, but now the others had outstripped them.

A tall, graceful, yet wrongly angled figure loped past them. He carried a caselike object with him. Rand spotted him out of the corner of his eyes and stumbled himself, drawing up against Alexa's compliant form, as the alien passed and made his way into the starship. It was their Choya pilot. The sight of him made Rand's stomach drop and his chest tighten.

"What is it?" Bevan asked, curious.

"The pilot," Rand said. They looked at him as if waiting for more. He shook his head, urging, "Come on!"

As they entered the loading tunnel ramp, Alexa reached out and gripped each of them by the arm. "Let's stay together," she urged.

That would be difficult as the crew had kept the students divided by sex. Bevan gave Rand another look, shrugged again, and said, "We shall try, my lady."

Relief washed over the girl's face. She stayed sandwiched between the two taller boys as they entered the belly of the starship. The crew counted them off, handing out paper cups with tiny pills in them.

"Take your meds and find your couches. Keep your safety webs on—we're making the jump immediately."

There was no time to separate the three of them. Randall made a rueful face and took all of his medication this time. He wanted to be aware and alert when they reached the College instead of sick with vertigo.

Alexa lay down, fastened her harness, and then put each of her hands out. Bevan took one and Rand, after a moment's hesitation, took the other. Her palm was warm and dry in his. He grew sleepy wondering how long he would have to hold her hand and if his would get sticky and sweaty, embarrassing him. The starship vibrated with power, thrusting them deep into their couches. Just before he lost consciousness completely, her slight voice said, "I want both of you to be my lovers."

He woke alone, his ears ringing, his eyes crusted. He knew the keen disappointment of having missed the flight, the eerie sense of reality twisted inside out, the awesome feeling of walking a corridor which might or might not exist in the same time-frame, all the sensations which toyed with human sanity. Most of all he mourned his inability to take part in the piloting, to understand what it was about the *tezarian* drive which transcended flight. He wanted to be at the helm, piercing Chaos, taking the starship down unimaginable pathways. He lay wrapped in half awake thoughts.

The burly crew men came through. "Wake up, sleepyhead. Breakfast is on and then we're disembarking."

The thought of food brought him out of his

safety harness and to his feet. There was a new world outside the skin of this starship. Rand hurried to meet it.

The Zarites at the port reminded him of walking hamsters, though sleeker, with big, round, transparent ears which flicked and blushed with emotion, and furred tails to give them balance. They worked to unload the starship, showing deference to both Choyan and human, their whiskers laid flat against their cheeks, their six-fingered, capable hands deftly working the equipment.

Rand caught one of them watching him surreptitiously. He grinned at the Zarite, watched the blush spread throughout its/his/her ears, and the piebald colored creature spun around in distress.

He caught it watching them again as they climbed into the shuttle which would take them to the College. Other sharp-muzzled, curious faces watched as well. Alexa laughed as she pressed her nose against the portal window when he pointed them out.

She turned her head sharply and their faces almost bumped. Randall drew back. She laughed again, her breath sweet with the aroma of the vegetable casserole they'd had for breakfast.

"They're beautiful." Her eyelashes lowered and rose, and she raised a hand idly to the curve of her neck, where she scratched a minor irritation.

The burly crewmaster had been striding past. He stopped, leaned past them, and saw what they were looking at. He laughed sharply. "Them? The Zarites are fast-fingered, grubby land workers. They'll have the flight suits off you and salvaged before you can blink. Watch 'em. You two settle in or Provost Gracet'll have my head for bringing you all in late." He brushed through.

Bevan leaned out of his seat and drew Alexa in beside him. Rand knew a certain sense of relief as well as irritation as he found an empty flight chair and sat down. Almost there. The goal he and his father had spent years working toward was almost within his grasp.

He was still woozy when they took the shuttle from the Arizarite port to the mountains where the upper and lower campuses of the College of the Brethren were located. He got an impression of a wilderness as varied and unpredictable as old North America used to be only perhaps a bit more lush and river-tracked. They were served mugs of something called *bren*, hot, thick, smoky tasting, like coffee or roasted malt . . . he wasn't sure. It woke him up and sat comfortingly in his stomach like a glowing ember.

Then the hills and mountains of the College rose before them. They were green up to the timberline, then purple and sheer, broken off as if whole cliffs had sloughed away under the pressure of reaching for the sky. Only the purest and sharpest made it. White clouds billowed in a sky of clearest blue. He could see the hilltop which had been leveled for the campus, and the biosphere units scattered across it. Rand sucked in his breath. The dream was real.

The Choya known as Provost Gracet met them at the front gates. Beyond her, Rand could see the faces of other students, young men and young women, most a little older, some a little younger, all on the threshold of their adult life, looking curiously at the new arrivals. Gracet arrivals. Gracet bore herself with great dignity, towering over the humankind. She looked once, over her shoulder, at the gate. Faces disappeared, then reappeared as soon as she had turned around again. Randall was reminded of the Zarites.

A great deal of the College was built of blue stone and red brick, except for the massive dome-halls which housed the biosphere's gardens, ponds, and aviaries. It looked as if it had been carved out of the mountains. Randall thought of Nepal, in the Himalayas, the Rooftop of the World. His world. This, he thought, was the rooftop of Arizar.

Gracet spoke in Trade, a language which he had spoken exclusively since leaving his home in preparation for this, but he still followed her laboriously.

"Twelve students," she said. "Hoping to become Brethren. We will lose at least four of you in the first few weeks. Over the next few spans, another two of you will leave us. Six then ... six graduates. Look at one another. Remember your faces and dreams. Either the one on your left hand or your right hand will fail."

Bevan stood to his left and Alexa flanked his right. They looked at him. Bevan shook his head and rolled his eyes. He was not going to be frightened.

"Only the successful will know what it means to become a Brethren." Gracet opened her arms, sinuous and graceful with their double elbows, beckoning them through the gates.

Rand found his duffel in a pile next to the gatepost and hoisted it over his shoulder. He was one of the last to enter. The gate swung shut almost on his heels with a heavy bang, closing away the rest of the world. The bars quivered with a sinister clang.

He was reminded that every dream carries a bit of nightmare within it.

Cleo stood like a mountain, not taller, but vaster, deeper and broader than he was. She kept her chestnut brown hair bound back, the gray streak over her right brow making her look like a thunderbolt had struck her. She moved gracefully despite her heft and embraced the four children put into her dorm by Gracet. Rand found an instant liking for her, though he was unsure of what to say or do, she was so unlike his mother, who wandered palely through his memories of the days before she had left.

Cleo pointed at Alexa. "A loft room for you, with a window seat, where you can curl up at night and read and write poetry."

The girl blushed, her lips half-opened in soft protest, then she hung her head, her curly fringe of hair curtaining her eyes.

Cleo continued briskly. "A separate room for you as well, Master Bevan. I recognize a charmer when I see one and I think you need to be kept alone if the others are to retain anything of theirs."

Bevan murmured half an objection which died softly on his lips. He shrugged in answer. "Your request, my lady."

Rand feared her look when she faced him, but her face softened. "Ah. The clear eyes of a seeker of truth. I'll put you in with Ahmad . . . no. Zain. Yes. That should do."

The fourth student who'd come in with them was another girl, dreadfully thin, freckled, with deep red hair. She had an astonishing birthmark on the nape of her neck, like a crescent sienna moon. Megan brightened as Cleo called her name. "I have a room, you might not like it, mind you, Stella is bossy and brassy . . ."

"I won't faint away," Megan said. Her voice, unlike her mannerisms, was coarse and deep.

"Good. Well, then, here are your maroons. There are two classes of students here, beginners in maroons, and those about to become Brethren, in the blues. Age doesn't earn you the blues. Going the course earns you that. Any questions?" Cleo held jumpsuits out, with zippers and buckles on them to take up, let out or lengthen almost any seam.

Bevan took his with a sigh, holding it up. He would have to adjust the leg length. He laughed as Rand held his up.

"Who wore that last? An elephant?"

Cleo narrowed her gaze. "Mind your manners, boy. That was mine when I was a student here."

Bevan's mouth snapped shut. He blinked a few times as if checking her credibility, then laughing softly at himself as her eyes crinkled.

The other students headed up the household hallways. Rand held back. "I have a question," he said hesitantly.

"Ask away." Cleo paused, her body quivering slightly, as if holding her back from motion took a great deal of effort.

"When will I meet a . . . a pilot?"

"A *tezar*? Well, my boy, you might never. The ones who come stay at the upper campus. You've got to earn the right." Her eyes misted slightly.

"Did you know one?"

"Ah, yes. I was bonded for . . . many years." Cleo's lips whitened. "Trust you to ask the hard questions. I can't give you those answers now. Maybe later."

"How much later?"

Cleo patted the suit over his arm. "When you've earned your blues." She looked up, saw a head peering over the banister. "Zain, get down here and collect your new lamb."

Zain was a dark-skinned man with cocoa eyes that slanted at the corners and an easy grin. He was tall, with long, gangly arms that reminded Rand of the Choyan he'd seen. Zain wore blue. The third floor room was cozy, two beds, two dresser compartments, two closet/bookcases. Zain's was neat, though obviously lived in, and he had books and manuals strewn all over the pull down desktop. Rand's half of the room did not look as if it had been occupied for some time.

Zain perched on Rand's bed. "Get into your maroons. There'll be a hazing muster any second now. You'll lose points if you're not dressed."

Rand skinned out of his clothes in response. The suit's zippers and buckles nearly defeated him until the darker boy came to his rescue.

"What hazing?"

Zain rolled his eyes. "You'll see." He stepped back. "Now you be good to our Cleo, hear? She's new, just come back to the College after a long, long time, but we like her."

His voice was full of island color. The deep rich sound of it filled the room. Rand grinned in spite of himself. Zain chucked his chin.

"You just a new kid," he said. "You'll see." His voice dropped. "You want to see a *tezar*, I know where there's one. He's been sick . . . he's staying at Dr. Ligo's. We won't go tonight, but if you're good and study hard. . . ." Zain rolled his eyes again, this time in promise.

A pounding at the door interrupted them. A gang of male and female students, myriad in their colors and races, pressed in, grabbed Rand up, and swept him out despite the fact he still had one bare foot, his shoe clutched in his hand. At the fringe of the gang, he spotted Bevan, who had his suit half-on, clutched around his waist, a white cotton shirt over his lean torso. Alexa was dressed, her thick, curling hair pulled back in combs. She waved at him as the mob swept along.

The spring night was cold, crisp, its air rich with a hundred scents he could not identify. Some of it might have come from the kitchen hall, but most from the makeup of Arizar and the campus itself. Bird whistles and calls stilled as the students mobbed into a large, concrete square, surrounded by buildings, and overlooking the biosphere dome. It stayed dark in the early evening, though he saw light sensor units. He wondered why. The students in blue carried an electricity, an excitement, with them.

Once in the square they began to sing. Rand recognized the ancient song from old videos. "We're poor little sheep who've lost our way, bah, bah, bah!"

Rand tried to sing while he jumped on one foot and put his other shoe on. The voices rose in volume, making up for lack of singing talent. Lights went on in the massive stone fortress they faced, and a tall, grave looking Choya came out.

As his gaze swept over them, the crowd quelled instantly. Zain had shouldered next to

Rand and elbowed him. "That's the Reeve. He runs everything."

He raised a hand. The silence grew so still, a blade of grass could be heard growing through a crack in the cement, Rand thought. His own heart seemed to thunder in his chest.

"A new class has come in and you rejoice because it is naming night."

Zain gave a little tremor next to Rand.

"Say hello and good-bye to your classmates. The following will report to upper campus in the morning."

Zain held himself tightly. His shoulder brushed Rand. If he were a cable, he would snap. Rand tore his stare from the Reeve and looked at the young man who'd been assigned as his roommate. "What is it?"

Zain shushed him, eyes never leaving the Reeve.

Upper campus meant meeting the pilots, Rand realized. He, too, held his breath.

"Listen: Darcy Fontiene, Hector Delrio, Uwe Luserne and Mitsu Tokagawa." The Reeve paused. "To the rest of you, congratulations in your studies." He turned and left, stalking away with that elegant grace indicative of his alienness.

Cheers and whistles broke out, with the exception of Zain, who stood in shocked silence. He looked to Rand.

"Noooo. . . ." It was more a moan than a word.

Rand knew then why Cleo had chosen Zain as his roommate. She had known the young man would not be moving up. Not yet. Maybe never.

Tears glistening on his face, Zain again cried,

"No," then turned and bolted, shoving students out of his way.

Instinctively, Rand raced after him.

Zain showed the fleetness of foot of a natural athlete. Rand's muscles cramped as he pounded after, stiff from the journey, from the medications, from days of lying in relative inactivity. His breath began to husk in his lungs almost immediately.

But he knew he could not let Zain out of his sight. Behind him, he could hear students shouting in alarm. Someone gave a high-pitched scream, a plea, "Zain!"

It did not slow him one bit.

They rounded a Zarite gardener, whose ears went up, then flattened in startlement. Rand skidded on a patch of mud, weeding thrown out on the walkway, nearly went to his knee, caught his balance and righted himself. Zain charged even farther ahead.

The thin mountain air, purer than he was used to, but thinner at the same time, burned in Rand's lungs. He began to wheeze as if he could not breathe deeply enough. He opened his mouth. Sweat poured down his forehead. He could hear Zain moaning with every hard footfall.

"Zain, wait! I don't know . . . where we're . . . going.

The dark student had begun to slow, but he did not respond. Then, suddenly, he leapt.

Rand could not see what it was. But he counted and then leapt, too, body straining in midair. He hit the rim of a massive ditch, clawed over it and staggered after Zain, who'd gone to his knees for a second but was up again.

Another broken horizon of tall buildings. One

was massive, its floors stretching high over the campus, its roof pitched steeply. Zain raced for it.

Suddenly afraid as well as weary, Randall followed. They burst into the interior of the building where the brightness of the lights stunned him a moment. Zain threw himself into an elevator. Rand jumped at its twin.

They paced one another in the transparent lifts. Zain would not look at him. He leaned against the glass wall, his chest heaving, his face wet with tears. Rand pounded on the glass between them, but the other student ignored him.

They got out on the rooftop. Rand nearly broke through the door before it released him, so certain was he of Zain's course. Zain jumped before he could reach him.

Rand lunged as well, and caught him by the sleeve. They both went sliding off the rooftop and down the steep pitch of the roof, stopping at the very edge of the eaves only by Rand's desperate efforts to slow them.

Rand's pulse thundered in his head. His arm stretched until he was certain it was coming out of its socket, every joint pulling, stretching, holding Zain's weight—for Zain seemed determined not to hold himself, but strained for the edge and the plunge to earth which would follow.

"Hold on," Rand pleaded. "Try holding on."

"It's no use any longer," Zain said. His arm slipped a little in Rand's hold. Fabric tore. Rand tightened his grip on the other's wrist, easier to hold than his forearm, but closer to the end. Zain gulped down a sob.

"Tell me," said Rand, "about the *tezars*."

Zain now dangled over the edge of the roof. The cords in his neck stood out as he looked up at Rand. "Let me go before I take you with me."

Randall countered. "I know it hurts. Don't let go. Don't make me drop you." He swallowed for breath. His chest stabbed with pain. "Tell me about the *tezars*."

Zain grimaced. "When you're a blue, you'll know. They come for you when they want you. They name you. You become Brethren." His voice disintegrated into tears. "There's nothing else I want to be." He opened his hand and began to twist, to wrench, within Rand's grip.

"No!" Rand began to slide forward on his stomach, over the eave, trying to catch Zain's sleeve with his free hand. He could feel his fingers going numb, coming open.

"Zain, stay with me!"

The other gave a violent lurch, tearing himself free. Rand plunged forward to recapture him and found himself yanked back in midair as Zain fell without a scream. His body made a heavy thud when it hit.

Rand began to shake. "Oh, God. Oh, God."

A deep voice said in his ear, "It's all right. I have you."

Rand felt himself embraced. He looked up. A Choya held him.

Palaton looked at the distressed youth within his arms. In the faint light from the steeple tower, he saw brilliant turquoise eyes, stunned by the tragedy they'd just witnessed, innocent in the ways of the worlds. Humankind, he thought. One of the children. Tragedy in his eyes echoed Palaton's memory of the children of Sorrow. The boy did not yet seem to realize he would have joined the other in death but for Palaton's intervention. His voices rumbled with unshed emotion as he repeated, "It's all right. I have you."

Chapter 24

"The boy is no longer your concern," the Reeve said. He sat back in his chair. He tilted his chin up as if to listen to whatever argument Palaton might make.

"He was subjected to an incredible shock."

"Which would have been far more injurious if Dr. Ligo hadn't sent you up to see who was tramping on his roof. The boy has been counseled and is back among friends."

The subtle undertone of the Reeve's voices were pitched to remind Palaton that he was *not* necessarily among friends. Palaton shifted his weight. "I'm aware that I'm a guest here, but even that caution can't keep me from asking— what drove the student to kill himself?"

Bryad examined a report on his desk. Without looking back up to meet Palaton's eyes, he said, "The process our students go through to become Brethren is arduous. One of the things we do is instill a great deal of pride in the accomplishment. Zain Ardoff had already been refused once in being moved to the upper campus. He could not take being refused a second time. Perhaps it's just as well. If the early courses are arduous, the balance of their duties are nothing less than an ordeal. You're not familiar with what we do, *tezar* Palaton, nor do I feel further explanations are possible at this point. If you wish to become committed to our program, then I can continue this discussion."

The Choya'i in the corner had not till now taken part in their debate. Gracet stirred now, drawing both Palaton's and Bryad's attention. She smiled briefly. "Perhaps our guest is asking questions so that he can make a decision."

Palaton answered, "It's difficult to make any decision blindfolded. What can you do for me . . . and what price do you ask in return?"

The Reeve said emotionlessly, "We can give you back your *bahdur*, *tezar*. We can restore it to you for a nearly infinite number of years. The process, once learned, can be repeated whenever your talent grows weary. As for the price— we ask that you renounce your House."

"You *what?*" The shock of the second outweighed the first.

The Reeve folded his hands on his desk. The confidence of the gesture was at odds with the tension in his body as he leaned forward. "Within Cho, the *tezars* operate almost outside the law, indeed, outside of society itself. They answer only to their flight schools and the emperor— and, historically, have even defied the throne. Your talents are what make space endurable. You and you alone keep Cho from being swallowed up. As a *tezar*, you don't need to be answerable to any authority but that of your peers."

Palaton could not sit. He got to his feet, paced a few steps, saw Gracet watching him closely, turned, and looked back at Reeve Bryad. "You're asking for treason."

"No. I'm asking for realism. You've already crossed the boundary. Your loyalties war with

the emperor who currently sits the throne."
Bryad stood up as well. "We have no quarrel
with him. We seek only to consolidate a House
which should have been, and isn't."

"And what position on the Great Wheel would
you take?"

"A position that is rightfully ours, when we're
ready." Bryad stepped to the window, which
offered a view of the campus. "We've much to
offer Cho. We can't cure the neuropathy *yet*, but
we can tame it so that it no longer cuts short
the lives of our most talented." Bryad looked
back shrewdly at Palaton. "I'm trusting you
with this. I think I can, if for no other reason
than that if you were to leave, you would leave
as a murderer of four hundred. If you stay, you
would stay as a hero, as a founder of new talent
and possibilities. You would know that the
Wheel turns for you, as it does for everyone."

Palaton swallowed tightly. He had no answer
to give the Reeve. "What about the children?"

"They," said Gracet triumphantly, "are part
of the process."

"But they can't know that. They surely cannot
be aware of our *bahdur* and how we function."

"There are rules," answered Bryad, "that
even we dare not break. And once partnered,
once made Brethren, the children won't either.
What I offer you, I'll only offer once. Our resources are limited and there are other *tezars*
who don't suffer the qualms you do."

Palaton restrained himself. Gracet's wide, calm
eyes considered him as he said, "I have to think
about this."

"Do that. Walk about the campus. Attend a
few classes, if you would. Watch the children of

another world. Then come back to me." The Reeve showed his teeth in a smile.

Palaton left the office.

Gracet stood as soon as the building monitors showed that the *tezar* had gone. Bryad said to her, "What do you think?"

"I think we have a case of natural bonding. We know such things do occur ... that's how Dr. Nuncia discovered the process. But there's nothing in her writings that tells us how he'll react."

"Then we have him."

"Maybe." She reached up and tugged on one of her hair ribbons, loosening a silky mane. She ran her fingers through it. "If we don't, he could be quite dangerous."

Bryad put an arm out to draw her closer. "One Choya can't bring us down. We've worked too hard and come too far to fall again."

Gracet arched her back in pleasure. She dragged a fingertip across Bryad's desk. Her voices partially muffled by Bryad's actions, she said, "We should have an answer soon. I don't think he can wait."

"Neither," answered Bryad, "can I."

Palaton strode across the campus, aware of the stir among the students. The population wasn't large, although the campus was. It had been made to house thousands where it now held dozens. He could tell by looking at it that it was meant to be the start of a House, of a colony independent of Cho, of all the things which Panshinea had hoped for and yet, if it occurred here, could be the death of him.

With his *bahdur* returned, his life once again held a realm of possibilities. One of those possibilities would surely be that he could redeem himself. He came to a halt under the large, spreading boughs of an immense tree at the corner of the quad. A group of children wandered past, gently herding a youth in the center wearing a deprivation helmet emblazoned with the Blue Ridge insignia. As he stood, astounded by the helmet, the blinded youth stumbled his way. The students parted and let him fumble toward Palaton. The student stopped just short and then removed his helmet.

He grinned to see who blocked his path. "I'm sorry, Provost," the humankind said. "Sensory deprivation class."

"So I see," answered Palaton with a certain irony. He watched as the helmet was handed over and the group made their way off in a different direction. They had mistaken him for a Choyan teacher and he was not about to correct their misperception. Why would the God-blind practice at being even blinder?

He left the shade of the tree. He also wondered how much time the Reeve would give him to make his decision.

Alexa came into the room quietly and shut the door behind her. Half the room looked incredibly sterile, where nothing remained but furniture and a bed.

Randall saw where her glance went and shrugged deeper into the covers of his own bed. He had gone cold and seemed unable to warm himself. Shock, the Choyan had told him. Dr. Ligo, a Choyan with a double horn crown and crisp chestnut fringe hanging from it, had told him so solemnly. He felt numb.

"You look better," the girl said softly.

"I don't feel better."

She sat on the floor next to him. "It sounded awful. I just wanted you to know I'm sorry."

Bevan had already been in. The Brazilian's skin had smelled faintly of her musky rose perfume, imprinted with her scent.

"Will you come to classes tomorrow? They've already started."

His dream of piloting nudged at him. He had left his parents, his home world, and his race behind to capture that dream. He'd been told he would make sacrifices and he'd expected to. But he'd never expected this. His silence woke something in Alexa's face.

She put her hand out and traced his jawline. Then she smiled broadly. "You're going to have to shave soon."

Rand grabbed his jaw where she'd touched it. Stubbly prickles met his touch and he could feel his face grow hot. He snatched her hand away.

But she did not let go of his fingers, catching them up, saying, "You're like ice!"

"I can't get warm. I keep thinking . . . I should have held on!"

"You tried." Alexa held his hand in both of hers, cradling it. She looked up at him, a distant look in her eyes, as if focusing inward even though she looked at him. The moment passed and she smiled again. "Let me help."

She stood up and touched her fasteners, opening up the maroon suit. Randall closed his eyes in instinctive embarrassment, and when he opened them, she was sliding out of the garment and kicking it aside. She wore precious little underneath and quickly removed that. "Move over," she told him, picking up the corner of his blanket.

He did.

She slipped in beside him. Her curves were warm and supple, where his were angular and bony. She wrapped a leg around him and put her palm on the flat of his stomach. He could not help his reaction to her, nor did he want to. Since her first touch days ago, he felt as if this moment would have to happen or he would burst. Her fingers encircled his hardness.

"Is this your first time?" she asked as she moved closer.

"No." The intensity of feeling brought heat gushing through him. His mouth half-opened in voiceless response.

Alexa smiled again. "Good." She pulled the blankets over their heads. "Then you'll know how to kiss me."

When they were done, she curled up like a kitten and went to sleep, taking up more than half the narrow bed, forcing him to sleep on his side. She'd been right, Rand reflected. She'd warmed him up. He listened to her deep breathing, knowing she'd been with Bevan during the night, thinking about how he felt about her.

Everything was too new to him. He still felt a certain numbness.

A curl of her hair tickled his nose. He moved it away carefully. The bed smelled of their lovemaking and his sweat and her perfume. He settled down into the nest their activity had made and slept.

Alexa woke, as she usually did, sudden and hard, gasping, eyes wide and staring as if they had opened before her conscious mind roused. She felt the lean body behind her and gathered her thoughts quickly. The darkness of her dreams receded as she forced them back.

She dreamed of hunting, and the kill, and even, God help her, the sweetness of human flesh. She dreamed of eating the helpless and reveling in it. A hot tear stained her cheek. She brushed it quickly away, determined not to let her dreams defeat her.

The small scar on the back of her neck, where her shoulder curved into it and then met her back, itched again. She rubbed it pensively. The moments of sexual passion and love pushed back her darker thoughts, but only temporarily, and now she wrestled with them again.

She wanted to go home. Her father would make a place for her, even though the Choyan had told her she'd been reported as deceased. She knew it was only to take her cleanly. Her father would know and his position and money would smooth the way.

And then she and the other would meet together and feast with the success of their hunt—

Alexa let out a sharp cry, then covered her mouth in dismay at the sound she'd let out. Her teeth felt sharp against her skin. She thought of biting deep, deeper, until the hot sweet metallic blood seeped out. . . .

The girl threw herself out of the bed and went to his bathroom. She ran water until it was as ice cold as Rand's hands had been and soaked her face. Then, as the dorm room darkened the shadows of dusk, she returned and dressed. She woke Randall, told him that the dinner bell would be sounding soon, and left him as soon as she could see he'd awakened. She would have to find another way to hold the darkness at bay.

*　　*　　*

Bevan pounded on the door at sunrise. "Classes, sleepyhead," he announced. His dark, thick hair was uncombed, looking as if he had just run his fingers through it. He had a shoulder pack slung over his back. "And goodies."

The Trade lingo did not translate quite properly. It came out as "barter bait." Rand walked out of the toilet, a towel around his hips, bare feet slapping on the cold floor, with shaving cream and razor to his face as Bevan opened his pack upon the unmade bed.

"What have you got?"

"This, my friend, is how a student survives." Bevan mulled over the loot. "A pot for grinding and brewing *bren*."

Rand shuddered. He was still not sure if he was going to develop a taste for that or not. He finished shaving—it was not a process requiring a great deal of precision for him yet—and wiped his face dry. Bevan tossed him a pair of shorts and the maroons. "What else have you got?"

"Waterproof styluses, pocket computers and various assortments of homeworld luxuries I don't think we'll be finding here." He held up a colorfully wrapped bar.

"Chocolate!"

Bevan snatched it out of Rand's reach. "Maybe later," he said with a flashing white grin. "But not now. You stole my lady yesterday."

Rand paused, jumpsuit half on, hanging about his hips. "She came to me."

Bevan shrugged. "I do not think she is the type of woman one can capture." Again, Trade did not quite translate the meaning, but Randall thought he knew what Bevan had in mind.

"I'm sorry," Rand added.

The other plied his attention to the goods strewn on the bed. He looked up, dark eyes intent. "Did she sleep well?"

"I don't know. *I* slept like the dead." Then Rand gulped, thinking of Zain. "That is—"

"Forget it. I know what you mean." Bevan began sweeping the goods back into the pack. "Stick with me, my friend, and you and I will earn our blues in record time."

"Are you in that much of a hurry?"

"Oh, yes. I have things to do and places to go." Bevan fastened the last two clips at his jawline and grinned at Randall. "Let's go."

Palaton watched the children of humankind. He became aware over days that most of them thought of themselves as grown, though they had height and maturity yet to be reached, that their temperaments ran like quicksilver, their tears almost as quick to surface as their smiles, that they had no real concept of the responsibilities that would face them as adults, though they thought they did. He found himself drawn to the tall, earnest boy with the turquoise eyes, watching him when he did not know he was being watched, thinking of the wrenching moment when their lives had collided with death.

He watched and considered, and he ached. They were alien to him, Arizar was unfamiliar, the Choyan of the College estranged and aloof and yet ... the most alien of all he saw was himself. He had no place in any of it, not even among his own people.

Chapter 25

Vihtirne of Sky drew herself up from the small throne of her Householding, a throne that was an exact duplicate of the much larger and grander one in Charolon. She was still stunningly beautiful, despite the stress of wielding power for Sky, and her looks held Nedar still, very still, in awe.

The corner of her mouth quirked, an indication that she was aware she held this power over him.

"Nedar," she said, her voices rich with welcome. "Thank you for answering my summons."

If he reckoned relationships, Vihtirne was probably a cousin three or four times removed. If he reckoned power, there was no one in Sky more powerful. She had been a Prelate, but her scientific papers had propelled her into industry and from there into patent ownership and from there into a position of wealth and influence. Choyan died for her love, hoping to prove themselves worthy of marriage, attempting terrible trials. Her love life was a thing of scandal and yet, oddly loyal, in that when she did marry, she never abandoned the Choya until his death. He had been much older. Nedar remembered, as he watched Vihtirne, that it was rumored she currently favored younger Choya.

She held out her hand and he helped her step down from the petite footstool at the throne's base. "You look well."

Nedar nodded. "I am, thank you." Although he had held out his hand to her she kept it, and now led him to a small table, offering intimacy in a shadowed corner of the audience hall.

He had no doubt that any recording devices were wired on her body, for her own private use, as his gaze swept the seemingly innocuous corner. She sat down. He sat across from her, feeling her sexual power as well as her worldly power. It struck him that she was radiating, enticing him, and then he realized that she was fertile, and wasting little subtlety in telling him so.

Nedar sat back in his chair and considered his options.

Two crystal goblets flanked the center course. Their pale pink liquids swirled as the Choya'i leaned over them. Vihtirne lifted the cover off an antique, etched gold plate. He'd expected dinner, instead, his gaze met an empty plate.

Vihtirne laughed at his expression. "Nedar! Would you feast on empty portions?"

"It seems not." He hung an elbow over the back of his chair as he relaxed into it.

"Yet I would give this plate to you if I could. Do you recognize it?"

He shook his head. His horn crown throbbed, but he did not reveal his weakness by raising his hand to his brow and massaging the base of it. Vihtirne was sharp. If she suspected any unwellness about him at all, there would be hell to pay.

"This," she said and stroked the golden platter, "was the dinner plate of Emperor Chasden, of the House of Sky."

He straightened then. Chasden was the last of the Skies to hold the throne.

Her eyes glittered as she looked back at him. "Need I say more?"

"Mistress. You honor me." His heart thumped a few times before he got it steadied, and he knew a tic in his jawline pulsed in sympathy. She offered him the prime candidacy of his House for the throne when it came time to force Panshinea down!

She smiled at the realization visible on his face. She replaced the domed cover. It clanged softly as she did so. "I trust you burn as brightly as ever. Cho cannot withstand another weak emperor. The Abdreliks and the Ronin wait to consume us, and the Quinonan and the Ivrians to lick up the crumbs."

He did not, but he would. Ah, but he would! "I'll serve the House well."

"You will have to. It's not enough to be a *tezar* any more. You need financial acumen and cunning. I will tutor you."

Nedar lifted a crystal goblet. "Then I cannot fail."

"We should both hope not." Vihtirne lifted her goblet, at the same time making an elegant movement and letting her gown fall from her shoulders, revealing a body that marriage and time had not yet diminished.

Bevan bounced on the bed, upsetting a pile of books that went thudding to the floor. He did not seem contrite as Rand swiveled around at his study desk and glared.

"Your Choya has been following you again."

"*My* Choya. What are you talking about?"

Their voices echoed in the still half-empty room. The extra bed had been pushed across it side by side to Rand's. Sometimes Alexa occupied it and at times Bevan joined them in sleep, the three of them curled up together "like a pile of puppies," Cleo said, having caught them at it once, heads pillowed on stomachs, study manuals in their tired hands.

"Don't tell me you don't know."

Rand mopped his sweating forehead. It was deep summer on campus and even though he had his window propped open, the afternoon breeze had not yet picked up and given relief to the sweltering dorms. "It's too hot for this." He turned back to the manual spread out on his desk.

Bevan said, "He follows you everywhere. Not all the time, but I've seen him. And so has our lady."

But Alexa wouldn't have mentioned it, used to secrets as she was, Rand thought. She would no more divulge his than her own. He wagged a stylus between his fingers. "I haven't seen him."

"Ummmm. Well, work as hard as I might, you'll be getting the blues before I will."

Rand cradled his chin in his hands. "I don't know. I can't get this."

Bevan got up and stood over him. "Your Braille?"

"Yes."

In the weeks they'd been there, Bevan had grown more quickly than Rand in height. He said it was because the food was better and more plentiful than he'd gotten in Sao Paulo. Alexa, with a giggle, said it was the loving.

Rand had no opinion except that now he could look the other right in his snapping, dark eyes.

"It's easy. We had to learn this at the Theresite. Because many of us would go blind from disease or deficiencies." Bevan reached out and shut the book loudly. "What does this have to do with the Choyan?"

"A pilot has to be able to deal with sensory deprivation."

Bevan curled his lip. "I didn't come here to be a pilot."

"I did."

"Nobody pilots but the *tezars*"

"I will." Quiet determination rang in Randall's steady answer.

Bevan waved a hand in the air. "Me? I want to rule Earth's finances. There's a real power."

"And never be poor again, eh?"

"And never be *sold* again," Bevan returned sharply. They looked at one another. Then Bevan raised and let drop his shoulders. "There's more to this than we were told." He summoned another mood out of thin air. "We need a carnival!"

"Oh, no." Rand raised his hands. "I've got studying."

"Nonsense, my friend. I'll have Alexa teach you Braille by anatomy, eh? In the meantime . . . it's too hot. I think a hike up the falls to the cooler climes of the upper campus is in order."

"What? Are you crazy? Maroons aren't allowed up there."

Bevan's teeth flashed. "I have not yet had time to read my rules book. So I don't know anything about this." His accent became honied. "Let's find Alexa and go."

*   *   *

The girl sat on her window seat, looking over the campus from her window, her hands in her lap, a faraway vision dazzling her. She visibly started when they crashed the door.

"Carnival," Bevan told her.

"What on earth?"

He pointed a finger. "Come, come, my lady. Having fun is serious business. Get dressed for the wilderness. We'll meet you downstairs. We have a guardian to distract." His eyebrows quirked, he threw back his head and Rand, with an embarrassed glance over his shoulder at her, followed their flamboyant friend out the door.

He not only got them off campus without anyone noticing, but stole a laundry sledge, a drudge hover, to carry them. It was made for weight not speed and slugged its way along the winding hillside pathways, the three of them riding its back as if it were a mythical flying carpet. In honor of the occasion, Bevan wrapped a scarf turban style about his dark hair.

"How will we get there?" Alexa asked breathlessly into the hot summer day.

"Believe it or not, the sledge knows the way. It was used at the upper campus before it was sent down here and repaired. It retains the directional memory."

Rand listened with a new respect for Bevan who ordinarily showed more inclination to sleight of hand than to mechanical acuity. He had to duck quickly as a low-slung branch came his way.

The trees grew sparse and the smell of their bruised needles faint as the sledge wheezed up the final incline, and they saw the upper campus, a massive, gray stone fortress carved out of a mountainside.

It looked like something out of King Arthur or some ancient feudal legend. Rand let out a whistling breath.

"It's going to be tough getting in there."

"On the other hand," Bevan said, "they probably aren't worried much about security. I doubt even the Zarites come up here."

Alexa had a hand up to her brow, shadowing her face. "It must encompass a couple of hundred acres, at least."

"Self-sufficient. It would have to be. Winters are tough this much higher up." Bevan abruptly unwound his scarf, keyed the sledge to a halt and slid off the hover. "I think we should walk the rest of the way."

"And keep to cover." Rand exchanged glances with Bevan. Both looked to Alexa.

She bristled. "Don't even say one word about my staying here."

"All right." Rand put his shoulder to the idling sledge. "How about helping push?"

They shoved the hover to the side and then killed the motors completely. It settled into the bracken with a heavy thump. Alexa dusted her hands on her hips. "I think we've reached the hiking part," she said, and strode off.

Deep purple shadows as cutting as blades were falling across the rock by the time they reached the lower foundation along the pathway the drudge had been following. They came upon a carven gate which was evidently used by service drones. Wheels had deeply rutted the immediate area. Bevan looked it over. The entranceway seemed to baffle him.

Alexa ran her fingers over the etched doorway. "Sensor operated. And none of us probably has the equipment it takes to trigger it."

Rand shouldered her aside. "There has to be a manual release in case of emergencies." He ran his fingers along the ridges. He found a niche. His nail broke with a nasty twinge, but as the pain jarred him, he felt something click even as it tore into the quick of his finger. He pulled back with a sharp word.

Bevan grabbed his hand just before he put it into his mouth to suck away the pain and welling blood. The other shook his head. "Tsk, my friend." He tore a ragged strip off his scarf and bound the finger. With a crooked grin, he added, "Pray they don't consider poison as an alternative security device."

Rand stared numbly as the two then walked past him into the opening grinding wide.

Down morbid stone hallways littered with the carcasses of failed machinery they walked. Rand caught up with them. Their steps whispered on the mossy flagstones. Alexa slipped once. Both boys caught her as she fell and she hung in midair between them. They set her down gently.

They passed a communications room, old, forgotten, its backup systems still blinking with power. Alexa turned to watch it as they passed, as if afraid it would sound an alarm. Then they climbed a back flight of stairs and found themselves at the outer corridor of a building which baked with heat. The smoke issuing from its vents choked them.

Bevan's eyes watered. He took Alexa's hand and drew her past, saying, "Crematorium."

"What?"

Rand had to run to catch up with them, upwind, out of the heat and stench.

"An oven for the dead," Bevan said. "It's hard to bury someone in the rocks." He went on without looking back.

"What dead?" Alexa said to Randall.

He shook his head, uncertain. Everybody died someplace, somewhere. But he wondered now why he had never asked what the College had done with Zain's body.

Bevan stayed in the shadows, in what was clearly an older part of the fortress. It was quiet and the stones showed little disturbance of the moss which coated them. They mounted a winding stair which took them onto a second thickly walled level. The rock left white powder as their maroons brushed it.

Alexa stopped, suddenly. "I don't want to go any farther."

Bevan urged her. "Come on. It's our only chance to see what the blues do."

She ran her fingers through her thick, curling hair. Then she shook her head. "I don't like this. If we're caught. . . ."

"I've never been caught on an open street yet." Bevan looked hurt.

Rand stood, torn between caution and curiosity. Finally he said, "Come on, Alexa. We're with you."

She turned wide eyes on him, deep in thought. She licked her lips, a furtive motion, then ducked her chin down, looking away. "All right. But not much farther in."

They drew her with them, hidden by the gloom cast by the massive wall, until they came to a break and boosted themselves up to a para-pet of sorts. It was an outer balcony wall and they faced a bank of windows. Now the late afternoon sun was at their backs, still hot, clear, bright. It pierced the polarization of the windows and they looked in.

Alexa gasped and Randall stared dumbly, uncomprehending. It was Bevan who said, "This is an asylum."

Humankind occupied the solarium. From the aged to the young, blues and maroons faded with time and disuse, the mentally disturbed rocked, walked, lay in the room. Slack faces with spittle drooling from their lips, or faces contorted with rage as they rocked violently, bang, bang, banging their forms against the chairs which confined them, to faces which alternated between knowing and blankness.

Alexa spun around, put her back to the wall, and took several deep breaths.

Rand could not challenge Bevan who had always had a knowledge of the darker side of life and poverty. These people were clearly not sane or functional. He could not tear his eyes away. As he watched, a Choya entered and came through the room, checking on several occupants, putting a hand out kindly and stroking brows. Bevan took his elbow and pulled him away from the window.

Someone inside let out a howl. It started up those who could still speak. Alexa shook, then bolted.

"Alexa!" Bevan called hoarsely after her. He turned to follow.

Someone caught Rand from behind. He felt hot breath graze his scalp as one hand slid about his waist and another around his neck, lifting him to his toes, pulling him back.

"Bevan!" He kicked and flailed but whatever

had caught him up grunted and tightened its grip. The arm about his waist pulled up into his diaphragm and it was all Rand could do to breathe.

Bevan faced him. He put a hand up, saying, "Put him down."

Rand was dragged back another foot. He sensed that his captor was taking him back inside, like dragging meat into a lair. He kicked again, hard, but his captor merely grunted again.

Bevan drew a step closer. He forced a smile. Rand could only imagine what held him. Whatever it was, it was big. He could not drop his chin to see the arms. It could be a Choya, or a good-sized human. The youth waved a hand gently in the air. "You don't want to do this. You want to be good. Put him down."

The hand on his throat grew hard, each finger like a steel band. Rand choked and knew panic. Whatever held him could kill him. Possibly meant to. Possibly did not know the morality of its actions.

Bevan put a hand in his jumpsuit thigh pockets. He came up with half a bar of chocolate— chocolate again!—and held it out. "I've something good for you, if you're good for me."

The grip on his throat and stomach loosened. "Put him down." Bevan waved the bar intriguingly.

Rand was freed. Bevan dropped the candy to the walk and bolted over the parapet side. With a gasp, Rand joined him. They ran until they found their escape corridor.

Alexa crouched inside the doorway which led to the old communications center, chewing on her fingernails. She surged to her feet as they pounded into the corridor. "Thank God!"

"Let's get out of here. We've been seen."

Her face paled further. "No—"

"It won't matter," Rand said. "I don't think anybody would believe it. We have to save them."

Bevan's eyes narrowed. "No. We have to save ourselves." The two faced off for a moment and Rand knew a thrill of challenge. Then Bevan flashed a smile. "We've got to get downhill before we're missed."

As they raced to the outside, Rand wondered what he himself believed.

Later that night, he could study no more, and he could not sleep. He padded quietly upstairs to Alexa's room and let himself in. The silhouettes limned by moonlight had not heard him. He stopped, seeing their outlines in movement and rhythm against the window's framework, knowing what he interrupted.

Alexa murmured throatily, while she traced kisses down Bevan's torso. "So good, so good. I could eat you. . . ."

His friend let out a groan and Rand hastily retreated out of the room, closing the door softly behind him, not wishing to be noticed.

He returned to his room and sat at his study desk, knowing he was a floor or two below Alexa's window, and knowing as he looked outward that he saw an entirely different sight, and that he was all alone.

Chapter 26

John Taylor Thomas fielded the late night call from his bedroom within the Ambassadorial offices. Since his daughter's taking, his wife had left, and his personal life had fallen into ruin. There was nothing left to sustain his existence except his work. He slept there and rarely left except to function as a diplomat.

The comline opened up through his private channels. GNask's low, gravelly, and smacking voice woke him up.

"Thomas. We've heard from your daughter."

He leapt up from the rumpled bed. "What?"

"We've heard from your daughter. I beg your pardon for the lateness of the call, but I knew you'd want to know."

"Is she all right? What did she say?"

"We haven't time to discuss that. She appears to be well. She wishes to be retrieved, but we knew that. The signal was weak. It will take some time for us to track it. However, we will locate it, and you will have her back."

Gratitude surged in his throat. He swallowed in order to respond. "What about the others?"

"She had little time to send much information. But, I think, ambassador, we will have our tampering charges substantiated. I think we finally have our Choyan in a trap of their own making."

Thomas' hand trembled. "Good," he whispered hoarsely. "And thank you."

GNask rumbled. "Thank you, Mr. Ambassador. We work together."

The comline went dead.

Thomas paced nervously, trying to absorb what he'd heard. The implications of it would sink in later. For now, Alexa was alive and well. He could not ask for more. He would never have the child returned to him that he had given GNask. But even a remnant of her would be welcome to him. Even that small, strange part.

Nedar left the auspices of his patron to seek out that which had been offered him so clandestinely. His *bahdur* continued to flicker, but he could control its burn by his own usage. Palaton had warned him and taught him an invaluable lesson. Ironic that it had been Palaton who'd disappeared, lost, gallantly sacrificing his own life to deliver four hundred medics out of Chaos to their destination. He had brought them through while losing himself.

But, reflected Nedar grimly, that left one less hero for him to conquer on his way to the throne.

He'd been offered hope, and healing, should he ever decide to pay the price. He would pay the price, his way. The secrecy served him well and intrigued him. He did not know who this splinter group of Choyan were, or what outlawed genetic experimentation they did, but they held out possibilities and he determined to snatch them up. Once he was rejuvenated, nothing could stop him. He journeyed to a base on the frontier fringes of the Compact and put in a call. He was answered promptly and told to wait.

Nedar would wait only for fortune and destiny.

* * * *

Alexa did not come to him again in those days of summer following their discovery. She found shelter in Bevan's company, and he in turn found strength from her, shutting Rand out. In classrooms they sat across from one another and as the provosts lectured on the wonder, the opportunity, the loyalty of companionship with the *tezars*, Bevan sometimes turned his handsome face to Randall and mouthed, *"Lies."*

The word pierced his chest like a physical wound. As they were taught more and more and yet learned nothing about the role awaiting them, Rand felt the wound deepen. Days passed. He sat in class, balancing his dream of piloting with the uncertainty that the Choyan would ever offer it to him. What was a Brethren? Were all the insane they had discovered the end result?

He could ask no one. If he did, he risked losing all that he'd worked for. And his uncertainties found no solace from his friends, for they had closed their circle, shutting him out. Bevan grew darker, more cynical, and Alexa withdrew into the shadow he cast.

On a hot day, when the thin mountain air seemed unable to slow the arrow rays of the sun, Randall snapped his book shut, threw his pocket computer in his pack, and left class. The provost stopped his lecture a moment in surprise, but said nothing as Rand hurried out the door.

Outside, he took a deep breath. The stifling

feeling did not go away. Perhaps it was not caused by the weather. Perhaps it lay deeper. He hoisted his pack and trudged across campus.

Cleo was not in her dorm office, an informal corner of the building's kitchen. That meant she was down at the biosphere, working in the organic gardens. Rand hesitated at the threshold of the kitchen. Finally, with nowhere else to go, he went to his room.

There was a sense of trespass when he opened the door. He couldn't place it until he saw the suit of blues laid neatly across his bed.

Rand put a hand to his chest as his heart began to race. He dropped his pack on the floor and hiked to Bevan's room. The suit of blues across his rumpled mattress was the only item of neatness within.

He took the stairs slowly to Alexa's. The door there was unlocked, slightly ajar. He nudged it open.

Blues hung from a peg on her closet door.

Rand backed out in confusion. What previously he had wanted most now frightened him. He went back to his room and stared at the uniform.

He was still staring at it when someone rapped at the door. Cleo put her weathered face in.

"Ah," she said. "You've come back early and discovered my surprise."

Rand turned to her. "It's the b-blues." He clamped his teeth shut on the unexpected stammer.

"What did you expect? You were made to wear them." Cleo beamed. "All four of you from this dorm were passed into blues. Unheard of, so quickly. But you've worked hard and earned them."

"Did I? And do I want them?"

Cleo looked puzzled. Then she nodded. "Boy, I think you should come down to my kitchen. I have tea brewing."

He followed her obediently, needing someone to talk to. The tea was a welcome change from the *bren*, whose strongness occasionally turned his stomach. He sat, nursing his cup, while watching her prepare peanut butter sandwiches to accompany it. The smell made him breathe deeply, savoring it. He hadn't realized how much he'd missed peanut butter.

"It's hard for me to digest at my age," Cleo said, lowering her bulk into a chair opposite him. "But I like the reminder of home."

He gulped down his first sandwich in agreement. The tea was sweet and scalding. He sipped at it cautiously.

Cleo rubbed her mug between her work-worn hands. Garden dirt was still embedded in her nails and cuticles. "Now tell me why it is that the sight of blues turns a healthy lad like you pale."

He shook his head.

"I blame myself," the dorm mother said. "I should never have bunked you with Zain. But I was fairly new myself and didn't know his mind like I thought I did."

The memory of Zain had faded considerably. "It's not that."

"What is it, then?"

"I still don't know what we do. I don't know what a Brethren is. I don't know what the Choyan want from us."

Cleo gave him a slight smile. "I do." She

folded her hands about her cup of tea. There was a bittersweet quality about her expression.

"Then tell me."

"There are new classes for that." The older woman leaned back in her chair. It creaked in response to her weight. "It's not my place. But I don't like to see a good boy troubled. I did it, you know." She looked away for a second, remembering. Her glance came back. "It was the best thing that ever happened to me."

"But what *was* it?"

"It's a spiritual thing. The Choyan come to us to be renewed. They choose companions and we share their lives, for a time. They become as children and we guide them until they are refreshed. The bonding is as close as any marriage, and more rewarding." Cleo looked up from his face to someone else standing at the rear of the kitchen. She smiled broadly. "Ah," she said. "I wondered when you would come asking questions, as well."

Rand turned in his chair and saw the Choya standing there, the *tezar* in his uniform, the one who'd saved his life once. He felt caught in the other's amber-eyed gaze. Emotions flecked the amber with liquid gold, holding him, but he found he did not want to be released.

"It's a telemedical function," Bryad said smoothly. "But it takes time. We ask our candidates to live on the upper campus, observing already bonded pairs, and learning about the humankind psychology."

Nedar's presence dominated the office. Bryad felt the force of his personality like a hammer. "I haven't time," the pilot said. "I'll meet your conditions, but you must meet mine."

"They act as filters. If you rush the process, you will be faced with returning to us sooner for a second treatment ... and possibly a third."

Nedar gave him a piercing look. "What does it matter, as long as it works?"

"Finding suitable Brethren is difficult. We must be ... cautious."

"Opportunity belongs to those who seize it," Nedar said, looking at the various documents studding the office wall. "You came to me. I think perhaps you need me as badly as I need you."

Bryad cleared his throat. His voices sounded weakened, obscured. "I have nothing to hide."

"Oh, but I think you do." Nedar approached the desk and leaned on it, his knuckles going white. "I think I know what you're trying to bring back out of the ashes, Reeve Bryad. And you need fresh genes to do so, to solidify the lineage and broaden it."

Bryad felt his eyes widen. He kept his face still, however, as the pilot neared mysteries he had thought hidden.

"The House of Flame was thought destroyed," Nedar continued. "But don't forget that we Skies experimented on our own. And we know that the Earthans gathered up what Flames they could to bolster their own weak line. They hid their specimens quite successfully from the rest of the Houses. They bred well and truly, outcrossing with their own blood. The revolt and destruction of the Householding of Tregarth within the Earthans was a subject of specula- tion and scandal for centuries. But within my own Householding, there were some who claimed to know the truth. It was said the Earthans of Tregarth were too successful in their experimentations. That 'commons, God-blind' they'd been working with revolted and set off on their own. Did they, Reeve Bryad? Or were they Flames, resurrected, and did they come to the stars to be free? Is this a College or a House, Reeve Bryad? And how much of the truth dare you tell me?"

Bryad got up, but he said only, "I offer you life, Nedar. *Bahdur.* I admit nothing of your speculations. Don't think I'm ignorant of your politics. You want the throne of Cho as much as we want new blood."

Nedar smiled slowly. "Then perhaps we shall come to an understanding. But we must do it quickly. I haven't much time," he repeated.

Slowly, Bryad answered, "I have three students who might suit your purposes. They're all strong candidates, although we've not trained them completely. Sit down, and we'll discuss our options. You may not have time, but what we do requires caution, else the humankind die or worse in the process. The bonding process infuses your *bahdur* into them, where they purify it by processes unknown to themselves, and return it to us, renewed and whole. They're not a psychic race, although they have a superstitious tradition of such abilities. The infusion of our talent is a strain many cannot bear. We chemically blind and restrain them during the purification period, so they cannot be aware or use the power we've given them. As they are dependent on you in this time, you are dependent on them. You must understand that. Your souls will be locked together. You must care for them as sensory deprivation sets in. It sounds a cruel process and, in many ways, it is. We've found over the years, however, that *bahdur* can

be overwhelming without these precautions.
Even with them ... occasionally a *tezar* must
be bonded with several candidates to find one
who is compatible and capable of holding the
bahdur."

Nedar quirked an eyebrow. "They're unaware
of the potential they hold?"

"Completely."

"Good. I'm ready when you are."

Chapter 27

Gracet stared at the Choya on her threshold. Interrupted from an afternoon of reviewing evaluations, her hair was mussed and her face drawn in irritation which lightened as she saw who the interloper was.

"Palaton," she said, and opened her door wider. "I was hoping you'd come to a decision." She let him in.

His voices died finally, and she was able to talk. She sprawled on the lounge in her outer lobby. "Often, there is a natural affinity between Choyan and their companions. We've not had an instance in decades, however, where Brethren were chosen before we'd attempted to match them up. However, I can see that this affinity has a great deal to do with your decision." She curled her legs under her. "I think I can persuade the Reeve to allow the partnership. If it brings you into our fold." She did not mention the expendability of the humankind. She'd already assessed Palaton as one who would not accept that inevitability. In fact, awareness of the difficulties of bonding might drive him from the program altogether. And she wanted him too much. She saw too much in him to let him go.

"Then you'll intercede for me with Bryad."

"Certainly. He'll be pleased as well." She hesitated. "There is the matter of renunciation. . . ."

"I'm aware of it." Palaton's voices had gone stiff.

She nodded, not wishing to push him further. She reached for her comline keyboard. "Bryad, I have *tezar* Palaton here in my office . . . he's ready to make a commitment."

The Reeve's voices came back, sounding drained but fulfilled. "Gracet, that will have to be delayed. *Tezar* Nedar has come in with an urgent request. We'll be bonding him to a Brethren as soon as you can have Bevan, Randall, and Alexa sent to the upper campus as possible candidates."

"What? This is unheard of. Even with preparation, Bryad—"

"No arguments. I want them summoned and in the Bonding Hall."

Gracet leaned back. She felt the color draining from her face.

Palaton said quickly, "I know Nedar. I'm going with you."

She turned her gray eyes to him. "How ruthless is he?"

Palaton did not answer.

The Bonding Hall stood at the cliffside of the upper campus. Its structure was ornate and imposing, the agate blue bands in its stone wall akin to the colors of Chaos, as the pink glow of sunset streaked it. The flying arch of its threshold stretched high over their heads as Gracet took Palaton in. The interior could encompass a far greater audience than the seven who awaited them, four Choyan and three subdued humankind in blues.

Nedar's expression opened as he saw Palaton. "I should have known," he said. "So Chaos spit you back."

"The experience," answered Palaton dryly, "is not one I recommend." He looked beyond, searching, found Rand standing a little to the left of the other two. The boy's presence comforted him. The humankind looked up, his face strained, the turquoise eyes shadowed by fatigue.

Of the other two, the young man had his arm around the young woman in a loose embrace as protective as it was sexual. She seemed unaware of the gesture, her attention on Nedar.

Palaton recognized Dr. Ligo, the waddling Choya who'd nursed him, as the physician moved among the three humankind, innoculating them for some purpose. The girl winced as the air needle punctured her arm briefly. Unshed tears sparkled in her eyes.

Behind him, Gracet said, "What we do here tonight may undo all we've worked for."

Nedar answered defiantly, "Or it may propel you into exactly the position you wish for yourselves." His voices rumbled arrogantly.

The Choya'i declined to answer. She stepped to the Reeve's side and merely set a restraining hand on the back of his wrist. Bryad shook it off. From her expression, Palaton could tell she was not used to being repulsed.

Bryad moved forward, Dr. Ligo at his flank. "Randall, Bevan, Alexa. You have been named and have come forward. You merit this, but I must also make you aware that this is because of necessity. The role of Brethren demands courage and sacrifice. We have a *tezar* who needs help and only one of your abilities can help. This is what you were chosen for, and what we've trained you for. Are you ready?"

Of the three, Rand said nothing, Alexa murmured a faint, "Yes," and Bevan said defiantly, "That depends."

Nedar's attention went to the girl. He stared intently at her. Palaton could feel his aura flare.

"The role of Brethren," Bryad continued, "involves the bonding of Choyan and humankind. We are alien to one another, yet we can help one another. To be bonded to a Choya is a potent experience. To withstand it, we have found it beneficial to dampen your own sensory abilities. We've already begun chemical blocking in your systems to accomplish this. Don't be afraid. The condition is temporary."

"What do you mean?" Bevan demanded. He dropped his arm from Alexa, rose on the balls of his feet, tense, ready.

Dr. Ligo said, "You will be blinded and deafened, to defeat the sensory overload of bonding."

The girl gave a tiny squeak. Rand moved closer to her in reassurance.

Bryad turned to Nedar. "You've had copies of their profiles. Have you made a choice?"

Palaton knew who it would be before the pilot spoke. Nedar would go for compliance, pliability. He would rape the soul of anything bonded with him and like most rapists wanted fire and yet ultimate victory.

"I'll take the female," Nedar said.

Alexa sank to her knees as the Choya reached for her. Bevan pushed his way between them. He glared defiantly into the pilot's face. "Take me," he said. "I can handle anything you give me."

Nedar hesitated. "Can you now?" he said softly, menace underlying his lower tone.

"Yes." Bevan threw his head back.

"The bonding procedure," Ligo said, "is a layer by layer process. You won't be instantly connected any more than you will be instantly blinded."

Nedar turned to look at the doctor. "Then," he surmised, "choices can be changed."

"At the outset, yes."

Bryad added, "And I recommend circumspection. Our procedures have been developed for the safety and care of all. Defy us, and we will ask you to leave the College."

Nedar and the Reeve traded looks. Nedar did not appear intimidated.

The Choya smiled at Bevan. "Then I will take your challenge."

Bevan took a step toward Dr. Ligo. "I'm ready."

Lights in the Bonding Hall dimmed. Bevan had gone down in a hypnotic state, and his limp body now lay draped on the sculpted couch which was at the center of the stage. He breathed evenly. One hand trailed to the floor, the other crossed over his chest. Alexa stood by fearfully, an unwilling witness. Palaton watched Rand closely. What happened here tonight would influence what would happen between them, what had already begun to happen. The ceremony aroused some suspicion in Palaton. He suspected that Daman and Cleo had not been subject to much of this, that most of it had been built up over the intervening years. How much

was ritual and how much was real . . . and what
was necessary to preserve the integrity of the
bonding?

How would it be to strip away the barriers
inbred in him and share his soul and his *bahdur*
with another, let alone an alien being?

Palaton stirred as Nedar was brought to his
knees beside the couch. Bryad led him into the
meditation exercises. Palaton had to distract his
attention to avoid going down into the same
maelstrom of mental preparation.

Nedar lay his hands across the boy's forehead.
Palaton's attention shot back, drawn by what
he felt was happening. He could see the other
Choyan, Gracet, Ligo, Bryad, and the unnamed
watcher, were not *tezars*. They had some awareness of what happened, but not a total understanding. Not the same awareness he did. He
could feel Nedar seep into the other's mind,
locking in, and then, like the backdraft of a
wildfire, flaming into his mind.

Bevan jerked awake out of his trance. His
mouth opened in a scream of agony. Gracet
jumped to her feet even as Palaton surged
forward.

"Stop him!"

Ligo paused, mouth gaping. "What are you
doing, Nedar?"

The pilot bore down ruthlessly, heedless of
the boy's convulsing body. Aurafire blazed around
them. It surrounded them like fire setting alight
a funeral pyre. Bevan began to flail at the Choya
with his fists, screaming hatred and defiance as
the pilot raped his soul. *Bahdur* flared.

Palaton tore at Nedar's shoulders. The other
was stronger than he, had not been ill, and
shrugged him away. Palaton came back, deter-

mined. He pried Nedar away from Bevan, gripped him by the shoulders, and yelled for assistance.

The boy ripped himself out of Nedar's grip. Something flashed in his hand. He screamed a last time in hatred and lunged. He stabbed twice, deep, into Nedar's chest. The Choya echoed Bevan's agonized pain and then fell forward, lifeless, in Palaton's hands.

Bevan froze. The knife slipped from his fist. He threw Alexa a look, then Rand. He turned and bolted from the hall as all the others remained motionless, immobilized by shock.

Galvanized, Rand went after him. Palaton lowered Nedar to the floor. His aura was fading. His *bahdur*, gone. Infused into the renegade boy who ran from his deed.

"God-in-all," said Gracet. "What have we allowed to be done?"

Rand raced after the sound of fleeing footsteps. He drew nearer in the darkness, his mind pounding with the memory of lost Zain. Don't let me lose Bevan, he pleaded. Don't let me lose Bevan.

He called into the night. The runner paused, slowed, then sped up again. Rand turned a corner and saw a portion of the upper campus he recognized, the massive squat building of the crematorium. He knew which way Bevan would go. He angled across the grounds, pressing, breath gasping, but now he was rested, acclimated. As fleet as Bevan was, Rand was more determined.

They burst one after another into the corridor which led to the servo exit. He could see Bevan now ahead of him, a dark ghost in the tunnel.

A peculiar halo seemed to outline his form, silhouetting him. As the door to the outside swung open and Bevan prepared to slip away, Rand sprang through the air and tackled him. Together they went rolling into the night.

"Don't touch me!" Bevan screamed into his face. They wrestled hand to hand.

"Bev," Rand gasped. "Come back!"

Bevan abruptly lay still under him. He took great, hulking sobs of breath. He shook with exertion. "I killed a *tezar*," he got out. "What kind of a future do you think I have?"

"I don't know . . . I don't know. But they saw what he was doing to you. . . ."

"It's what they do to all of us. Don't you see? We saw the crematorium, the asylum. We're used and tossed away. No one misses us. No one ever comes back, Rand. No one ever comes back."

Rand's thoughts swam. "Cleo did," he said finally.

"Only one you can name. One against all the others." Bevan kicked out from under him and sat up, chest still heaving to breathe. Rand was breathing hard, too.

Bevan made a fist and raised it in the air. Sparks shot upward, sparks with heat and light and fury. Rand shrank lest one touch him. They looked hot enough to burn. They showered sizzling to the ground.

Bevan looked at Rand. "I'm running. Don't try to stop me again." He got to his feet. He stood a moment, knees shaking, as if waiting for Rand to protest.

Rand got up. His mind was filled with mistrust, his dreams split by a radius of doubt about what the Choyan intended, and what they achieved. "Go on," he said. His voice choked.

Sudden light illuminated the massive fortress wall above.

Bevan fled into the night before Rand could say or do anything else.

Chapter 28

GNask stood before the general council of the security hall of the Compact. He bowed in formal greeting. "It grieves me, fellow ambassadors and members, to do what I must do today. But I have incontrovertible evidence which must be introduced. I have had brought to my attention a plot against the Terran world which involves subjugation and interference of the deepest kind instigated by Cho."

He paused as gasps and reaction drowned out his speech for a moment. He then added, "I ask that my evidence be reviewed and that the wrongdoers be brought to justice. Exploitation of a Class Zed planet is a most despicable action and cannot be left unpunished. In the interest of equity, I will also request the president pro tem of the Compact resign his position in favor of a disinterested party." GNask bowed in irony to the recently elected Choya who currently wielded the power of the office of president.

The Choyan ambassadors, their Ivrian allies, and others surged to their feet in protest. Havoc roared through the general council. He caught a bemused glance from John Taylor Thomas. The Choya Firendan pointed at him and guards swept the Abdrelik from the speaker's podium and followed him outside. He said to his secretary as they moved through the shouting throng, "We've got the coordinates we needed. I want a move on that hidden base. Find me a renegade *tezar* who will fly us in. Evidence or not, I want to level that base before anyone else realizes what the evidence points to and gets there."

The secretary nodded wisely. He left his ambassador's side, making an exit corridor with his own bulk, his *tursh* sitting up in excited style above his left ear. GNask watched him go, a grin revealing his tusks. He had finally found a chink in the Choyan armor. If only to protect themselves, a *tezar* would step forward to pilot him in, to betray and destroy a splinter group whose actions jeopardized the whole of Cho. He had driven a wedge between Choyan factions that might well shatter the whole planet.

He had no details of the Choyan operation but he had a location where the children of Earth were being taken. For what purpose, he still had no inkling. Alexa had not been able to communicate with him that fully. But when they went in to destroy the location, he hoped to pull her out.

The downfall had begun.

Panshinea sat at the *lindar* keyboard, his fingers searching out idle melodies as Gathon told him what news had just been sent in. The emperor did not pause, though his face creased heavily.

"Where," he mused, "is my hero in exile now? Who in Cho will stand beside the Great Wheel descendant as it brings down the House of Star?"

Rindalan stood, the Prelate reedy with age to the point of gauntness, his massive crown fully revealed by the advanced thinning of his hair, and his face no less grim than it ever was. "Get command of yourself, Panshinea. What could the Abdreliks be referring to?"

Gathon said, "We know there must be a splinter group colonized elsewhere. We've had hints of it for decades."

"Cho does not colonize!" Panshinea said. His fingers danced, jerked, upon the keyboard. "I sent my hero for a cure. Ten long years he's been gone. . . ."

Rindalan looked across to Gathon. "He's hopeless in these moods. Do what you must."

The disapproving Choya gave a half bow and left. Rindy stayed by the *lindar*, saying, "You know Palaton's dead."

"If he's dead, so is all my hope." Panshinea stopped playing abruptly and rested his hands upon the mantleboard. "Vihtirne is supporting Nedar to supplant me. Do you think we can face such a challenge, dear Rindy, you and I alone?"

"Not in this state."

"No, neither do I. If I vacillate, the best I can hope to gain is time while the Skies decide whether to wait for me to die on my own . . . or to wrest the throne by force. What good it will do either of us to play for time, I cannot know. But it seems to me to be the only thing we can do." With a sigh, Panshinea dropped his hands down upon the keyboard again, searching out a melancholy tune.

The Prelate stood in silence, a thoughtful expression upon his aged face. He had not known the emperor still had it in him. Perhaps there was hope yet.

* * *

The Reeve summoned their shuttle *tezar* to his offices. Staden was a Choya of limited *bahdur* even after all their efforts to renew him. He had retired from Chaos piloting to run the shuttle for them from the Arizar port. He appeared in Bryad's office promptly, his mane disheveled at this early hour.

"I want his body off-planet. Take it up until I can tell you where to dispose of it. Maybe Chaos. I don't know yet."

The aged Choya stared at the blanket-covered body of Nedar.

Bryad turned about as Staden shouldered it, wrapped in the blanket, and prepared to carry it out. "Tell no one of what you do. *No one.*"

"I understand, Reeve," Staden answered, even though the expression on his blunt face plainly said he did not. Bryad watched him go.

He did not understand his own actions, but he did not want the ashes of a *tezar* mixed with the remains of the humankind at the crematorium. It was dishonorable and Bryad felt estranged enough from his people.

They had found the one humankind and brought him back. He waited now in solitary for them to decide his disposition. Gracet, as usual, had had her own opinion on it. The other provosts were more pliable to his will. "Think," she had said, "what you destroy with Palaton if you destroy the boy."

Now that they had lost Nedar, Palaton's contribution had more import. But there were always other *tezars*, there would always be burn-out, there would also be other candidates whose vulnerability led them to this world. Bryad did not feel kindly toward Palaton. He keyed Gracet. "Let's take a look at the boy again."

They walked to the cell together, Gracet saying little. She wore her hair down, clipped at the nape of her strong neck. Palaton rose as they approached. He had been holding vigil outside Rand's solitary confinement. Of the girl, there had been no sight. Cleo reported she'd returned to her dorm and stayed there. The girl would have to be moved, lest she contaminate the other students. Bryad made a note to have that handled.

Palaton stopped Bryad before he entered. "Has Bevan been located yet?"

"No." There was a distinct possibility the Zarites could be aiding the humankind, but the Reeve did not tell Palaton that. The growing current of unrest was one Palaton might sway in his favor, and Bryad had no desire to have his efforts further undermined by trouble. The control they had exerted over the Zarite civilization's growth and expansion had been a careful one, and necessary, if the two groups were to coexist. The colonizing Householdings across the continent would have to be mobilized. The humankind had to be found and hunted down at all costs. Zarite interference was a complication they could do without.

"Send Rand after him."

Bryad measured the *tezar*. "I have resources. The humankind will be found and dealt with."

"There are consequences here," Palaton responded. "There are consequences which neither of us can predict. Send the one to bring back the other. Then justice can be served."

"Bevan is afoot in the wilderness. If he has any destination in mind, it must be to get to the port, to flee. If my guards can't find him, there's a good chance Arizar itself will kill him."

"He has *bahdur*. If he can control it, or worse, if he can't, he can affect the whole countryside. Rand told me some of Bevan's background. He comes from a city teeming with crime and poverty and he knows his way around. He has resources neither you nor I can guess at." Palaton added, "we seem to be adept at underestimating the humankind."

"And how do you propose to have one boy catch another?"

Palaton paused. Then he answered, "Because he has my *bahdur* as well. Because he's asked to do it. Because he's our only hope if you wish to keep the College intact. I don't know the full extent of what you do here, or where you come from, or what destiny you have proposed. But neither am I vulnerable enough to accept any crumb you hand me unwittingly. As Nedar died, he burned a single thought into my mind. 'Is this a College or a House?' It's a question worth remembering. Do you wish me to seek an answer?"

"No," said Bryad quickly, then blanched because he had answered too hastily. Palaton smiled.

The Reeve drew himself up with dignity. "Do what you must," he said then. "You hazard the bonding." He spoke to Gracet. "Deal with them." He left.

Gracet's mouth fell into a sad line. "You've risked much," she remarked. "In this stage of bonding, his life is tied closely to yours."

"I know that." Palaton put a hand to the

locked door, pointedly waiting for her to open it. "I have no choice."

He had enough God-sense left in him to see the boy's aura blaze as he entered the small storage room where they'd confined him. Rand looked up, face a pale moon in the dimness, and then smiled. As Rand stood, Palaton weakened visibly and the boy caught him, awkwardly lowering the much taller Choya onto a crate.

Rand kept his embrace about Palaton for moments longer than necessary. Gracet looked away, pretending not to see. Palaton craved the touch. It was not a physical thing, it was beyond that. When Rand let go, Palaton reached up and combed his hair away from his turquoise eyes.

"They're asking you to go after Bevan."

"I know."

He would, of course, now that he burned with Palaton's power. And he knew that was what infused him, knew when all the Brethren from all the years before had never known what it was they carried.

"This College, misguided as it is, could be a vital step in curing the disease that kills us all."

Rand nodded again. "I'll help," he whispered. "For you and for Bevan. Just ... don't let me fail this time. Help me hold on."

They entwined fingers. Palaton felt a surge of courage and determination, as well as of fear. He squeezed back tightly. "I'll be here. And I've got you."

Bevan's numbed feet went out from under him. He fell with an "Oof", rolling down a scarp of dirt and gravel. His skin came off in patches as he slid to a landing and then lay panting. He could barely see. His head throbbed. He fought to stay awake, alive, moving. He'd run all night.

As he lay, the sharply blue sky of Arizar canopied him, and he focused on it. He wouldn't be safe until he got off-planet. Once off-planet, he could go anywhere. He had the power. It tingled in his veins. It pounded in his eardrums, slinked through his heart chambers, rasped in his lungs.

He knew it.

No wonder the Choyan had resorted to blinding and deafening them, cutting off as many senses as they dared, confusing the poor Brethren who carried and purified this burden. He'd never imagined such a power existed, let alone that it could be transferred. It was the power Rand had thirsted for, and now he had it.

And they'd kill him for it. That he knew as well.

Bevan forced himself to sit up, ribs aching, skin raw where his slide had torn it. The world tilted and then righted itself.

He had to find sanctuary before the drugs they'd given him had done their job. He had to survive!

As Bevan's emotion flared out, the brush he sat in caught fire spontaneously, roaring up. He leapt out of the bracken, swatting at it with a cry of astonishment. The flames licked out as he kicked dirt over them.

Had he done that? Bevan closed his eyes wearily, chest pounding with the jolting excitement, now calming. He remembered the sparks flowing from his hands in the night.

He could have. He had no way of knowing. And if he had, could he do it again, on purpose? He pointed a finger. Nothing happened. Bevan grinned raggedly. "So much for burning bushes."

His voice sounded hoarse on the morning air. He stumbled into motion heading in the direction of the sun.

Sometime in the heat of the day, he fell face forward on the dirt and gravel bank of a small brook, inches from the water he craved. He reached a hand out and dunked it, drawing his fingers back to his mouth and sucking the coolness from them desperately, too tired to crawl any closer. He did that for long moments, dunk and suck, dunk and suck. Then, finally, he heaved himself up and crept close enough to put his face into the water and drink. Different yet similar enough, it flowed lifesaving goodness down his throat.

With a sigh, Bevan curled up on the bank to sleep.

He woke to the sound of curious voices. Furred, sleek forms stood over him as he rubbed his eyes and propped himself up on an elbow. Curious Zarites surrounded him. Their ears went back, then came forward slowly as he greeted them in Trade. He held out a bloody and skinned hand, then passed out entirely.

Palaton showed Rand the hand brakes on the jet sled. He had brought up the runners to fit the humankind's shorter leg length, but the boy still seemed too small to be riding the powerful machine. He leaned over. They touched foreheads. "You remember how to ride it."

A shared memory, Palaton riding into the wind, taking the bridges of Sorrow at breakneck speed, defying the rain and gravity. A fleeting glimpse of the alien race trapped to their deaths in the crystal. . . . "I remember," said Rand shakily.

The boy was not yet used to their communion. He understood. Neither was he. He was weak in a way he did not understand, as though his heartbeat were only an echo of Rand's. It was more than the loss of his power. A single thought passed through their minds: *He only knew he was alone no longer.*

Chapter 29

Staden had seen a lot of happenings at the College over the years, but he had never seen one of his people die. He carried the body out as Bryad bade him, loaded it in the ground shuttle, and made the journey to port. The Zarite crew watched him curiously, obsequiously, with their furred and whiskered faces, as he moved the body to the transport and waited for them to load the berthing cradle.

One of the Zarites patted him on the leg. "Where are you taking the master?"

Where, indeed? Bryad had not sent him word. He wondered idly if there would be a reward for taking him home. Staden had been away from home all these years.

"I don't know," he growled in answer. "Just do your job."

The creature ears pinked. "Yes." He ducked his sharp muzzle face and turned away.

Staden oversaw the crew's work for a few moments, then boarded his ship. He had set the still form down in the main passenger fuselage and the knowledge that it was there prickled the spiked salt and pepper hairs about his horn crown. He had spread a light tarp over it, but a hand remained free of both blanket and tarp, the cuff of its uniform bearing the braided insignia of Blue Ridge. Staden himself had come from the Commons. He'd always thought Blue Ridge produced the best.

The Zarite crew signaled that they'd finished. He strapped in and took the ship up, found an inconspicuous orbit, put the vessel on automatic, and opened communications to await Bryad's signal. He read a bit, played the computer simulated gameboard a while, practiced his reed flute. Time grated by with the thought of the dead body in his passenger lounge.

Staden had never been very talented. His abilities, both as a Housed Choya and as a *tezar*, had been strictly limited. But his *bahdur* prickled with the presence of the other in the transport.

He got up and walked out uneasily. The form seemed still as death. Blood had begun to stain the tarp deep crimson, marking the wounds.

Even dead, a *tezar* carried some residual power until the power was consecrated and given to the God-in-all. Or so the Prelates said. The power resting in them had been given and would be taken back. But, and Staden quivered with the thought, what would it matter to the God-in-all if a little had been drained off for the needy?

He knew it could be done. He understood the transfer through bonding. The mystery of what the humankind did to purify corrupted power was another matter. But, as far as he knew, dormant *bahdur* lay in front of him with no one to claim its remains but he and God-in-all. And surely God-in-all had enough.

Staden approached the form. It took all his nerve and the hairs on his arm stood up edgily. But the wish to go home once again and the inability to make the chaos journey to do it spurred him. He lifted the corner of the tarp. He put his hand out to the dead Choya's forehead and opened himself.

The dead one's hand shot up to his throat and closed, tight as steel cables. The eyes burst open, alive and angry.

"Get me," the dead Choya rasped, "something to staunch the bleeding. And then you had better pray I let you live to serve me longer."

Bevan woke in a nest. His arms and legs had been folded gently to accommodate its size. The soft coverlets and herbs scenting it wafted about him gently as he straightened his legs, letting them hang over the edge, and gingerly stretched, every muscle bruised and cramped.

He looked about a small cottage, mud-brick and straw, a pleasant home employing some minor solar technology, including a hot plate, but other items hanging on the walls he either did not recognize or they were primitive at best. He yawned and the noise sounded like an alarm.

Instantly the room was filled with wide-eyed whisker-quivering bodies.

They fed him only after taking him to see the battered jet sled they intended to give him. It had been repaired with homemade wire and cog pins, and he only wondered what the circuit chips looked like, but it had started when he turned it over, and it would make the journey.

And it was his gift. So, as he sat hunched on a stool too short for him and ate the vegetable stew and unrecognizable patties, he thanked the Zarites for their help.

The elder, his jaws graying, nodded in turn. "We help when we can. The star masters have been good to us—but we know they take as well as give."

Bevan paused, spoon in hand. "What do you mean?"

The elder pointed to his daughter who busied herself in the kitchen corner. "She married despite their recommendation. When the time came, they came and took her kits before they could be born. That happens here. The masters are wise, yes—but her kits were healthy. I saw the bodies. Why then did they force her to give them up? Why, then, was the marriage unwise?"

He had no idea. The Choyan forced abortions on the native population? It sounded as if they were manipulating the gene pool. But to what purpose? The Zarites seemed a willing and ingenuous people.

Perhaps too willing. Bevan's glance flickered over the technology they had quickly picked up and incorporated. He did not know how long the Choyans had been on Arizar ... but he did know it was difficult for two equal races to split a planet. Much easier for a worker/slave relationship. The colonial history of his own country had been checkered. Bevan hid his thoughts behind a chunk of dark bread.

Then he said, "Perhaps the masters are worried you grow too fast, learn too quickly. The land can be poisoned, the air poisoned, by cities which grow too fast."

The elder nodded wisely. "This we know. The masters are counseling us in these ways."

Bevan relaxed. Perhaps there was nothing sinister about the Choyan Households here, after all. He smiled. "Perhaps," he said, "the kits would have become ill later. I'm sure they'll let her have a family. She is young and healthy."

"Perhaps." The elder sounded dubious, both about Bevan's answer and the future possibility. He patted the table with clawed fingers. "You're being hunted. It's best that you leave soon."

That caught him by surprise and he choked, spitting, and then mopping it up hastily. "What do you mean?"

"Another student from the College. Tall, pale, light eyes. His jet sled is better," the Zarite answered matter-of-factly.

Rand. Still on his heels. But why?

Bevan stood, feeling a darkness grow inside. Why would Rand seek to stop him? What had the College promised him to bring Bevan back? The thought of betrayal took his appetite away. He would have to find a way to deal with his former friend.

They brought him a new jumpsuit, blues, faded and patched, but clean and whole. He dressed quickly, making the adjustments to zippers and straps. Then they ganged outside to watch him take their jet sled. They pressed a map and woven sacks with food into his hands.

Bevan paused on the sled. Technology, even this battered, had to be worth something to the family. "Can I leave it—if I get to the port—can I leave it somewhere where you can pick it up?"

"Our family will take care of it for us."

"Yes, but which family?"

The elder tilted his head. "All of Arizar is our family," he said solemnly. "No one will steal what you put into their care."

Bevan shrugged. He could not comprehend a theftless society. The jet sled came alive when he asked it to, and vibrated between his legs.

The young Zarites scattered, paws over their ears, faces trembling.

He left in a cloud of dust and vapor, their shouts of farewell drowned out by the roar of the machinery.

Distance did not dim the link between Rand and Palaton. Palaton rested in Gracet's quarters and tried to deal with the backlash of sensory information, the overlay of Randall's perception of the world flooding him. To avoid sending the same sort of confusing images outward, he sat, a cold cloth binding his eyes, sounds dimmed, not moving, just being. Inside his mind, timber and brush roared past as the jet sled sped and skidded down treacherous logging roads as Randall searched for Bevan. The search pattern took tedious, looping turns since the other had been on foot, but little sign had been found of him.

Palaton mused. Gracet entered quietly. He lifted his compress. Her expression voiced the question. "No sign of him yet," Palaton answered.

"Bryad will call the Household guards out. He'll have no choice. The humankind can't be allowed to reach port, to get off world, with *bahdur*. . . ."

"I understand the calamity." Palaton paused. "Nothing of this sort has ever happened before?"

"No. Usually the tragedy befalls the students. Sudden death, occasionally insanity. We've had Choyan die, too, but never has one been killed." Gracet took up a chair and sat, rubbing her arms as though chilled. "The process still takes a great deal of experimentation. Its worth is best measured by the alternative."

Palaton opened his mind to disagree, but then sight and sound and taste and touch flooded him.

Rand paused the jet sled on an overlook. The cliff point hung over the foothill, where the terrain would eventually smooth out before it roughened again. He thirsted. Dust hung at the back of his throat. Sweat soaked his torso and he could smell himself. He pulled the water bottle off the sled frame and aimed a cool squirt down his throat.

Then he saw it. And smelled it, too, faintly. Smoke on the air, a thin gray trailing. Death in the forest. His vision went suddenly spotty and then dark and Rand panicked, dropping the water bottle. He clutched his hand over his eyes.

After a blurred moment, his vision came back. The spilled water pooled at his feet as he bent to retrieve the water bottle. The smoke trail still rode the air as he blinked to see it.

It might be Bevan. It might be Zarite loggers or beekeepers. Rand brought the power back up and headed toward the trail. Riding the sled was like riding a cycle and he leaned into it, taking the curves at breakneck speed. Bevan could be hurt, even dying, in the mountainside wilderness. Branches grabbed and tore at his cheeks as he bent over the handles. The jet sled hit a hump of dirt and he sailed out in space before it hit, hovers complaining, and rose again with an angry whine. Something in him pulled for caution. It felt foreign and he realized it must be Palaton. Rand smiled grimly.

* * *

He reached a clearing where black-edged grass still smoldered and hung in the air. He looked about and then saw Bevan ducking into a growth of shadow ferns, the canopy of trees dense and green about them. He could never take the jet sled in there or it would foul. He killed the engine to dismount.

"Bevan! Wait."

The other stilled, stalled, blurred in motion. Rand halted in confusion. Then, from the corner of his eye, he saw another Bevan, in furious movement, diving at him.

The impact of the hit knocked him away from the jet sled and into the tall grass. The breath left his body with a whoop. Bevan bore him to earth and sat astride him, fists in the air.

Rand managed to gasp for a choking word. "Why—"

Hatred darkened the other's expression. "Judas!" He swung at Rand's face. The blow hit his cheekbone with an astonishing pain. Skin split and swelled almost instantly. He fought back out of instinct.

The two wrestled in the grass, their blues trampling what the wildfire hadn't burned. The smell of seared foliage stained his senses. Rand managed to get on top a second and hold Bevan's fists back.

"I came to help you!"

"Then let me go!"

Rand took a shaky breath. "They'll never let you go this way."

Bevan freed a hand and aimed it at his face, Rand met it in midair and as their hands met, sparks clashed. *Bahdur* against *bahdur*. Bevan groaned, saying, "You let them do it to you. You believed them!"

Bevan's cheeks puffed out. His dark eyes blazed. "You can believe their lies." He heaved, throwing Rand aside. He kicked, hard, the point of his boot thudding home just below the rib cage. Rand curled in pain.

He forced himself to his knees as a jet sled started up. It was not his machine, that lay where he'd left it. He got to his legs, quivering, bent double in agony.

The machine sounded behind him. Rand turned and saw Bevan aiming at him. He stumbled and the sled clipped him as he passed.

There was no remorse on Bevan's face, Rand thought, as it sent him sprawling into darkness.

Hurt, agony, misery, betrayal, fear, bewilderment. . . . Palaton lay in pain as well. But his was faint, pulsing, an echo of his Brethren's. He reached out, along the connection, and urged Rand to get up.

The boy refused, curled about the core of his misery, mourning the death of friendship.

Get up.

Rand sat up shakily. Blood covered his wrist. He looked at it, unseeing. The image shot through Palaton's vision as clearly as if he'd stood over the humankind.

Stop your bleeding.

Wearily, Rand tore off the tattered cuff and wrapped it back around the gash in his forearm as a pressure bandage. The bandage provided some comfort for the throbbing pain. He felt sick to his stomach. Every breath brought a sharp stab. It helped as he got to his feet.

Go after him.

Rand bent over. His blues were torn at the knee, the skin scraped sharply and already showing purple bruising, but the injury seemed no worse. He vomited and then stood, dry retching, and staggered back against the jet sled when he was done.

The movement seemed to help. He wiped his hair from his forehead and eyes. He didn't want to go after Bevan.

You must help him.

Rand uttered a humorless laugh. He leaned against the jet sled for dear life, too weak to mount.

Palaton pressed along their linkage. *Rand, Brethren, the fire . . . he did not start it on purpose. He has* bahdur *he cannot control. Do you understand? It will destroy him. It could well destroy Arizar.*

The thought sickened him. But his guts were dry and he could do nothing more. "All right," he said aloud. "All right." He got on the machine and started it up. He needed no map. Bevan shed aura and he could read it, its sickly green hue hanging in the pure air like a poison.

It must be a poison. Look what it had already done to his friend.

The jet sled plunged out of the clearing.

Chapter 30

Gracet brought him food after dark. She knelt beside him. "What's happening?"

"It's too dark for the jet sleds to be used safely. Bevan has succumbed to fever and is sleeping. Rand, too, I think. The *bahdur* uses humankind badly."

Provost Gracet smiled ruefully. "Does it use us any better?"

He looked at her. "I would like to think so." She was stern, not a beautiful Choya'i. He felt no attraction to her, but he admired her temperament under pressure.

"You should call him home so you can proceed with the bonding."

Palaton made a noise. "I should think we're bonded enough."

"No . . . I mean, you need to know how to seal yourselves away . . . how to keep from draining each other completely. How to protect yourselves. Bonding to a Brethren is a step by step procedure. You and Rand have given yourselves to each other naturally. Now you need to learn how to stop giving."

He sipped wearily at the cooling *bren*. "There will be time enough for that later. For now . . . the boy is hurting. Soul shock. Rand must find him."

"I know," she said. She left him in the company of her many books and her paintings of Cho, the paint crackled with age, but the vision still as pure as when the artist had painted it.

Rand slept badly. He ached and his face burned with heat, and he'd little water left after spilling most of it. The ground dug into his back and bugs crawled and bit with annoying regularity. Finally he fell into near unconsciousness and in that black inescapable sleep, he found dreams.

Palaton had been half-dozing. He jerked awake. "God-in-all." He grabbed for the arm of the chair to steady himself, his mind flooded with images being sent him by Rand—with no earthly idea of how Rand dreamed what he did.

Panshinea, shuttling down to the surface of Sorrow, gaunt Rindalan in tow. An emperor under siege, coming to protect the position of his representative at the Halls of the Compact. Enemies in position, awaiting him. The Abdrelik mission in triumph. Cho in turmoil without an emperor, without an heir. The House of Sky poised to attack the House of Star.

And Sorrow with its crystal rivers and streams beckoned to Panshinea. The emperor paused at the memorial in front of the Halls, and wept. So also did crusty Rindalan. And, like a plea to God-in-all, his name echoed from the lips of the emperor.

Palaton knew the Halls well, knew the emperor well—and knew that Rand did not.

Yet what he saw was not his memory being bounced back at him.

Foresight. The boy had to be blatantly precoging all that he dreamed.

Even Palaton had not had those talents, beyond a whisper of foreboding. What floodgates had they opened by fusing a humankind with a Choya?

If the premonitions were true, Panshinea walked into havoc created to bring him down, Palaton's name on his lips.

Palaton stood up. His body swayed unexpectedly and he righted himself. He found Gracet's bedroom and woke her, half-dragging her from the bed.

"I need a starship and a pilot."

Her face was creased with sleep, but all she said was, "We have an upper campus full of them. And there must be a ship or two in port."

Later, when she realized the import of what he planned, she protested. "This will be the death of you, and the boy, too."

"It can't be."

She shook her head. "I can't tell you what it will do to traverse Chaos in your condition. The *bahdur*, your soulstrings—you're already frail. And Rand needs whatever support you can give him."

His voices husked in answer. "I must be in two places at once. I've no choice in this. My world and my Brethren both call me."

Gracet had no further argument. She clasped his hand tightly, saying only, "The College has much to ask forgiveness for. If you cannot come back . . . remember us well."

Fatherless, lineage obscure, he had never known the depth of his potential. But now the feeling lay about him like a pall. He was heading into his destiny, whatever it might be. Palaton answered her handclasp before turning to the *tezar* waiting for him. "From Blue Ridge?" he asked, as the Choya wore a plain flight suit.

The Choya grinned back. "Salt Towers."

Palaton murmured. "Well, someone has to be." He mounted the two-seat shuttle and waved the pilot on.

GNask watched the raiding flight take off from base. The dark velvet of space delineated their silvery forms well, he thought. He mopped the corner of his mouth from habit, catching up a string of drool. The Choyan would never know what hit them. And there would be ruins enough to document his claims, ruins and skeletal fragments, and perhaps, if they could be persuaded, evidence from the mouths of survivors. The Choyan would never again be the respected, prominent race they had been.

And he, GNask, would make sure of it.

He would have to break ties with the man, of course, but that would be a welcome break. The constant whining, pitying litany of the human had become annoying. *Help me, help us* . . . the man could not possibly know the disgust and contempt in which GNask held him. The humankind came from a species which plundered its world and soiled its waters almost beyond redemption. Humankind deserved to be wiped from the face of their Earth.

He sharpened the focus on his view screen so as not to miss the sight of his fleet going into Chaos.

Rand woke, heart pounding. He leapt to his feet in the moonlight of the twin silvery disks hanging low overhead and he let out a cry of abandonment.

Then his answer, thin, faraway, but there. *I'm here.*

"Don't leave me," panted Rand. He put a hand to the rough bark of a tree to steady himself.

Palaton only answered, like a faint whisper within, *I'm here.*

Rand could not pull him back, he could only accept. But as shadows clouded his vision and his hearing dimmed, he knew a keening fear. Would it be enough? He was not alone . . . but would it be enough?

Alexa woke, restless, rousing to see the pale wine-colored sky of near-dawn. Dreams of muddy water and heavy bodies sliding through them to kill disgusting things in the silt, then swallowing them down raw haunted her.

She went to the toilet, put a finger down her throat and vomited. Nothing came up but thin, yellow bile. If she had eaten, there were no vestiges of it in her system. But she knew she hadn't. She never had, no matter how much she tried to vomit it up. It was just dreams.

She put her face against the cool tile of the wall. She was evil and knew it. Her mind reveled in thoughts she could never dare reveal to anyone, least of all someone who might love her. She lifted her face and looked in the silvered pane of plastic which served as a mirror.

Human on the outside, but a disgusting, maggot-ridden evil inside. No matter who loved her. No matter who curled up with her in the night. She had sought innocence from Rand, whose earnestness shone like a beacon through any darkness, and when that failed, understanding from Bevan who like herself often stood poised on the brink of good and evil. But no soft murmurings, no gentle stirrings of passion, no heated ruttings could save her.

She needed to go home. She needed to find that other half of herself, to be one thing or the other. Alexa put out a trembling hand as she left the toilet, found her blues, dragged them off the peg, and began to dress. An urgency rode her. She needed to be whole, whole and away from there.

Letting the twilight of early dawn and its still heavy shadows hide her, she left the dorm.

She was outside the gated wall, beside the broken slabs of granite, when the raiders came screaming in, their silvery skins red-hot as they hit the atmosphere and rained destruction upon the College. She ran for high ground, away, as far away as she could get from the screams and the fire.

Her limbs trembled with the horror of the raid and with the eagerness for the rescue she knew was coming. She flung her arms up into the sky and prayed for wholeness, for oneness with the Abdrelik awaiting her, and she remained that way until the sky hook plucked her up.

As soon as the dark thinned enough, Rand got back on the jet sled. He ate as he rode, one-handed, steering through broken terrain that showed some traces of the Zarites' efforts to tame it. The port of Arizar glowed on the horizon, shedding the light of civilization like a homing beacon. He didn't know if Bevan had also risen early although he could trace the aura

hanging like a fog in the morning dew. He also
didn't know what he would do when he reached
Bevan again without Palaton to aid him. Would
Bevan come with him? Or would they destroy
each other?

Such thoughts seemed impossible, but even
as he tossed the last of his breakfast to the dirt
and wiped his hand on his trouser leg, the sky
opened up and began to rain death.

He slewed the jet sled off the road, but kept
going as he looked overhead. He thought of the
campus guards Bryad had threatened to use,
but knew the look of starships when he saw
them, even fleetingly, red-silver splinters against
the morning sky. Someone or something else
had brought tragedy to Arizar.

His heart in his throat, he also realized that
their main target had been behind him, in the
mountains. His eyes clouded as he mourned
Alexa and Cleo, Gracet and his fellow students,
the funny Zarite gardener, and all the others
who had had no warning.

Thank God, Palaton had gone.

The screams of the raider ships passed overhead again. Rand leaned over the frame of the
jet sled and asked the engine for more power,
his shadow racing the shadows of impossibly
quick ships above.

Summer embraced the Hall of the Compact.
Fruit trees laden with both flowers and their
ripening burden hung over the walkways. The
oppression of threatening thundershowers lingered in the air. Rindalan made a wheezing
noise and Panshinea halted in his tracks.

"Are you with me, old Choya?" the emperor
whispered.

"I am . . ." Rindalan returned. "But you must walk a little slower."

"I walk to my death," Panshinea answered lightly. "How else would you have me go? Would you drag me?" He turned and waited.

Every inch the Star, his hair red-gold in the summer light, his clothes of the richest thread, cut to mold to his still elegant figure, his horn crown undulled by age, the emperor paused for the shambling figure of the Prelate. He held out his arm.

"Are you prepared, Rindy?"

The Prelate shook his head. "I think not. This is a foolish thing. You cannot supplant your representative with yourself. You lay yourself open to Ronin assassination, humiliation, Abdrelik manipulation—"

"They'll not replace us as head of the general council," Panshinea interrupted, repeating his earlier vow. "Not unless it's over my dead body."

"Such a thing," wheezed Rindalan, "might be just what GNask hoped to set in motion."

Panshinea clucked. "You have little faith. As long as a single spark of *bahdur* burns in me, I shall hold the enemy at the gate."

Despite the emperor's support, Rindalan still shuffled with the effort to keep up. "Only remember, Panshinea, that our power is our secret, and you must not reveal yourself before the Compact."

Panshinea looked down. He said nothing in answer, but there was a blaze in his forest green eyes. The Prelate had no inkling whether it was determination—or insanity flaming within. The council doors opened to admit them.

*   *   *

GNask shifted impatiently. In the hours before the council had admitted no less than the emperor and High Prelate of Cho, he had called in favors and kept them at bay. No word had come on the efforts of the raiders he'd sent out. He could stall no longer. When the secretary called to order the question of the day, he bowed graciously, giving way, and the emperor and his fellow Choya were let in.

He listened as Panshinea reclaimed the office which the emperors of Cho normally held only figuratively, through nominated ambassadors. He watched the Choya closely, knowing that the being could be brilliant and charismatic as well as wildly erratic. If Panshinea stayed steady, he would hold the voters with him. If GNask could send him veering off target, he would be removed just as his representative had been removed.

He had only one objection he could make without censure. As the vote came to him, all but nominal in allowing Panshinea to take the office, he raised an objection.

The emperor stood on the central dais. He turned and raised an eyebrow in inquiry. "What does the ambassador of Abdreli have an objection to?"

"Not to your good person, Panshinea," GNask answered smoothly. He disliked Trade, it did not have the nuances of his own language, but he was forced to use it and made do with it as best as he could. "The only objection I have is for the welfare and the stability of the government you leave behind. The emperor, as I recall, has no heir. . . ."

The prime directive of the Compact was stability. Any world left unstable, or allowed to continue in an unstable direction which might affect other worlds, other races, other civilizations, was either cut off—or assimilated by races which could give it stability. Even Cho was held to the criteria. Panshinea's mobile, handsome face froze.

"As I understand it," GNask said, moving to the edge of his diplomatic dais, "there is some discussion about your health and the ascendancy of another House to power. While your internal politics are none of my affair, there is the question of stability. *Tezars* are our lifeline, the support of each and every space-going member. Your responsibilities are immense."

"Our responsibilities—" Panshinea choked to silence. The gaunt Choya with him tugged on his sleeve and said something, his words lost to GNask through white sound muffling.

GNask waited, certain that he had precipitated events in one way or another. The emperor had no heirs—he had rivals in the Houses of Sky and Earth, but that ascendancy to the throne might well cost the Choyan a civil war. And no candidate had surged forward from the House of Star, a House plunging into descendancy.

Panshinea shrugged off his adviser. Agitation clear in his posture, he strode forward and opened his mouth to speak.

The council doors opened. Another Choya entered, the natural light from the backdrop of Sorrow outlining him against the artificial, dimmer lights of the inner halls. But GNask knew him, knew him from his bearing and his voices as they rang forth. The Abdrelik clashed his tusks in frustration.

"I am the emperor's designated heir. I'm prepared to take his place either here at the Halls or at home, wherever I am most needed."

Palaton strode to the base of the dais, looked up at his emperor, and extended his hand.

Murmurs ran through the assembly. Panshinea took the hand and helped the other up to stand beside him. "The heir of the House of Star," Panshinea said. "You know him as the *tezar* who saved four hundred when Chaos swallowed him up, sacrificing himself. He found his way out of the patterns. No *tezarian* drive has ever burned as brightly. He honors me by accepting as heir."

Rindy put a shaking hand on his arm. The eyes of the old Prelate misted as he said, "Where have you been? You put out distress signals—we knew you thought the medics lost— we could not locate you to tell you the truth—"

"The truth is what you make it," Palaton answered. Panshinea had sent him out into the Chaos of the unknown, into uncertainty and failure, hoping perhaps to temper him, and hoping as well that Palaton would fight to find his way back. This was not his father, and he was not the emperor's son, but they were Choyan, and for destiny and the future of their planet, they would accept each other.

Panshinea smiled broadly. "Vihtirne is going to be very disturbed. We've a hard fight ahead of us."

Palaton said dryly, "I've never known you to be afraid of knocking heads."

There was a lull as Rand brought the jet sled into the outer city rim of the Arizar port. Zarites scrambled through streets broken by cluster bomb fire, their furred hides streaked with blood and soot, their voices high with terror.

He dropped the vehicle, searching for Bevan's aura, which had grown wispy thin and threatened to disappear completely. He rubbed a hand over his eyes, trying to clear his vision and knowing it would do him no good. Alarms began to wail again. Raiders screamed close.

He was running to a concrete bunker when the world exploded and he felt himself thrown into the air.

"Rand. Rand."

Cold hands upon his brow. He woke from an odd dream of Palaton, speeding his way home, like a comet streaking through the sky, and looked into Bevan's face. Rubble piled around them. The other was battered and dirty, and blood splattered the front of his blues.

Rand hurt everywhere and he lay in the hands of a person who had become his enemy. He licked chapped lips. "Don't run."

"I have to." As an attack began again, Bevan glanced overhead, even though they were either underground or buried. "But I can't . . . I can't leave you here like this."

"I'm dying."

"I think so." The softly accented words were almost obscured by Bevan's emotion. "But you didn't let go of me. You never let go of me."

"No. I—I couldn't." The ground shook. Cement slabs around them trembled. Dust sifted down on them. "Come back with me. They need our help and . . ." Rand sucked in his breath sharply at a pain arcing through him. Bevan answered the pain by stroking his forehead again. A warm drop splashed down upon his cheek and slid

away. "The power is different with every Choya.
Come back and they'll teach you. Palaton will
show you—" *Palaton was so far away, so faint.*
Rand fought to stay awake.

"I can't!" Bevan bit his lip. "You know where
I come from, my friend. I smile to survive, not
because I have happiness in my heart. I don't
have trust inside of me. All I have is doubt and
fear. It grows, like a cancer. There's nothing
that can cut it away."

"Friendship can. Love." Rand reached up and
grasped the other's hand tightly. "It cuts across
anything . . . against time or space . . . we have
the power."

And between their clasped hands a light grew.
It grew in intensity from the green and amber
of their auras until the darkness of the rubble
filled with it. Then it shrank into a ball and
dove, straight at Rand's chest.

He gasped as it penetrated. The pain radiated
everywhere, incredible, unbearable. His flesh
shone translucently. Bevan echoed his pain and
fear, their hands squeezed together.

It went out. The shelter went black and even
Bevan's face could not be seen. A tremendous
BOOM! sounded nearby and a cement slab went
sliding again, opening up the ceiling of their
meager hiding place. The Arizar sky, streaked
with soot and flame and smoke, shone in.

Rand let go of Bevan and sat up. The agony
had gone.

Bevan paled. He brushed his thick, dark hair
from his dark eyes. He looked at his hand.

"What did we do?"

Exposed, they whispered. But the wonder in
their voices shouted.

Together, they had healed. *Power untold.*

Rand sobered suddenly. He got to his feet and pulled Bevan up. "Get out of here," he said. "Do what you have to."

Bevan ran to the edge of the shelter. He looked back. "My friend?"

"You're right. They'll hunt you to get their power back—and maybe worse, because they don't even know what you can do with it. But I won't ever let go of you, understand?"

Bevan smiled. "I understand." He turned and raced from view.

Rand dropped suddenly to his knees. He was not as well as he'd hoped he was. He curled to his side and wondered if he would live until Palaton found him.

Palaton had his *tezar* bring the ship in despite the damage. Raiders had cracked the port like an eggshell. He already knew there were survivors at the campus, that they had fought off infantry as Households across the continent came to their aid, but massive destruction had been wrought. Abdrelik, he thought. It was their style, although the ships had not been marked. But none of that was his concern. He held the weak thread of Rand's life pulsating in his mind as it spun out, and he was out of the ship before the loading ramp was even fully lowered, casting along that lifeline.

Even then it took him hours. The aura drawing him grew so weak it was a bare glimmer among the smoke and ashes. He stalked along broken streets, listening to the wail of weeping Zarites and the grunts of work parties searching the houses and factories for the living. He reeled it in, his own essence, searching for it, praying for life.

The trail ended at the city's edge. Palaton paused uncertainly among the broken towers of concrete. He wept at the sudden realization that he was alone, powerless, but the loss of his *bahdur* was as nothing to the emptiness of losing Rand. His voices broke with sorrow.

A husking whisper penetrated his grief. *"I'm here."*

Palaton dropped to his knees in the rubble and began to dig. The cement tore at his hands, pilot's hands, the tools of his trade, until the blood ran freely.

He was rewarded by the sight of a pale, alien face smiling at him from the wreckage. Palaton drew him out gingerly, and then cradled him. This was his strength. His compass to his destiny. The child he could pull safe and alive out of the crystal of disaster.

Palaton put back his head and shouted for joy.

DAW

Charles Ingrid

THE MARKED MAN SERIES

☐ **THE MARKED MAN** (UE2396—$3.95)
In a devastated America, can the Lord Protector of a mutating human race find a way to preserve the future of the species?

☐ **THE LAST RECALL** (UE2460—$3.95)
Returning to a radically-changed Earth, would the generational ships aid the remnants of a mutated human race—or seek their future among the stars?

THE SAND WARS

☐ **SOLAR KILL: Book 1** (UE2391—$3.95)
He was the last Dominion Knight and he would challenge a star empire to gain his revenge!

☐ **LASERTOWN BLUES: Book 2** (UE2393—$3.95)
He'd won a place in the Emperor's Guard but could he hunt down the traitor who'd betrayed his Knights to an alien foe?

☐ **CELESTIAL HIT LIST: Book 3** (UE2394—$3.95)
Death stalked the Dominion Knight from the Emperor's Palace to a world on the brink of its prophesied age of destruction. . . .

☐ **ALIEN SALUTE: Book 4** (UE2329—$3.95)
As the Dominion and the Thrakian empires mobilize for all-out war, can Jack Storm find the means to defeat the ancient enemies of man?

☐ **RETURN FIRE: Book 5** (UE2363—$3.95)
Was someone again betraying the human worlds to the enemy—and would Jack Storm become pawn or player in these games of death?

☐ **CHALLENGE MET: Book 6** (UE2436—$3.95)
In this concluding volume of *The Sand Wars,* Jack Storm embarks on a dangerous mission which will lead to a final confrontation with the Ash-farel.

DAW

C.J. CHERRYH
THE ALLIANCE-UNION UNIVERSE

The Company Wars
☐ DOWNBELOW STATION   (UE2431—$4.99)

The Era of Rapprochement
☐ SERPENT'S REACH   (UE2088—$3.50)
☐ FORTY THOUSAND IN GEHENNA   (UE2429—$4.50)
☐ MERCHANTER'S LUCK   (UE2139—$3.50)

The Chanur Novels
☐ THE PRIDE OF CHANUR   (UE2292—$3.95)
☐ CHANUR'S VENTURE   (UE2293—$3.95)
☐ THE KIF STRIKE BACK   (UE2184—$3.99)
☐ CHANUR'S HOMECOMING   (UE2177—$4.50)

The Mri Wars
☐ THE FADED SUN: KESRITH   (UE2449—$4.50)
☐ THE FADED SUN: SHON'JIR   (UE2448—$4.50)
☐ THE FADED SUN: KUTATH   (UE2133—$4.50)

Merovingen Nights (Mri Wars Period)
☐ ANGEL WITH THE SWORD   (UE2143—$3.50)

Merovingen Nights—Anthologies
☐ FESTIVAL MOON (#1)   (UE2192—$3.50)
☐ FEVER SEASON (#2)   (UE2224—$3.50)
☐ TROUBLED WATERS (#3)   (UE2271—$3.50)
☐ SMUGGLER'S GOLD (#4)   (UE2299—$3.50)
☐ DIVINE RIGHT (#5)   (UE2380—$3.95)
☐ FLOOD TIDE (#6)   (UE2452—$4.50)
☐ ENDGAME (#7)   (UE2481—$4.99)

The Age of Exploration
☐ CUCKOO'S EGG   (UE2371—$4.50)
☐ VOYAGER IN NIGHT   (UE2107—$2.95)
☐ PORT ETERNITY   (UE2206—$2.95)

The Hanan Rebellion
☐ BROTHERS OF EARTH   (UE2290—$3.95)
☐ HUNTER OF WORLDS   (UE2217—$2.95)

DAW
Epic Science Fiction Adventures
C.S. Friedman

☐ **IN CONQUEST BORN**   (UE2198—$3.95)

Braxi and Azea, two super-races fighting an endless campaign over a long forgotten cause. The Braxaná—created to become the ultimate warriors. The Azeans, raised to master the powers of the mind, using telepathy to penetrate where mere weapons cannot. Now the final phase of their war is approaching, when whole worlds will be set ablaze by the force of ancient hatred. Now Zatar and Anzha, the master generals, who have made this battle a personal vendetta, will use every power of body and mind to claim the vengeance of total conquest.

☐ **THE MADNESS SEASON**   (UE2444—$4.95)

He'd had many names over the centuries. Now he was Daetrin, a name given to him by the alien conquerors of humankind, the Tyr. Three hundred years ago, the Tyr conquered Earth, isolating the true individualists, the geniuses, all the people who represented the hopes and discoveries of the future, imprisoning them in dome colonies on poisonous worlds. There the Tyr, a race which itself shared a unified gestalt mind, had left these gifted individuals to work on projects which might reveal all of humankind's secrets. Yet Daetrin's secret was one no one had ever uncovered, for through the years he had buried it so well that he had even hidden his real nature from himself. But, taken into custody by the Tyr, there was no longer any place for Daetrin to hide. Now he must confront the truth about himself—and if he failed, not just Daetrin but all humans would pay the price.

DAW